# THE HUNTER'S QUARRY

A totally gripping suspense thriller

## MARK WEST

THE
BOOK
FOLKS

Published by The Book Folks

London, 2022

© Mark West

ISBN 978-1-80462-014-4

www.thebookfolks.com

*For David and Pippa*

# Prologue

The man was going to kill her.

Barbara Gilbert had expected to be pursued but not that he would be so quick off the mark. Her anxiety levels were high when she sneaked out with the package, but seeing him on the corner of Duncan Street had pushed them through the roof. The man wore a dark blue peaked cap, dark trousers and a red puffa jacket, and stared at her.

Thinking a public place might be safer she ran into The Newborough Centre, a shopping arcade brightly lit against the encroaching twilight. A glance over her shoulder confirmed the man had followed her in. Heart racing, she looked around frantically for somewhere to hide. To her left was a clothes store spanning two floors, the windows mostly obscured by banners advertising seasonal offers.

She rushed into the shop and up the back staircase to the first floor where she crouched down to catch her breath and keep an eye out for the man. He didn't come up the stairs. She looked across the shop floor which was dotted with small islands of clothes racks and saw him walk past the windows looking in.

Fear pulled her scalp tight. Did he know she was in here? Was she being tracked on CCTV? Were other people, even now, coming up the stairs to trap her? She tried to take a deep breath but couldn't and it felt like anxiety was squeezing her lungs.

The man stopped to look through the window, cupping his hands around his eyes to see. She pressed herself against the wall, trying to stay out of sight, her mind racing. If she managed to get out somehow, would he risk chasing her through the centre? Stupid question – of course he would because he knew what she had in her handbag.

\* \* \*

Keel scanned the shop floor but saw only a mother and daughter checking a display of costume jewellery and a man who looked nervously at racks of bras.

He took a small handset from the inside pocket of his puffa jacket and held it to his ear.

"Mr Wilson?"

"Mr Keel?"

"Are you sure she's here? I'm at the doors but can't see her at all."

"She entered at the ground floor and went towards the back staircase."

"I'll do a sweep of the upper floor then head down."

"Keep me informed."

"I will," said Keel and slid the handset back into his pocket.

\* \* \*

Barbara willed herself to take deep, steady breaths. It wasn't helping to panic – she'd got this far and simply needed to keep her cool. She slowly counted to three in her head then peered around a rack of shirts.

She saw the man slide something into an inside pocket then zip up his jacket as he stepped away from the windows. He moved out of sight towards the doors.

Barbara rocked back on her haunches. If he came into the shop he'd be able to peer into every nook and cranny. Panic gnawed at her. If he did come in, that would mean the doors were clear, and so long as she could avoid him before she reached them, that could be her escape route.

Someone moved behind her and Barbara gasped. How could he have found her so quickly? Holding the rack for support, she turned her head slowly.

"Can I help you?" asked a female voice.

Barbara hissed out her breath. A woman wearing a polo shirt in the shop colours leaned forward.

"Are you okay?" Her identity badge swung on its tabard.

"I'm fine, thanks."

The woman's frown created harsh lines between her brows. "You don't look it. Have you lost something?"

"Sort of," said Barbara. She peered around the rack to make sure the man wasn't coming then stood up and smoothed her skirt against her thighs.

"Are you sure you're okay?" asked the woman.

Barbara favoured her with a smile and shook her head briskly. "I'm just having one of those days."

The woman's face brightened. "Aren't we all, love?"

If only you knew, Barbara thought. Keeping close to the wall she moved away from the assistant and kept looking around the shop. Through the wide windows she could see people strolling and talking on the upper walkway. A harassed-looking young mother walked by. The child strapped into its pushchair was merrily eating a bag of crisps while the toddler attached with a Day-Glo harness held a foot-long rubber skeleton that still had the 'Reduced' sticker attached to its forehead.

Barbara hadn't seen anything of the man by the time she reached the windows. The doors were ten feet away and she took big steps towards them, trying to look confident. She glanced out through the window again. The mother with the pushchair had stopped outside a small toyshop window and the toddler clutched his skeleton tight as he peered in at the display.

Half a dozen steps to the door. Barbara held her bag tight to her side and tried to watch every inch of the shop at the same time. She still couldn't see the man.

\* \* \*

Keel reached the back of the shop without seeing any sign of Barbara. There were three changing rooms in front of him but all three had their doors wide open. He walked towards the staircase and saw one of the assistants looking towards the front of the shop with an unreadable expression on her face. Could be something, could be nothing.

He angled towards the doors.

* * *

Barbara took another step and saw the man coming towards her. Their eyes locked.

She kept moving as panic radiated through her. She tried to ignore it and concentrated on walking. Now wasn't the time to be scared; now she had to get out of the shop and into the crowds to lose herself.

"Excuse me, madam," the man said as he pushed past two teenaged girls.

Barbara was at the double doors now.

"Excuse me," the man said loudly.

She went through the doors. Nobody paid her any attention. She glanced left and right, trying to figure out the best way to go. Escalators ran down to the ground floor at either end of the walkway.

"Excuse me," the man called loudly, and the young mother jerked around to look at him.

Barbara kept moving and looked around constantly as she planned her next move. The escalators would get her down to the exits but he'd easily be able to keep up with her and, perhaps, call for assistance.

"Excuse me." His voice was quieter, as if the reaction by the young mother had made him realise he didn't want to call too much attention to himself. "Madam, I need you to stop."

The corner of the walkway was fast approaching, the glass barrier making a ninety-degree turn before leading towards the escalators and the other side of the centre.

Barbara glanced back. The man had moved towards the barrier, as if to cut her off.

4

"Shit," she hissed.

There were three shop units in front of her. The coffee shop and charity outlet appeared to be on this floor only. The Zap! games store might be on both floors but she couldn't be certain.

A narrow and unremarkable door stood between Zap! and the coffee shop with a 'No Admittance, Access Stairway' sign stuck on the upper panel. Not ideal but the staircase might lead her down to the ground floor.

Barbara drifted towards the corner and looked over her shoulder to make sure the man had followed her move. She darted left at the last moment and cut in front of two mothers with laden pushchairs talking over their sleeping infants.

She rushed towards the door but couldn't see a handle. Barbara ran her hand down the gap between the door and the jamb, hoping to feel something she could use to pull it open but felt nothing. A glance showed the man was less than ten feet away. She turned back to the door as her mind raced.

"Excuse me, madam." He sounded like he was right behind her.

She felt sweat on her upper lip as she pushed the door. It seemed to give slightly but not enough. Did this all end with her foiled by a door she couldn't open?

"Hey." The man gripped her elbow, his fingers pressing against the bones.

"Let me go."

"This doesn't need to get unpleasant." He stood so close she could feel his breath on her neck.

"If you don't let me go, I'll scream rape."

"You think that'll make people come to help you? I'll tell them I'm security and check your bag…"

Panic almost overwhelmed her and she struggled to think as his calm but insistent voice burrowed into her head.

"If I shout rape, who'll care what's in my bag?"

"Why don't I just take your bag?"

She hit the door hard with the heel of her hand and with a metallic popping sound it moved away slightly from the jamb.

"Come on, love," he said.

Barbara drove her right heel back and it connected to his shin with a resounding crack. The man yelled and let go of her arm. Half-turning, she shoved him and he staggered back several steps. Yanking the door open, she rushed through and pulled it closed behind her.

She stood on a dark narrow landing with poured concrete walls. Concrete stairs dropped in front of her. Dim strip lights on the ceiling struggled to light the space and angled down with the staircase.

Behind her, the man pounded on the door. Barbara knew she might only have moments before he managed to open it, so she held her bag close to her hip and rushed down the stairs. She paused at the first landing and her breath burned in her chest. The door finally gave and light flooded into the stairwell.

"Give it up," the man called.

She ran so fast it felt like she wasn't in control of herself. Panic swarmed around inside her head and she tried to shake it away but the movement upset her balance. She slipped and only just managed to hold herself up and jarred her arm in the process.

"Shit," she said and started again.

There were voices from below. The staircase ran down to a doorway through which light glowed. She kept running and the sound of the man in pursuit – his heavy footsteps and breathing – filled the narrow space.

"Stop!" he shouted. "Stop!"

She came to the bottom of the staircase in a rush, misjudging both the distance and her speed. She staggered on the flat surface but kept her balance and clattered into the wall. She took a moment to catch her breath then went to her left.

The underground car park had a low ceiling and beams of concrete criss-crossed over her head. Voices and engine sounds echoed around her. A painted walkway led across the roadway to another door which stood open, stairs leading up. Several cars were parked close by but she saw no one.

There wasn't time to consider her options and she ran for the other stairs.

Suddenly, someone was in her way and they collided heavily.

* * *

Keel moved quicker as the woman disappeared from view.

From what he could make out, the stairs led to some kind of underground parking area, which shouldn't offer too many options of where to run. If she hesitated, he had her. People always dithered.

Above the engine noise, he heard a thud and something slap hard against the floor. Keel heard a man's voice, muted, and the woman said...

* * *

"Sorry!"

"Don't worry," said the man in a suit she'd bumped into. "It was an accident."

The force of their collision had pushed him back towards the roadway and he'd dropped the armful of files and paperwork he was carrying. He crouched down to gather them together.

"Sorry," she repeated and edged around him onto the roadway. From the right she heard a heavy bass pounding and an engine revving.

Her pursuer had reached the bottom of the stairs. He looked at the man kneeling and picking up the paperwork. She took advantage of his distraction to move.

A horn blared and startled her. Adrenaline surged as she saw the red Audi coming at her, surely too fast for this car park.

Her pursuer yelled "Hey" but she couldn't tell if he meant her or the car.

Barbara ran, all her efforts focused on the exit ahead.

* * *

An annoyed-looking man knelt in front of a briefcase as he gathered sheets of paper.

Keel clocked him instantly – early fifties, slightly heavy, grey hair cut short – before glancing at Barbara who was halfway across the roadway. A horn blared from a car he couldn't see. Keel looked beyond her, trying to second-guess where she was going, and spotted the door.

Jumping over the man, Keel ran onto the roadway. A red Audi came at him and he knew there'd be an impact. He flung himself onto the bonnet and his elbow caught a windscreen wiper. The car didn't slow and Keel's momentum carried him over. He saw the driver, hands braced on the steering wheel, mouth open and then Keel was weightless. The car went by dangerously close as he landed in a heap on the rough concrete and he rolled away from it, not wanting the tyres to catch him.

He came to rest against the support of a crash barrier. The driver didn't even brake. Keel got to his feet slowly. He braced his legs to make sure they weren't damaged and breathed deeply to check his ribs were okay. Everything felt alright apart from his throbbing elbow.

"Fuck." The woman had gone. The door to the stairwell swung lazily closed. "Fuck."

* * *

This staircase clung to the walls with a narrow gap between the flights. Barbara went up quickly, pulling hard on the banister. The first flight was fine but her calves were burning by the second.

Behind her, the man came through the door holding his elbow. Barbara looked down at him and he glared at her. She kept moving, breath hot in her chest and throat.

A slim redhead with a big handbag draped over one shoulder was making her way down the flight of stairs. Barbara, moving too quickly to properly get out of the way, caught the woman on the arm with her elbow.

"Shit, sorry!"

The woman, wearing a baggy T-shirt and leggings, looked surprised. "Sorry, I was miles away."

Barbara took the last two steps slowly, momentum gone, legs heavy. The redhead continued down the stairs without looking back as the man came up them at full speed. The sight of him urged Barbara on and adrenaline allowed her to trot up the next flight.

By the time she reached the landing her legs and hips were on fire and the taste of hot bile filled her mouth.

She couldn't keep going.

\* \* \*

It didn't take Keel long to catch the woman.

He watched her energy deplete with each flight and when he caught up with her on the fourth, she was struggling to breathe.

He grabbed her and with a strangled cry she stumbled but he kept her upright.

"Don't…" she said.

"I warned you," he muttered and walked them up the stairs.

Near the top he shoved her and she sprawled onto the landing. The impact knocked her head onto the smooth concrete and her eyelids fluttered for a moment.

"Get up."

"I can't." She clutched her bag tighter to her.

"Get to your feet."

"I can't…"

He grabbed the neck of her blouse and it ripped as he pulled her up and pushed her against the wall. He held her up until her legs did the job.

"Give me your bag."

"Why are you doing this?"

"Missus, I'm going to look in it one way or the other, so let's play nice, eh?"

He grabbed for her bag but she held it tight. With her free hand she slapped his face and the surprise was far worse than the sting because he hadn't anticipated it.

"I'll use my nails next time," she promised him, her lips a thin line.

"I'll hit you back next time. Give me the bag."

She raised her hand to strike him again and he grabbed her wrist, pushing it back hard against the wall. Her body contorted as she cried out.

He pulled her bag off her arm then released her wrist. She cowered down, arm clutched to her chest, as tears ran down her cheeks.

He stepped back into the middle of the landing and held the bag open, rooting through it – make-up, tissues, a glasses case, a pad, a wallet and an umbrella. Frowning, he checked again but found nothing that wasn't there before. He upended the bag and toed through the scattered contents to spread them out.

"Where is it?"

She looked at him with wide eyes. He checked the bag for hidden interior pockets but couldn't feel any.

"Where is it?" he asked again, slower this time but she only stared at him.

Frustrated, he looked up and saw a thin banner highlighting winter activities in the Centre. It was held to the wall with nylon cord. He quickly unwound the nearest end and wrapped the cord around his fist.

The woman frowned and when he threw the empty bag at her she turned her head. The bag bounced off her chest and skidded onto the first stair. He pulled the woman roughly to her feet.

"Last chance," he said.

"I don't–"

Quickly, he twirled his fist to release some of the cord and wrapped it around her neck. She gagged and tried to get her fingers under it, but he pulled her away from the wall. She staggered into the banister and he pushed her until she was hanging over it. Her legs kicked as he hooked the cord around one of the metal balusters. With a final shove she went over.

The woman shrieked until the cord snapped taut and he heard the crack of her neck.

Breathing deeply, he turned to the scattered contents of her bag and searched through them again. He took the handset from his pocket.

"Mr Wilson? The subject is terminated. Unfortunately, she didn't have the item."

"Did she drop it?" The voice held a brittle snap of annoyance.

"Not that I saw but there were two points of contact. A man in the car park and a woman on the stairs."

"We'll check the CCTV. Clear the scene and await further instructions."

Keel slipped the radio into his trouser pocket, took off his jacket and hid her handbag inside it. He walked down the stairs. The woman hung in the void between the second and third flights, swaying gently. One of her shoes had come off. Her toenails were painted purple.

# Chapter 1

Rachel Turner opened the car park's pedestrian door onto the plaza behind the Newborough Centre. The chill air cut through her damp T-shirt and made her shiver so she pulled the hoodie from her gym bag and slipped it on as the door closed behind her.

She shouldn't use the shortcut through the car park – all the signs proclaimed 'No Unauthorised Access' – but it seemed like she'd got away with it again. She cut across the plaza with a smile.

Today's self-defence class had been hard work but good fun. Kim, the instructor, pushed as hard as ever, and since none of the regular blokes had turned up, the session quickly descended into the 'how hard should you kick a man in the knackers to drop him?' discussion. Despite Kim reminding them it was more effective to go for kidney shots, the overall consensus was "as hard as possible".

Someone across town, well away from the centre of Hadlington, had taken advantage of the fading light and set off fireworks. The starbursts drew excited coos from the children around her. A few of the adults grumbled about how early it was but the spectacle made Rachel smile. She'd promised her daughter Tilly they'd go to the big display on the common at the weekend and was already looking forward to the toasted marshmallows Tilly had suggested they make.

Rachel wasn't particularly looking forward to tonight. Her friend Nat had invited her to a party and since Glen had Tilly overnight, Rachel had been persuaded to go. At the time, deep into a wonderful bottle of white, it seemed like a great idea. Now, heading for the car in sweaty clothes that didn't keep out the wind, all she wanted was to go home to luxuriate in the peace and quiet, and have a long hot bath and catch up on some TV.

* * *

It took Peter Lewis five minutes to gather all the papers he'd dropped after that woman ran into him as she came out of the stairwell like an express train. It capped off a shitty afternoon and the fact she immediately ran off – then a bloke, ten seconds later, had walked over the paperwork – didn't improve the situation.

In the end, with annoyance fizzing in his head like an angry wasp, he'd simply opened his briefcase and stuffed the papers inside. He could sort through them tomorrow and knew half were already going to end up in the bin. As usual, the planning proposals meeting with some of the idiots from the council had quickly turned into a slanging match. It was only the thought of relaying the story to his colleagues that kept him sane.

To make himself feel better he checked the package was still tucked neatly into one of the briefcase pockets. It was.

Peter stood up and brushed off the knees of his trousers. He walked to the car and dumped the briefcase on the back seat. Before he turned on the engine, he took out his phone and opened Val's last text to him. He'd already read it but wanted to de-stress before his drive and this was the best way he could think of doing that.

> *Hey, hope your day's going well. Have booked a table at Cosa Nostra, will meet you there at eight. Love you.*

The message had come during his meeting so he hadn't been able to respond. Now he did.

*Day has been up and down, mostly down. How was yours? Thanks for booking the table, can't wait to see you there. Love you xx.*

Feeling the weight of the day lift, he backed out of the parking space and drove out of the car park.

\* \* \*

Keel sat in his Range Rover on the second floor of the car park behind the centre. He hadn't encountered either point of contact on his way here but he'd passed on the descriptions of the male and female in as much detail as he could. For the last half hour, he'd watched people come out of the lift across from him but hadn't seen either of the marks.

His handset beeped. "Mr Wilson?"

"Nothing from the shop CCTV but we tracked the male contact from the car park. I'm just running the details from his car registration and I'll message the information through to you."

"And the female?"

"Nothing yet. She parked elsewhere but we've tracked her out of the centre and will get back to you."

"Thank you."

"Head out now, it shouldn't be long before we have both sets of information."

"Agreed."

The call ended as the lift doors opened. Two families came out, with half a dozen excited-looking children clutching boxes of fireworks. Last out of the lift was Munro, carrying two large cups of coffee. Her short white-blonde hair caught the light as she nodded at him, even though he knew she couldn't see him through the darkened glass.

He leaned over to open the passenger door, took the cups she handed him and waited until she'd climbed into her seat. She was slight enough that the car barely moved.

"Anything?"

He held the two cups up and handed her the one with 'Carrie' written on it.

"I've just heard we have the male, and the female detail is coming soon." Keel lifted his cup and turned it until he saw the scrawl which read 'Geronimo'.

"Running out of ideas?" he asked with a smile.

"Something like that." She favoured him with a sideways glance, the hint of a smile at her lips.

"Any issues getting rid?"

He'd kept the jacket and bag tucked under his arm as he went back into the Newborough Centre, removing the cap as he took the stairs to the second-floor car park. Once in the Range Rover, Munro already had the bright yellow 'Clinical Waste' bag open and Keel put the prop clothing and bag into it, sliding his own parka on before he got into the driver's seat. Munro had put the bag into one of the waste bins behind the centre before she got their coffee.

"Not one," she said. "Everything sweet as a nut."

He nodded and turned the ignition on, the engine coming to life with a muted roar.

"That's the way I like it," Keel said and pulled out of the parking space.

# Chapter 2

Rachel's house keys were missing.

She'd parked in her designated space at the side of the converted house and rushed around to the front door, but when she reached into her bag and the pocket where she kept her keys, she couldn't find them.

Rachel held her old Radley bag open under the white glare of the security light over the door and searched it. She shrugged the gym bag off her shoulders and checked it but there were no keys, just her day clothes and heels.

She knelt down and re-checked the key pocket. Probing with her fingers, she felt cool air then the cold stone of the step. There was a hole in one corner and she felt a flash of panic.

"Shit."

She cast her mind back over the day. She'd finished work at lunchtime then got Tilly from school and dropped her with the child-minder before running some errands and going to self-defence. Her keys could have dropped out anywhere.

The bag had seen better days but she was reluctant to let go of this faithful companion which had lasted almost as long as her marriage. She sorted through the clutter of her life, essential items like tissues to packets of wet wipes and everything in between. She noticed a brown box in one corner and frowned but decided it was one of Tilly's Little Buddies sets. Her daughter loved the little figures beyond reason and they were everywhere – all over the flat, in the car, in Tilly's school bag. But while the Little Buddies were there, her keys clearly weren't.

Heart thumping now, Rachel opened the torch app on her phone and worked her way back across the gravel to the car park, hoping to find them on the way. They weren't there. She checked in the car and relief flooded through her when she spotted the bunch in the passenger footwell.

She locked the car and walked back, the keys firmly gripped in her hand. She picked up her gym bag and unlocked the front door.

\* \* \*

Peter Lewis dropped his briefcase by the wall and clicked on the hallway lamp. He took off his coat and hung it up then went into the lounge. Four lamps, already lit on timers, lent the room a cosy air.

He'd never intended to live in a flat, which this was however much the estate agent had made a point of calling it an apartment. Before the divorce, when Maxine walked out on him because she was 'so deeply in love' with a tennis coach almost twenty years her junior who'd inevitably buggered off with all her money after he seduced her into marriage, he'd had a nice place in The Hills, one of the finer areas of Hadlington. The divorce had really tarnished his comfortable life and left him without much to show after working bloody hard for almost forty years.

He shrugged off his suit jacket and draped it over a chair back then closed the curtains. He felt the need to calm himself now. The meeting had been bad and the collision with the woman frustrating, but he wanted to be bright and relaxed when he saw Val later.

* * *

Rachel leaned against the front door to close it and dropped her gym bag. She put her keys on the small bookcase that had slowly been overrun by Little Buddies books.

She flicked on the hall light and kicked off her trainers, flexing her toes with relief. Walking into the lounge, she put on the lamp and closed the curtains. Tilly had been working on a school project this morning and her pencil box still spilled pens and crayons on the coffee table, an easy mess to tidy. Rachel wished her daughter was there now, the tip of her tongue poking through her lips as she carefully coloured in her latest picture.

Glen had Tilly as per the custody arrangements – two nights a week then every other weekend. As much as he said he loved his daughter – and Rachel believed he did –

he seemed to find a lot of reasons not to look after her. Even tonight had been touch-and-go until she put her foot down and said she'd been invited to a party so he didn't have a choice.

Rachel went into the kitchen and took off her sock to massage the sole of her foot as she waited for the kettle to boil. It ached from standing in a meeting room most of the morning and the gruelling session Kim had put them through in class. She idly wondered if it was better to wear heels or flats tonight and, as she kneaded the ball of her foot with a forefinger knuckle, she decided on the latter.

She poured her coffee then made scrambled eggs in the microwave and ate them from the bowl as she stood by the window. Various lights were coming on in the houses over the back and the garden security light came on as Mr Johnson from the corner ground-floor flat walked his arthritic little dog. Tilly loved the manky pooch and it liked her but always growled at Rachel.

As she rinsed the bowl her mobile rang. Picking up her coffee, she walked through to the hall, found her phone in her bag, looked at the screen and smiled.

"Hi Nat."

"Hey, are you at home?"

"I am."

"Getting ready, I hope?"

Rachel nodded to the empty flat. "Of course."

"Glad to hear it."

Nat had often expressed her worry that divorce and single-motherhood might turn Rachel into a hermit and wouldn't be swayed from the opinion. As such, she'd seen it as her mission to make sure her old friend went out often, even if Rachel really wasn't keen. Tonight was one such occasion.

"I'll get you on the way. I'm just heading to the Hadley Hall Hotel to pick up a few people from my course, then heading to the party."

"I've literally just got in, had a bite to eat and now I'm going to have a shower."

"Okay, okay, I know I'm nagging. You have the address?"

"I have the address, Nat. I'll see you later."

"It'll be good to see you."

They said their goodbyes and Rachel went into her bedroom, peeling her T-shirt over her head.

\* \* \*

Keel's phone beeped while he sat at traffic lights and he flicked the screen to read the message.

"Okay, we have both contacts."

"Good," said Munro, looking out the window at the firework blooms lighting up the sky. "I'm fed up with watching the fireworks."

"You don't take enough pleasure from the mundane."

She offered a thin smile. "I don't get paid to."

He typed the first postcode into the satnav and a route appeared taking him to the eastern edge of town. The other was off to the north-west.

"Got them," he said. The lights changed and he put the Range Rover into gear. "Let's go and see Barbara's friends."

\* \* \*

Peter went into the bathroom. The taps were at full strength but the water level wasn't quite deep enough for him. He liked a full bath. He sprinkled some salts into the water and went into his bedroom.

He stripped off his work clothes and hung up his suit then put on his dressing gown and went back into the bathroom.

\* \* \*

Keel pulled the Range Rover to the kerb outside the address.

Munro reached behind the seats for her backpack then she opened the door and got out, her breath instantly visible in the night air.

"Keep me informed," he said. "If we can avoid any unnecessary culling, it'll be better."

They smiled at one another. She liked and respected Keel a great deal. He'd taught her well, but she'd never quite grasped his concept of not eliminating loose ends if you didn't have to. "Of course."

She closed the door and looked up at the target building as Keel drove away. From her vantage point, she could see a lot of windows spread over four floors, half of them lit and shielded by curtains. She couldn't see any CCTV which didn't mean there wasn't any. She adjusted the backpack and walked confidently up the gravel driveway, a young woman coming to visit a friend – nobody to pay attention to, nobody to remember.

In the brickwork beside the front door was a brass plate with twelve buttons, each with a little card underneath labelled with a name. Munro found the name she wanted then began systematically pressing the buttons, waiting ten seconds before pressing another.

The fourth button struck gold. "Yes?"

"Hi," she said and made herself sound perky. "Sammy?"

"No, you've got the wrong flat."

She pressed five more buttons until another answered. "Hi."

"Hello," she said, still perky. "Is that Sammy?"

"No, sorry, nobody called Sammy here."

"Damn, she said she lived here as well."

"Sorry, love, can't help you. I haven't been here long myself so I don't really know any of my neighbours."

"That's a shame. She's on the first floor, so I can't even stand under her window to try and get her attention."

"No," said the voice. "I don't suppose you can. I tell you what, I'll buzz you in."

"Oh really, would you mind?"

"Of course not, push the door."

Munro pushed the door when the buzzer sounded and it swung open easily. She stepped into a carpeted hall. A wide staircase ran up the back wall.

She unzipped her backpack and took out a pair of latex gloves then put her backpack over her shoulder before pulling the gloves on. She went up the stairs two at a time without touching the banister. The exercise felt good as did her sense of purpose.

\* \* \*

The long hot shower did Rachel a world of good.

These days, the chance to get a twenty-minute shower was rare and she'd turned up the temperature until her skin turned pink with the heat. When she finished the mirror and window were frosted with condensation, and droplets of water ran down the stainless-steel towel rail.

Now she stood in front of the mirror in her bedroom, wearing underwear with a towel wrapped around her head. She'd already tried on a dress but decided against it and tried on another. Then a blouse and jeans. It wasn't going well.

Nat had assured her the house party was nothing special, just a chance for people on the course to have a drink and a laugh. It had been so long since Rachel last went to a house party though that she didn't know what to wear. A dress would be nice but it was going to be a chilly evening and a blouse and jeans would work equally well and be a lot warmer.

She stared at the clothes on the bed.

"It shouldn't be this complicated," she said.

\* \* \*

Munro stopped outside the door. She took off her boots, shrugged the backpack off and put her boots in it. She took off her jacket, undid the top two buttons of her blouse and hoped that now, in socks, she looked like a neighbour just back from work and kicking off the uniform of the day. She took a small cup from the backpack then slipped off her gloves, put them in her pocket and pressed the doorbell with a knuckle.

She put the backpack on the floor and stepped into the middle of the corridor where she could be easily seen through the peephole.

* * *

Rachel's doorbell rang.

Surely Nat hadn't come to pick her up? She pulled on her dressing gown and tied its belt as she walked to the front door.

* * *

Peter sighed when the doorbell rang. He wasn't expecting anyone but that didn't mean it wasn't something important.

With another sigh, he padded through to the hall.

# Chapter 3

As Sergeant Ken Maley drove them into the underground staff car park at the Newborough Centre, PC Pippa Vincent wished she'd managed to get the leave form in for today.

A full moon always brought out the crazies, which was not only scary but also made a shift feel twice as long. Combining that with Bonfire Night was a recipe for disaster. Unfortunately, she hadn't been quick enough with the paperwork and others had beaten her to it, including her regular partner.

Maley braked to a halt in a disabled bay and was quickly out of the car. Pippa kept pace with him. He had a good reputation but didn't like to be slowed down and she didn't want to make the night drag any more by having him get onto her.

"Are you ready?" he asked.

He had a lot of experience on the job and seemed concerned that Pippa might not be able to keep her head.

"I think so."

He nodded. "Is this your first jumper?"

"No," she said and blinked back memories.

That honour belonged to a poor man who'd landed on his head. When she arrived on scene, he was lying at the base of the multi-storey car park with not much recognisable above his shoulders. She'd been sick on sight.

"First one indoors though."

"Fair enough," said Maley. "Just be ready for the smell."

"Yeah," she said and rushed around the car to join her superior.

A man who'd been guarding the doorway and diverting the public, came towards them. He held out his hand and Maley shook it.

"I'm Chris Wood, security supervisor for the centre."

Maley introduced himself and Pippa. "So, what've we got?"

Wood turned on his heel and led them to the door. He shooed the rubberneckers away and, when satisfied they wouldn't be able to see anything, pulled the door open. Maley went through first. Pippa followed him and the sharp unpleasant smell hit her almost immediately, bringing tears to her eyes.

"Do you ever get used to the smell?" she asked.

"I never have," Maley said.

Wood closed the door behind him and rushed to catch up, holding a hand against his nose as if that would help.

"One of the cleaners called it in. I got down here as soon as I could but we'd already drawn a bit of a crowd."

"Bloody ghouls have their own jungle drums," muttered Maley.

"Nasty business," said Wood.

"Where's the cleaner?" asked Pippa.

"Up in the management offices drinking lots of strong sugary tea."

Pippa followed Maley along a narrow corridor, the concrete walls making it feel horribly enclosed. They walked at a brisk pace. She took a notepad and pencil out of a pocket on her stab vest so as not to hold anything up when they got to the scene. The corridor opened into a wide, brightly lit space with a staircase across the way. She could already see a mess on the floor in the area between the flights.

"I asked for an ambulance too," said Wood.

"One'll be on the way," said Maley. "They'd usually beat us but we happened to be about a minute away."

"I'm not sure which of you she'll have more use for," said Wood.

Pippa frowned and glanced over her shoulder at him. He offered her a queasy smile and looked as if he'd rather be anywhere else than here with this sight and smell.

Maley moved with purpose and went up the first flight of stairs. He stopped at the landing and looked up. Pippa was just behind him and looked up too.

The woman hung between the second and third flights, swaying gently. Her face had turned a pale purple and her neck a livid red where the cord had dug in. Her eyes bulged and blood ran down her chin. Her head had canted at an obscene angle and a bone pressed up through the skin of her shoulder. One of her shoes had come off and bounced away under the first flight of stairs.

"Oh," Pippa said.

"Oh indeed," said Maley. He turned to Wood. "How many flights are there here?"

"Six up to the offices."

"How many doors do we have leading off the stairwell?"

"Three off the upper floors only. I've got them covered from the outside."

"Good. Has anyone been through here since the cleaner?"

"Not that I'm aware of."

"Okay." Maley looked at Pippa. "You sure you're okay?"

"I'm fine," she said. She wasn't okay but she knew she could deal with it. "What do you want me to do, Sarge?"

"Go with Mr Wood to the offices. Get a statement from the cleaner and then see if there's anything on the CCTV."

"There won't be," Wood interrupted. "The service only covers the centre itself and the car park. This area is basically access so it's a bit of black hole for surveillance."

"That's understandable but there must be something in the centre itself."

"Of course."

"So in theory we can track people in and out of the stairwell?" Maley waited for Wood to nod. "Go and get your cleaner sorted and have the CCTV ready for my colleague."

"Yes," said Wood and went back the way he'd come quickly, as if eager to be away.

"What do you think?" Pippa asked.

"Don't know. Could be a jumper or it could be something else entirely. What do you think?"

"I agree with you." She took one last look at the swaying body then snapped her notebook shut and put it away. "I'll go up to the offices."

Maley nodded without looking at her, staring at a point on the stairs where Pippa couldn't see anything.

"I'll wait for the ambulance," he said.

# Chapter 4

Peter didn't recognise the young woman with short white-blonde hair he saw through the peephole.

He set the chain, opened the door and peered through the gap. "Hello?"

The young woman smiled.

"Hello," she said. Her voice was strong and upbeat. "I'm really sorry to bother you but I'm Mrs Maxwell's niece. From downstairs?"

She phrased it as a question but since he didn't really know any of the neighbours on other floors and couldn't be sure he'd know Mrs Maxwell if he tripped over her, he kept quiet.

"You know," she said. "Lovely old lady, she lives in the corner flat."

Not wanting to be rude, he nodded. "Oh yes."

"Anyway, long story short, we're doing some baking and she's run out of sugar. I've tried other neighbours but nobody's answering and I don't want to go out in the cold just to get some so could you lend me a cup please?"

She fixed him with a broad, friendly smile and he felt his reserve go.

"Of course, I'll just…" He gestured at the chain and closed the door enough to unhook it, then opened it fully.

"You're a lifesaver," she said.

"I wouldn't go that far."

"You've never tasted my aunt's cooking."

He gestured her to come in and was about to ask her remove her shoes when he saw she only wore white socks.

"This is bigger than my aunt's," she said.

"Really? I thought they were all pretty much the same size."

"I don't think so." She held out her hand. "I'm Carrie, by the way."

"Peter," he said and shook her hand. She exuded a positive energy he liked. "Go through."

She went into the lounge and looked around. "This is very nice. I do love this building and the size of the flats."

He edged around her and went towards the kitchen. "I like it a lot too."

"Nice and quiet?"

"Generally. Lois next door occasionally practises the cello but it's a nice sound and in the summer, if she's playing, I have my window open and sit near it to listen. It reminds me of the writer listening to Holly Golightly."

"Audrey Hepburn and George Peppard," she said. "One of my favourite films."

"The book's better." He paused at the kitchen door. "So, some sugar?"

"Yes," she said and handed over her cup. She stood in the doorway while he found a bag of sugar in a cupboard and emptied some into the cup.

"I understand we have a mutual friend," she said.

"Other than your aunt?"

"Yes. I thought I recognised you anyway but your name tipped it."

"Small world."

"It is. So have you seen Barbara Gilbert recently?"

The name didn't immediately ring a bell.

"Barbara?" He tried to think of all his friends even as far back as school. "No, I don't think I know her."

"Maybe I'm wrong but she said she saw you today."

"You must be mistaken." He hadn't seen anyone out of the ordinary today, either in the office or at the meeting.

Carrie's smile slipped and she frowned. "I'm afraid not."

He frowned now, her words not making sense. Had she implied he was lying?

"I'm sorry," he said and held out the cup but she didn't move to take it. "You must have me confused with someone else."

"I don't think so."

He felt disorientated and didn't like it. "I'm sorry, Carrie, but this doesn't make sense." He held the cup closer to her. "Here's your cup. I need to take a bath as I'm going out."

She didn't reach for the cup but looked towards the bathroom door.

"I didn't realise," she said carefully.

"That's okay but if you wouldn't mind leaving."

"Of course." She stepped back from the doorway. "Sorry to have bothered you."

The mood and attitude had changed and now he felt guilty for thinking the worst. "You haven't. Here, take the sugar."

"You're so understanding," she said and stepped into the kitchen. She took the cup. "I mean, I could be anyone, couldn't I?"

His suspicions raced back. "Eh?"

"Who's Barbara Gilbert, Peter?"

A chill rippled up his arms. Who was this woman and what did she want with him?

"I don't know Barbara Gilbert."

Carrie flung the cup and it hit him just below his left eye.

He staggered back. The cup smashed on the floor. He put a hand to his eye and his heart hammered. Fear fogged his thoughts and his throat constricted so he couldn't take a full breath. Everything felt confused, like he'd stumbled into something while only being half-awake. He moved his hand and opened his eye carefully. It stung.

Carrie stood right in front of him smiling and punched him hard in the gut. He folded over her arm as his breath whooshed out. He coughed.

She stepped forward and he dropped to his knees as he desperately tried to suck in air. The edges of his vision darkened. He gasped and watched her socked feet, the right one quietly tapping out a rhythm.

"I punched you in the solar plexus so your diaphragm's gone into spasm and you're winded. I didn't hit you hard but you're not in the best of shape so if you calm down, it'll steady and you'll be able to breathe again."

He couldn't calm down because he couldn't draw in enough air. He felt panic fizz through his head. Tears ran down his cheeks.

"While I have your attention," she said, as calmly as if they were in a coffee shop deciding what to drink, "I'll ask you again. Who's Barbara Gilbert?"

Peter looked up but couldn't speak.

"Wow, you're in worse shape than I thought. I'll make my questions yes or no answers, so either nod or shake your head."

It hurt to breathe in. He nodded gently.

"You collided with her today in the Newborough Centre car park." She pulled on a pair of latex gloves she'd taken from her pocket.

"I did collide with a woman but I have no idea who she was."

"Did she give you the asset when she knocked the papers out of your hands?"

He shook his head. She kicked him and her left heel jabbed his knee. Pain shot through his leg and if he'd had the breath he would have howled. Instead, he fell onto his side, one hand on his belly, one on his knee. He swallowed back bile, worried he'd choke if he vomited.

"Try again," she said.

He shook his head and watched her foot move. He let go of his belly to hold his hand up in defence.

"Please," he whimpered.

"Barbara had an asset in her possession and we want it back. When my colleague caught up with her, she no longer had the asset. You were a point of contact."

"She didn't give me anything," he gasped. He took a few breaths as the pain in his stomach eased. "She bumped into me and knocked my stuff flying then ran off."

"Well that's a shame. Come on, let me help you up." She held out her hand and pulled him to his feet. "How are you feeling?"

"How do you think? I want you to go now." He propped himself up by holding the worktop. Just out of reach was a small plastic tub filled with kitchen utensils.

She pursed her lips. "That's not very neighbourly."

"Neither was the punch."

"They never are."

He swept his right hand along the work surface and pushed the plastic tub at Carrie. Some of the utensils – a couple of wooden spoons, a potato masher and a spaghetti fork – came loose. Carrie shielded her eyes then grabbed his wrist and yanked down and sideways. Peter felt something snap in his wrist and cried out in pain. She pulled him across her and turned her hip, catapulting him out of the kitchen. He hit the back wall hard enough to dislodge a picture.

She grabbed the lapels of his dressing gown and pulled him to her. Peter didn't know whether to defend his face or hit out. He swung a punch and it jarred against her temple. She grunted and pushed him away but held onto his dressing gown and it slipped off his shoulders. He staggered naked into the bathroom and the backs of his knees hit the edge of the bath. His centre of gravity shifted and he cried out as he fell.

* * *

The man went into the bath and Munro pushed against his shoulders. His head went under and he tried to writhe free but had no leverage. She counted to twenty then pulled him up. Spluttering, he spat water at her.

"You dirty bastard," she said and wiped her face angrily. "Where is the asset Barbara gave you?"

He shook his head and grabbed for her hands. "I don't know who you mean."

She pushed him under again and he thrashed futilely for another twenty seconds. When she pulled him back up he gasped in breath, coughing and choking.

"Where is it?"

"I don't know," he yelled.

He went for her face and she felt his fingers press against her cheeks and temples. She pushed him under again. His movements were sluggish now and when she pulled him back up, he coughed out even more water.

"I don't know," he gasped. "I really don't know."

She could see in his eyes he wasn't lying.

"That's a shame," she said and pushed him under again. It didn't take long for him to stop thrashing.

Munro stood up and smoothed her blouse. She checked her reflection in the mirror to make sure he hadn't marked her face but it seemed clear.

Although she believed he'd told the truth, she checked through the flat thoroughly and methodically. The kitchen, lounge and bedroom were all clear. The package wasn't there.

She checked the bathroom last but the sickly-sweet smell of death and shit was almost overpowering. She went into the hall and saw his briefcase against the wall. She opened it and pulled out a messy sheaf of papers then checked the pouches. One held a small box. She took it out and opened it to find an expensive-looking engagement ring glittering at her.

"Poor Peter's girlfriend," she muttered and took her phone from her pocket.

Keel answered immediately. "And?"

"Mr Lewis doesn't have the asset."

"Did Mr Lewis tell you this?"

"I asked him and I checked."

"And where is he?"

"Cooling off in the bath."

"Right. I'm about ten minutes from the second contact, the traffic is a bitch."

"Must be people heading for the fireworks."

"That's what I thought. Make your way to me and I'll see you later."

Munro slipped the mobile into her pocket and went out into the corridor. She pulled Peter's front door closed, put on her boots and jacket, picked up her backpack and went downstairs.

The pavements were busy with families walking towards the town centre and the roads were crammed like rush hour. She walked three hundred yards and passed two bins before she disposed of the latex gloves.


# Chapter 5


Rachel opened the door to see Tilly beaming a smile.

"Hi, Mummy, can I do some more colouring for school?"

Confused, Rachel stepped to one side so her daughter could come in. Tilly held up her left hand and Rachel absently high-fived her, casually hooking her right forefinger through the loop on the top of the little girl's backpack. In a well-practised move, Tilly put her arms back so she could keep going.

Holding the bag, Rachel leaned into the corridor. Glen leaned against the wall to her right with a sheepish expression on his face.

"Hey," he said.

The disappointment felt physical, as if she had to swallow it down before she could speak.

"What?" she said.

He shrugged and his sheepish expression faded into a grin. "Something came up."

Disappointment morphed into anger. "Came up?"

He rubbed his hands together. "You know how it is."

"No," she said slowly through clenched teeth. "I don't."

Glen came towards her. "It's only one night."

"It's my night, Glen, to do what I want and for you to take some parental responsibility."

She saw his eyes drop to take in the open neck of her dressing gown and she pinched it together.

"I know that," he said. "I'll make it up to you, I promise."

"When did a promise ever mean anything to you?"

"Ouch." He feigned surprise but she'd seen that hurt expression before and it didn't phase her in the slightest. It might have, once, but too much water had passed under that bridge.

"Don't bother, Glen, seriously."

"Are you going to invite me in?"

"Do I have to?" she said and then felt Tilly against her leg.

"Come and see my colouring, Daddy."

"Sounds good, princess." He smiled at Rachel and edged past her through the door.

With a frustrated growl, Rachel closed the door and followed her daughter and ex-husband into the lounge. Tilly stood by the table.

"We could have a tea party if you're thirsty?"

"Oh God, no," he said. "Let's just see your drawing."

Tilly looked first at her Little Buddies tea set then her drawings and finally at Glen. He smiled at her. She sat on the floor with her feet under the coffee table as she spread some drawings out for him. He knelt beside her.

"That's an excellent unicorn," he said. He didn't sound enthusiastic.

Tilly looked up at him and frowned. "That's Ellie, from my class."

"Oh," said Glen. He looked at Rachel and raised his eyebrows. "Looks like a unicorn to me."

Rachel glared at him, wishing he'd just bugger off.

"I suppose I'd better ring Nat then, eh?"

"Why's that?"

"Because I'm going out with Nat."

He looked vaguely interested. "Anywhere nice?"

She leaned closer to him and whispered. "It could have been the greatest place ever but since its contingent on you looking after your daughter like you're supposed to, we'll never know."

Tilly looked at him and waved her pen.

"Like you were supposed to," she said with a big frown. "Now I can't sleep in the special bed."

Glen held his hands, palms out. "I'll make it up, princess, I promise."

"Don't…" said Rachel quietly.

Glen shifted so he held his hands up to Rachel. "I'm sorry, okay?"

She couldn't hide her annoyance that he seemed to be treating this like some big joke.

"No, it's really not okay. What's so bloody important anyway?"

Tilly shot her a disapproving look. "You said a swear, Mum."

"I'm sorry."

"Shouldn't do it," Tilly said and went back to her drawing.

"So what is it, Glen? Old friend in town for the night or some mate hosting an open mic?"

"Oh," he said and nodded as if he'd expected the comment. "Now you're knocking the comedy?"

"No, I'm knocking your ability to apparently only find gigs when they inconvenience me."

"Not cool, Rache. Anyway, can't you ask someone else?"

His casual disregard never failed to astound her.

"Oh yes, just ring them up at seven o'clock and see if they're willing to take my daughter for the night?"

"Naomi would help out."

Tilly looked at Rachel with a big smile on her face. "Can I stay with Naomi and Anya?"

Rachel rolled her eyes at Glen. "Nice one," she muttered.

"Please?" Tilly begged.

Glen looked at his watch. "Listen, girls, I have to get going. I'm really sorry to drop you in it like this but, you know…"

"Please can we call Naomi? Can I call her?"

Glen got to his feet, dropped a kiss on Tilly's head and stood in front of Rachel.

"Go on, give Naomi a ring."

Rachel narrowed her eyes. "You never told me the reason," she said quietly.

"Open mic night," he said and stepped around her. "I'll see myself out. Catch you at the weekend, princess."

Tilly jumped up and raced out of the lounge and, as Rachel listened to her daughter plaster kiss after kiss on Glen, she got her phone from her bag and rang her friend.

\* \* \*

Keel's progress slowed considerably when he began to see signs for 'Fireworks On The Common'. He checked Hadlington Common on his phone and realised the road went straight by it.

He took a side road in an effort to keep moving, because the sooner he got to the woman, the better.

The traffic came to a standstill and Keel drummed his fingers on the wheel to calm himself. He'd been in this profession long enough to know that the minute he allowed base emotions to take hold he was done for. Control allowed him to make the necessary clear-headed decisions. He'd seen too many people – friends and colleagues as well as enemies – collapse when they needed to be strong; getting hurt or, on occasion, killed. His first mentor, an ex-SAS sergeant called Llewellyn, had taught him this and Keel was there when the man forgot his own advice. Seeing Llewellyn's body slump against the wall, a spray of blood painting the brickwork in an arc from a large hole in his head, haunted Keel's snatched moments of sleep for days afterwards. Sometimes, even now years later, the image still had the power to wake him.

Munro, his apprentice of sorts, hadn't quite got it yet and still fed on anger which sometimes pushed her into situations she didn't need to be in.

* * *

"Rachel, it's fine."

Rachel sighed and took a deep breath. She knew Naomi, one of her oldest and dearest friends, didn't mind and her daughter, Anya, got on well with Tilly but it still felt like admitting to some kind of personal failure.

"You're a star."

"Hardly," Naomi said. "You'd do the same for me in this kind of situation. My only plans for tonight were to take Anya to the fireworks and then perhaps toast some marshmallows when we got back. Tilly will fit right in. Anyway, I'm fully aware of Glen's shortcomings. So where are you going?"

"Nat's taking me to a party to do with a course she's on at work."

"What time are you going?"

Rachel turned so she could see the clock on her bedside cabinet. "I need to be there for seven thirty."

"Not a problem then. I'll be there in ten minutes, okay?"

"That would be wonderful, thank you." Her friend couldn't be any more of a lifesaver if she tried.

Tilly came into the bedroom. "Are you going to the party dressed like that?"

Rachel looked at herself in the mirror. The towel was still wrapped around her head.

"Hardly, sweetheart."

"Good. Can I borrow your phone? I want to take a picture."

"It's in my bag but make sure you put it back, you forgot last time."

Tilly tilted her head and frowned. "I do know, Mum. I'm six, not five."

"Of course you are."

\* \* \*

Keel was stopped at a zebra crossing which seemed to have a steady stream of people using it.

He'd been so sure the contact would be Lewis, especially with the man's briefcase a textbook drop – casual flick of the wrist, paper distracting attention – people wouldn't see unless they looked intently. Barbara Gilbert's only other point of contact was the woman, Rachel Turner.

Keel's phone rang.

"Mr Wilson?"

"What's the situation, Keel?"

"Munro intercepted Peter Lewis but he didn't have the asset. She's dealt with him and I'm on the way to Rachel Turner."

"We've tracked her across social media but it appears she and Barbara Gilbert don't have a link."

"Not at all?" Keel frowned. "That doesn't make any sense."

"Maybe once she realised you were after her she just wanted rid of the asset. Perhaps Ms Turner might not even know she has it."

"Unfortunately for her."

* * *

"Naomi's here! I'll get the door!"

Rachel stared at herself in the mirror as Tilly rushed into the hall and pulled open the door. After a moment of silence, she and Anya shrieked each other's names and then the footsteps pounded back towards the lounge.

"Alright?" Naomi called as she walked into the lounge.

"Be out in a sec," Rachel said.

"Naomi, did you want a cup of tea?" Tilly said. "And look at this picture I've done."

"That's very nice," Naomi said. "I like her dress."

"It's Ellie, from school, but Daddy thought she was a unicorn."

"That's because daddies sometimes can't see things like little girls can."

"I took a picture of it so I can email it to Ellie."

"Couldn't you take the picture in to school tomorrow to show her?"

"But then she can't see it tonight."

"Of course."

Rachel went into the lounge. Naomi knelt between the two little girls while Tilly showed her the drawings and Anya poured pretend tea into small plastic cups.

"So," Rachel said and all three turned.

Tilly stuck up her thumb and went back to her drawing.

"Very pretty," said Anya and Rachel smiled. It appeared her black dress and black tights combo was a winner.

"You look fine," said Naomi and stood up. "How are you getting to the party?"

"I was going to book a taxi," Rachel said. "It's on the other side of town."

"Well I'll drop you off. Come on."

"Really?" Naomi's lifesaving skills had moved up a class now.

Rachel grabbed her handbag and made sure her keys were secure. "Have you got your bag, Tilly?"

As if taken by surprise, Tilly gasped, jumped up and raced into the hall, coming back with her Little Buddies backpack.

"Ready to go," she said.

"Come on," said Naomi as she favoured Rachel with a smile and herded the girls out of the door. "We'll let Mum lock up while we go to the car."

* * *

Keel made up time once he'd passed the Common and barrelled along the centre of the road on the back streets pushing the Range Rover hard.

Bursts of fireworks lit up the sky, a jolly battle painting the car bonnet in an array of colours.

He glanced at the satnav, saw how close he was and put his foot down.

* * *

The evening had got colder.

Naomi had the engine running with the girls strapped into booster seats. Rachel got in, relieved the heater was on.

"Who wants to go to the fireworks then?" Naomi asked.

As the girls cheered, Naomi pulled out of the parking space and drove down the driveway. At the pavement she indicated left and stopped. Rachel watched a black Range Rover come racing up the centre of the road.

"Bloody hell, he's moving," she said.

From the back seat she heard a whispered "You said a swear."

At the last moment the Range Rover pulled in quickly and rushed by Naomi's car.

"He's in a hurry," Naomi said and pulled out into the road.

\* \* \*

Keel pulled on latex gloves as he walked from the car park round to the front door. He checked the bell panel and pressed the top four buttons. No response. He pressed the next four.

"Yeah?"

"Hi, is that Jamie?"

"No, it's Michael." The voice sounded very young.

"Hi, Michael, how're you? This is Oliver. I live in the flat below you but I've forgotten my key. Can you let me in please?"

"Yeah, okay."

"Thank you, Michael."

The door buzzed and Keel opened it. He quickly went up to the third floor and stopped outside Rachel's flat. He pressed the doorbell and counted to ten. There was no response. He tried again, counting to thirty. No response.

He checked his watch. If she'd taken her daughter to the fireworks he might have just missed her. Perhaps she'd been in the car he passed as he pulled in.

He rang Munro.

"Did she have it?"

"I don't know. I got caught in the traffic and her flat is empty."

"Maybe she's out with the kid."

"Could be. Are there any good pictures of Rachel on her social media?"

"Two or three full face ones."

He retraced his steps back to the foyer. "She has no apparent connection to Barbara Gilbert which might suggest the package was planted and our lady has no idea what she's got. I think the best way to proceed is to make that assumption."

"Assumption is–"

"What's going to get us through this evening," said Keel. "You're local. Do you know a team you could pull together quickly?"

"How many would you be thinking of?"

"Two or three? Smart people who are good and sharp if they need to move quickly."

"I could get some names. Are we anticipating violence?"

"From the profile I'd say no but it wouldn't hurt to be prepared." He opened the front door. "Pull off the most recent picture you can find, ideally with both Rachel and her daughter, and send it to your crew. Tell them to get to as many displays in town as they can. Walk the crowds and keep their eyes open. Bonus for the one who spots her."

"And what're we going to do?"

"After you get here, we're going to wait for Rachel to come home."

# Chapter 6

Maley didn't join Pippa in the management offices of the Newborough Centre until the body had been taken away by the ambulance. From the bag found nearby it appeared she was Mrs Barbara Gilbert, but until there was a formal identification that couldn't be confirmed.

Pippa had already interviewed the cleaner and now Olga Bisera sat at a desk in the corner, hunched in on herself with a blanket over her shoulders. She held a cup of tea with both hands and looked terrified. A worried-looking first aider hovered behind her.

Olga didn't have much to tell. She had taken her usual shortcut down the stairwell, been alerted by the terrible smell and found the body. She'd rushed back upstairs to report it to her supervisor who'd informed Chris Wood.

Pippa sat with a CCTV technician who seemed very squeamish about the role she'd been asked to perform. It took them almost half an hour before they saw Barbara Gilbert make her entrance into the centre. Different cameras followed her up the escalators and into a shop.

"Does it look like she's hurrying?" Wood asked.

"Hard to tell," Pippa replied.

"She's not dawdling," said the technician.

Maley leaned in to get a better view.

"She looks like someone who'd rather not be shopping whilst the place is packed," he observed.

It took a while to find her again on one of the upper-level feeds. When she came out of the shop there was a man close behind her wearing a cap and dark winter jacket.

"Who's that?" asked Maley. "Centre security, perhaps?"

"No one I know," said Wood. "That's not our uniform."

"The hat hides his face well," said Pippa.

Maley turned and levelled his finger at her. "Good call. Can we track back to see him come into the centre?"

"Are you suggesting he might have something to do with it?" asked Wood.

Maley shrugged. "It might be a coincidence but it's always worth following these things up."

"It might just be a member of the public who spotted something, got curious and followed her," said Pippa.

"I'll check," said the technician.

It didn't take long because the man in the cap occupied the same catchment areas as Barbara, just a few seconds behind her. Unfortunately, the hat brim hid his face all the time. They went back to the upper-level footage but the door wasn't used again in the hours' worth of footage the technician sped through.

"He didn't come back out that way then," said Pippa.

"What about the CCTV on the other side?" asked Maley. "I know there are no cameras in the stairwell but can we see the entry points from the outside, who went in and came out?"

"Certainly," said the technician. Knowing the timestamp of when Barbara went through the first door, she checked the cameras on the other side from the same time.

"Nobody should really be in there," said Wood. "It's not a public thoroughfare."

Maley nodded but didn't say anything. Minutes passed as the technician fast-forwarded through the footage and then stopped suddenly when Pippa said, "There!"

A woman appeared in a corridor with curly hair and carrying a handbag. She wore what looked like leggings and a T-shirt. The woman came down the corridor towards the camera then opened a door and disappeared from sight.

"Who's that?" asked Maley.

"I didn't recognise her," said Wood, "but that doesn't necessarily mean anything."

"She looked like she was dressed for the gym," said Pippa.

"Maybe she'd just been," said the technician and looked sheepishly at Wood. "I go to the place next to here sometimes and when I'm done with my classes, I cut through and use the stairs down to the car park."

The tape played on until Olga appeared. They didn't find any more CCTV footage of the man in the cap.

# Chapter 7

Jack Martin was trapped.

The woman who might have been called Ellen or Helen – he hadn't caught it properly over the sound of the stereo even though he'd asked her twice – had cornered him near the top of the stairs. He had his back to the wall and she wobbled between him and the banister so anyone coming along the landing had to negotiate around her.

"So what is it you do?" she asked.

"I work in finance, that's why I'm on the course."

"What course?" As she leaned closer, her wine glass tipped at such an angle it seemed only a matter of time before her entire drink slopped onto the carpet.

"At the college," he said. "The one that's almost finished so we're having this farewell party."

He hadn't wanted to come up for the course but the company he worked for had just been swallowed up by an American concern, so he wasn't given the choice. Which is how he found himself staying four lonely nights at the Hadley Hall Hotel while attending a five-day course at Hadlington Technical College.

Nat had arranged the party as they sat in the refectory and tried to eat the lousy lasagne. He liked her, a funny and flirty thirty-something who'd impressed him with her knowledge of the Sarbanes–Oxley Act and he got caught up in her excitement. He'd had to make his nightly call to Luisa earlier but now wished he was back in that boring hotel room.

"I don't know what you mean," said Ellen or Helen. Some wine escaped to stain the carpet.

"You're, um…" he said and pointed to her hand.

She looked and shifted the glass.

"Thanks," she said, the word tapering into a sibilant sigh.

"Our course finishes tomorrow." Why was he even bothering to explain?

"I'm not doing a course."

"I know."

She frowned. "My head aches a bit."

"Did you want to sit down, Helen?"

"Ellen," she corrected him. "I think I'll go to the loo. Hold my wine."

He only just caught it. She staggered along the landing towards the bathroom door so he put her glass down against the skirting board and went downstairs.

\* \* \*

Nat had properly undersold the scale of the party.

Half a dozen people stood in the small front garden of the mid-terrace house and Rachel could hear the music pumping from inside even from across the road. So much for the "small gathering". Rachel manoeuvred through the front door and pushed her way past the knot of people in the hallway. She checked the lounge and dining room without finding Nat so she went into the kitchen and saw her friend though the window as she stood in the yard.

"Hey, Rachel, so glad you made it."

Waving her cigarette like someone trying to guide in a plane, Nat pulled Rachel into a heavy embrace and Rachel held her, enjoying the closeness. She missed adult-sized hugs. Tilly did it often, as hard as she could, but each one felt fleeting and never long enough for Rachel to properly enjoy.

"I said I would," she said into her friend's frizzy blonde hair.

"It's good to see you."

They caught up while Nat finished her cigarette then went back into the kitchen and got a glass of wine each. The combination of a drink and standing out in the cold had got to Rachel and she excused herself to go to the toilet.

By the time she'd got back, threading her way through more people than she'd have thought possible to be on a college course, Nat was standing by the sink and pouring a drink as she talked to a tall, thin man with dark hair greying at the temples. He wore a long-sleeved checked shirt, black chinos and dark trainers.

\* \* \*

The chill of the night air pinched at Keel's cheeks as he stood at the kerb. There were no pedestrians on the street. Cars lined both sides of the road and most of the houses had lights in their ground floor windows. A few bedroom lights were on. There was a pocket park situated across the road from Rachel's building. Beyond the park he could see houses on the next street over and what appeared to be an old factory of some kind. To his right, Moore Avenue rose up to meet another road. All the streetlights he could see worked.

He pulled his hood up and walked to the end of the street checking for CCTV cameras. None were immediately visible but they might be hidden and he couldn't afford to take any chances. He walked back to Rachel's building and stood in front of it.

Converted from what had once been a grand residence, it looked sturdy and imposing. The top floor flats had balconies and the corner one closest to him had what looked like a tent set up behind the railing. Most of the windows had the curtains pulled across them. Thin trees had been planted at the inside edge of the pavement, along the property line, and a scruffy hedge grew wildly just behind them. A wide driveway led to a car parking area on the left of the building where a row of trees marked the border of the house next door.

There was a lot of potential for him to be spotted and he didn't like it.

* * *

Jack had found Nat in the kitchen pouring a generous glass of wine while holding a bottle of Magners. Half a dozen people he didn't know milled about. When Nat saw him she smiled widely.

"Hey, you." Her eyes were bright. "Drink?"

"Not for me thanks, I'm driving remember?"

"Of course, you're heading home tomorrow."

"I am."

"I've been looking for my friend. I appear to have lost her." She looked around as if searching for the missing person.

Jack looked at his watch and was surprised to see it was after ten. Ellen or Helen had obviously talked for longer than he'd thought.

"I'm going to get off."

"Why?" Confusion flashed across her face. "Aren't you having fun?"

"Well, I don't really know many people here."

"You know me," she said.

"I do, but unless that Magners is also for you, you're taking it to someone."

"Might be." She giggled. "Actually, maybe you could do me a favour? Could you try and find Rachel?" He must have looked blank. "You know, my friend?"

"Rachel, you said. But I don't know who she is."

"We're supposed to go home together but, well, Al and I have hit it off and I might not be going home tonight. I don't want Rachel to walk or get a taxi on her own."

"So how will she get home?" he asked, though he already thought he knew.

"Could you take her? I know I'm being annoying but you're a good bloke and you're safe."

"Oh." The word had an oddly deflating feel to it. "Nat, I really don't know what she looks like."

"Lovely curly red hair. She's about five eight or so and slim. Pretty too." She looked over his shoulder. "Like her, in fact."

Jack turned to see a woman answering Nat's description looking at them quizzically. He smiled.

"Take care of her, won't you?" Nat said. She put down the wine bottle and picked up her glass.

"I'll talk to her," Jack said.

"You're a good man," said Nat and then she was gone.

Jack turned. "Hi," he said. "This honestly isn't a chat-up line but are you Rachel?"

"Who wants to know?"

"Me. Nat was just saying about you."

"Has she hooked up with someone?"

He nodded. "Someone called Al. I think she took his drink out into the yard."

"Marvellous," she said and shook her head. "Yes, I'm Rachel Turner, professional gooseberry. Nat's having a year as a dedicated singleton."

"And you keep getting caught out by it?"

She smiled and he liked it. "More often than you'd think."

He laughed and she joined him. Her laugh was soft and melodic. If the situation were different, he could imagine being interested in her – a pretty woman with high cheekbones and gleaming eyes.

"I'm Jack," he said, "Jack Martin."

"Hello, Jack Martin," she said and they shook hands. "So are you on this mythical course?"

"I am. I'm a stranger in a strange land. I sit next to Nat and she convinced me to come but I don't really know many people."

"So where are you from?"

"Bristol. How about you?"

"Hadlington born and bred. Nat and I have known one another for years and usually go out for a drink or a meal when I'm child-free, but tonight she invited me here."

"At least you know people then."

She smiled again. "No one other than her."

"And now me," he said and held up his glass of Diet Coke. "I'm Jack."

"Cheers, Jack." She touched his glass then took a sip of her wine. "So, what about you? Are you married?"

"I am." He held his left hand up for her to see then immediately felt stupid for doing so. "To Luisa, for ten years. How about you? You mentioned being child-free this evening?"

She pursed her lips. "Divorced."

"Sorry to hear that."

"Don't be. Compared to some horror stories I've heard, I had it painless." She finished her wine. "I'll be honest, I noticed your ring when you were talking to Nat and it's nice to talk to someone not angling for a date."

He frowned. "You're the second person to say I was safe in as many minutes."

She tilted her head and pulled a face. "Oh dear."

"I know," he said, nodding gravely. "It feels like I'm going to seed or something."

"Sorry," she said with a smile.

"Forgiven. I am safe but it'd make me feel cooler if you didn't point it out."

She laughed. "I'll try to remember."

\* \* \*

Keel stood at the entrance to the park.

He'd left the Range Rover a few car lengths down and debated getting back into it to wait for Munro but knew he wouldn't have as clear a sight on Rachel's building. The park would be better. He gently pushed the gate open and it squeaked slightly. A border of grass led to dark spongy flooring and he could make out the shapes of a see-saw, roundabout and a small slide. Ahead, three swings hung on a frame. There was a gap where the fourth should have been. He sat on the swing nearest to Rachel's. In the dark with his black Parka, he'd be as good as invisible should anyone walk by, though no one had since he'd arrived.

A rocket screamed into the air from behind the factory and dogs barked at its progress. It exploded and the lights cast his flickering shadow across the grass.

\* \* \*

Rachel enjoyed the evening despite herself.

She and Jack clearly felt at ease with each other and their light conversation was peppered with laughs.

They'd moved out of the kitchen and ended up in the hallway. Rachel tucked herself into a corner near the understairs cupboard and Jack stood in front of her, close enough to put off blokes looking to practise their chat-up lines but with enough distance for her to feel comfortable.

When she yawned, Jack checked his watch.

"I'm not usually this much of a lightweight," she said.

"I am." He smiled. "It's late. Would you mind if we called it a night?"

"Of course not."

"I've enjoyed chatting with you but the course starts at nine and I have trouble keeping my eyes open to the end of the lectures at the best of times. Then I've got a long journey ahead of me."

"With Nat buggering off, I'd have left a while ago if I wasn't chatting to you."

His eyes widened in surprise. "If you'd said, we could have both gone."

She laughed.

"Nat suggested I might give you a lift home," he said.

"I don't mind getting a taxi."

"So long as you tell me how to get back to the hotel from your place, I'll drive you."

Rachel patted his arm gently. "That's the least I could do, I'll get my coat."

"I'll find Nat, tell her I'm taking you back."

She went upstairs, eventually found her coat under the pile in the front bedroom and Jack stood by the front door waiting when she got back.

"I can't find Nat anywhere," he said.

"Don't worry, I'll text her later."

"Let's go then," he said and pulled open the front door.

# Chapter 8

Keel watched his breath cloud and fade. It felt like he'd been sitting here for hours and he was beginning to feel the cold.

A car pulled up and he snapped to attention. He couldn't see the vehicle but it had come up Moore Avenue from the right and stopped somewhere before the park, perhaps behind his Range Rover.

A door opened, creaked, and then closed quietly. The faintest of footsteps, no more than the sound of gravel under soles. Someone was moving carefully and clearly trying to be quiet.

Tensed, Keel stood up and held the swing so the chain didn't make any noise.

The footsteps came closer. He waited.

Munro came into sight through the railings. Keel moved across the safety matting and onto the grass as she stopped and looked around. He cleared his throat quietly and startled her. She turned quickly to look into the park but it was obvious she couldn't quite see him.

"How did you get here?" he asked.

She let out a breath. "Too far to walk," she said, her head still moving as she tried to spot him. "A friend of mine runs a ringer operation and I know where he keeps the keys so I helped myself to a vehicle."

"Inventive."

"Always," she said and smiled as she finally saw him. She came into the park and they moved towards the swings together. "Any news at this end?"

He shook his head as she checked her watch. "No and you'd assume they'd be back by now. Even if she didn't go to the fireworks and Rachel went out with friends, it's a school night so chances are she's probably going to come home."

"Unless," said Munro and looked squarely at him, "she gets lucky."

"In which case she enjoys a very pleasant evening and we have an uncomfortable one sitting here."

\* \* \*

Apart from a few pubs they passed with knots of people having a smoke break outside, the centre of Hadlington seemed as though it had closed down for the night. Some hardy revellers made their way home sharing the pavement with dog walkers but the streets were increasingly empty.

Rachel directed well and Jack tried to keep certain landmarks in mind – a big old boarded-up cinema along one street and a church on another that appeared to have been converted into a pub – so he could retrace his route. His hotel was on the other side of town and the one-way system seemed to follow little, if any, logic and he didn't want to spend his night driving around in circles.

They passed a taxi rank on Market Street. Two people stood under the canopy smoking cigarettes and watched the car go by like wolves tracking prey. Behind them a firework exploded over the buildings in a silent mass of colours.

"Fireworks go on late here," he said.

"Just the idiots." She glanced at the dashboard clock. "Oh God, it is late isn't it? I feel really guilty getting you to drop me off. You'll be like a zombie tomorrow."

He smiled. "Don't worry. I'll pretend I'm working and bluff my way through any questions. We're finishing at lunchtime."

"And you're heading straight home?"

"Absolutely. If I can skip the traffic at Oxford and Swindon, I should be on the M4 before rush hour starts."

"You have it all planned out then?"

"To the second. I like a good plan."

"Me too," she said and smiled at him. "So did the week go as you'd planned?"

"Not really. I didn't want to come. I don't like being away from home and, to be honest, if Nat hadn't taken me under her wing, I'm not sure I'd have stayed." He wanted to say more but didn't know if he could. "In fact – and please don't take this the wrong way, I'm really not hitting on you – but meeting you has been a real highlight. Chatting with you has probably been the easiest conversation I've had all week."

"Oh," she said, clearly touched. "Thank you. If it's any consolation, I didn't want to go to the party either. I've had a crappy day so meeting you has been my high point too."

"Look at us, a couple of highlights."

"We could be hairdressers!" she declared and they both laughed. "Have you always lived in Bristol?"

"For a good while. I went to university there and it's Luisa's hometown."

"So what do you do in your spare time?"

"I do a bit of fell running and orienteering."

"That's very energetic. I manage the odd parkrun."

"It's all exercise," he said. "I've just joined a group that organises night runs through woods, which is quite exciting. Often, all you can see is what's in the beam of your torch and it's both bloody frightening and weirdly exhilarating. You have to sign a disclaimer first, in case you break your leg."

"I'm not sure exciting and exhilarating are words I'd use."

He laughed. "And how about you?"

"Work and being a mum accounts for a huge amount of my day but I've been taking self-defence classes for a while."

"Not a bad idea. To look after yourself or to keep fit?"

"A bit of both." She paused and looked up. "I had an incident a while back and decided I wasn't going to get caught out like that again."

He glanced over. She had a faraway look in her eyes and he decided not to push it.

"So you were at the party because of Nat too?"

Rachel looked at him slowly as if coming out of a trance. "Uh-huh. We've been friends for years. Her relationship ended last year and she took it much more in her stride than I did. Though she doesn't have any kids."

"Can't have been easy, especially with children."

"Child," she corrected him. "My little girl Tilly."

"How old is she?"

"Six."

"Was she out at a fireworks display tonight?"

"Yes, with friends." She pulled her lips tight. "Glen, my ex, had planned to take her but like he often does, he found a reason to cancel."

"That doesn't sound good."

"No, it's… He's her dad, you know, so I have to be careful what I say, but he wore the tarnish off the 'great bloke' label years ago for me. Unfortunately, I can now see a similar kind of disregard creeping in with how he treats Tilly."

"That's a shame."

She shrugged as if to say 'what can you do?'. "Do you have any?"

"Not yet, but they're definitely part of our plan."

"They're definitely worth it," she said. "Turn right here."

Jack indicated even though he hadn't passed another car for some time. Montagu Street was short and narrow with traffic lights at the end.

"You won't be able to come back this way," Rachel said. "But the road we join, if you follow it back, will take you through to the hotel."

"Thanks."

* * *

Keel checked his watch and wondered how much truth there might be in Munro's earlier flippant comment. If they were going to pull an overnighter then now would be the time to get some stimulants.

"How are you feeling?" he asked.

Munro jumped at the sound of his voice. She'd been sitting quietly on the swing with her arms folded and now dry-washed her hands as she fought back a yawn.

"Okay," she said.

"Why don't you grab us some coffee? I noticed a Costa drive-through near the cinema on the other side of the centre and that'll probably still be open."

She held the swing chains steady and got up then rocked her head from side to side.

"Good idea."

"I'll call if I need you."

"Please do. After freezing my arse off all this time, I want to be here when we recover the asset from Rachel Turner."

# Chapter 9

An explosion of colour caught Pippa Vincent's eye.

Glancing out of the window of the police station at the fading splendour, she saw other explosions light up the sky as if trying to create a pattern. The great and the good of Hadlington had clearly come home from the pub and decided now was the absolute perfect time to set off their own little displays. The idiots.

Pippa sat alone in the open-plan office. Most of the shift had been called out to deal with the usual Bonfire Night chaos – fireworks used as weapons; displays getting out of hand and fires being set deliberately by little toerags who wanted to ambush fire engines. She'd spent the evening at her desk on the third floor. Three walls of windows gave her a panoramic firework display people would have gladly paid to see, and she still hated the whole thing.

She touched the two-inch length of scar tissue on the back of her left hand and felt a shiver run through her. It was ten years ago when she was in her early teens. Her mum and dad let her go to the display on the common and some lads threw a firework at her friend Sonia. Rachel put out a hand to save her and the fuse burned her hand badly. The boys ran away and Pippa had hated fireworks ever since.

"Working hard?" asked Maley as he came through the double doors carrying two plastic cups of tea.

He'd gone to see the inspector on their return to the station while she started to write up her notes. He put a cup on the corner of her desk and settled himself in the chair across from her. He sipped from his own cup and winced.

"What do they make this stuff with?" he muttered. "Blood, sweat and–"

"Tears?" she finished for him. It was an old joke he made almost every time he got her a drink.

"You know me too well," he said with a broad smile. Another firework went off, drawing his attention. "Still not enjoying them?"

"Not in the slightest, Sarge."

He glanced quickly at her hand. "My kids used to love the pretty lights and loud bangs."

"I didn't and now I always seem to pull duty on Bonfire Night."

"It's like you're cursed, Pippa." He nodded towards her desk. "So how's it going with our suspected suicide?"

"I'm almost done with the report."

"The inspector's moving things along," said Maley. He tried another mouthful of his tea but it still made him wince. "I really should wait until this crap cools down."

"Family Liaison has been on. They spoke with Mr Gilbert and, as you could well expect, he took it very badly. He had no idea why she would do it and wasn't aware of any issues in either her private or professional life."

Pippa's radio squawked out a hiss of static and she touched the volume button. A pickpocket had been caught working the big display at the common.

Maley raised his eyebrows. "If they caught him, think how many they missed."

"You're such a cynic."

"I've been in the game too long."

# Chapter 10

Jack turned into Moore Avenue.

"If you go to the end," Rachel said, "you'll get to the link road. Or you can head back the way you came and follow the signs for the train station."

"I'll do the latter. I might recognise landmarks then."

"Anywhere around here would be great," she said.

He saw a couple of spaces ahead and pulled in at the kerb just in front of a park entrance.

"I'm over there," she said and pointed.

Jack looked across the road at a large townhouse set back with a short gravel driveway.

"Very nice."

"It's not all mine," she said and unclipped her seatbelt. "You can't even see my windows from here."

"Do you want me to walk you over?"

"No, I'll be fine, there's no one around. Anyway, you need to get back to get some sleep."

"Don't remind me," he said and she smiled. "Take care, Rachel. It's been nice to meet you."

"And you." She opened the door and the interior light shone brightly onto her cheek. "I'm sorry about calling you safe too."

He put his hand on his chest. "I should survive," he said theatrically. "But just know I was mortally wounded."

"I thought that. And thank you for not making this weird."

"Already spoken for," he said.

"That's not always the barrier you'd expect so thank you for bucking the trend. Luisa's a lucky lady." Rachel kissed him lightly on his cheek. "Thanks for the lift."

"You're welcome."

She got out and shut the door. He pulled away and she waved. He watched in the rear-view mirror as Rachel crossed the road and disappeared from sight behind a fence. At the end of the road he did a three-point turn and drove back, glancing at her building as he passed. Rachel stood on the steps at the front door, holding open her handbag as she looked into it.

A sense of movement caught his eye and he looked towards the park, swathed in the pale white-blue glow of the moon, but he saw nothing in the shadows.

He stopped at the junction to let a lone taxi rumble past then turned towards the town centre. He switched on the radio as he passed a sign for the train station and sang along with Warren Zevon about werewolves of London.

\* \* \*

Keel listened as a car pulled up just outside of his line of vision.

The engine didn't stop. A door opened and he heard the murmur of conversation, then the door closed and the car moved away. It passed by the park with a man behind the wheel. Footsteps sounded on tarmac and he watched a woman cross the road. She had curly hair.

The Vauxhall Insignia came back and slowed slightly before driving out of sight. It wasn't a taxi. Had Rachel been dropped off by a friend?

The car's engine note faded into silence and Keel stood up, holding the swing chain so it didn't rattle.

\* \* \*

Rachel was standing under the security light when she realised her keys weren't in her bag.

Her stomach dropped and she squatted on the step to check again. The keys weren't there. Neither was the Little Buddies case she'd noticed earlier or, worse, her phone.

She checked again. Had she used her phone at the party then put it down and forgotten? Did she even have her phone on her? She cast her mind back and remembered Tilly asking to send a message to Ellie.

Her finger found the tear in the seam and Rachel groaned as she sat on her haunches. Her keys could have fallen out anywhere. Did she hear them rattle when she got into the car? If they'd fallen out in there, Jack might find and return them. Or maybe they'd survived the car ride and fallen out on her walk up the driveway. It wouldn't take long to retrace her steps to the pavement and check.

\* \* \*

Keel could see Rachel on the front steps of her building. He smiled and walked briskly towards the driveway.

# Chapter 11

The traffic lights were on Jack's side and he made good time. No cars passed him, not even taxis, as though the town had decided to collectively go to bed.

A small dark shape darted from between two parked cars and he reacted on instinct to stamp the brake pedal. The tyres juddered against the tarmac and something rattled in the passenger footwell.

The cat safely raced out of sight on the other side of the road as the Insignia came to a stop. Jack gripped the steering wheel with his heart racing and realised he was lucky nothing had been behind him. He slumped back and rubbed his face then leaned across the passenger seat to see what had made the noise.

A set of keys were in the corner.

Pulling the slack in his seatbelt, he reached for them.

A PVC key ring – a colourful if badly drawn woman with the words 'Best Mummy In The World' written across the figure – held several keys and a door security fob.

Rachel was the only person who'd been in his car since Bristol. Any of the keys could be to her front door and, if they were here, she was potentially locked out.

Jack did a quick three-point turn and headed back to her house.

\* \* \*

A man came from behind the trees at the edge of the pavement and startled Rachel. She put a hand to her chest and stepped back.

"Sorry," he said. "I didn't mean to scare you."

"I know," she said, willing her breathing to steady. She felt a tingle of fear but he could be a neighbour, this wasn't necessarily a bad situation. "I just didn't expect anyone to be there."

The man held up some keys and rattled them. "Have to live somewhere."

She couldn't see clearly enough to recognise him as the nearest streetlight cast his face in shadow.

"Of course," she said cautiously.

"Do you live here too? I haven't lived here long so I hardly know anyone in the building."

"It happens." She looked back at the building. "Unfortunately, I've lost my keys."

"I can let you in, if you want."

"You're very kind, but it's all my keys."

"Well," he said. "That's careless, Rachel."

His use of her name set off a prickle of fear across her shoulders and she wished she could make out his features.

"Sorry, I can't see properly because of the light but who are you?"

"You don't know me," he said lightly and tilted his head. "But I think you have something I want."

She heard him but the words didn't make sense, each one feeling like a punch. Fear raced through her and burned out her breath. She blinked and tried to clear her mind; to keep in mind Kim's mantra from the self-defence class to stay positive. As Kim kept saying, you couldn't expect victory if you planned for defeat.

Rachel looked around desperately for options and tried to stay focussed. She could run back to the door and ring all the intercoms in the hope someone would answer but she knew it wouldn't be quick enough. She took a step back and the man matched her move. The security light came on and bleached his face white. He had short black hair, dark eyes and high cheekbones. She didn't recognise him at all.

Terror wrapped around her like a foul blanket and her skin felt clammy. She took another step back. How could she plan for victory here? She couldn't get to the road without the man being able to easily grab her and she couldn't get into the building.

But she could go round it.

Clutching her bag to her chest like some magic talisman that would shield her, she walked briskly to the corner of the building.

"Where're you going, Rachel?"

She ignored him and, once around the corner, ran. She kept to the path that hugged the building and led to the shared garden. If he chased her, she could try to outrun him and get back to the road. If he waited for her, she would try and get over the fence into the neighbours' on the next road over.

The man came after her and his heavy footsteps echoed. The sound drove her on.

Deep shadows made the block paving almost invisible and she hoped no one had left anything against the wall she might trip over. There was a slight drop from the path to the lawn at the back of the building and she jumped it to land on the grass. She kept her footing and hoped the man would fall. A compound fracture would slow him down nicely.

It wasn't until the security light – which she'd forgotten in the heat of the moment – clicked on that she realised how far across the lawn she'd run. She skidded to a halt and heard a laugh.

Rachel stood still. Her heart seemed to be beating twice as fast as usual and she couldn't get enough air into her lungs.

"Where are you going, Rachel?"

She muttered Kim's mantra and tried to remember the breathing exercises; to keep her mind clear so the moves came naturally. This is what she'd been going to the classes for, but she was terrified and all she'd learned felt just slightly out of reach, like a page that wouldn't come into focus.

Someone on the next road over set off a rocket and it soared into the air with a whine and exploded overhead. Should she call to them? What did she have to lose?

"Help!" she yelled but they let off another rocket and the scream of it buried her shout.

She would never reach the fence without getting caught which left her with the option of running again. But he was so close and with the shoes she wore she'd never outrun him.

Rachel took a deep breath in through her nose and exhaled from her mouth. She repeated it until her breathing steadied and her heart calmed. Concentrate and focus. She heard the man step off the path and knew she had to act quickly.

She feinted left but went to the right and glanced over her shoulder as the man reached for her. His flailing fingers just missed as she ran to the path. He was so close she could hear him breathing. She ran close to the building and the security light went out leaving the moonlight to paint the garden in a pale glow.

Something brushed the back of her neck and she cried out. Her breath was hot in her throat. Fingers grabbed for her shoulder but didn't properly connect. A surge of terror coursed up her arms and she pushed herself on.

Another rocket was launched and it lit the garden in a variety of colours when it exploded. The block paving shifted from orange to blue to white before the pale darkness reclaimed it.

The man's foot caught her right ankle and her feet tangled together. She stumbled and threw herself to the right, away from the wall.

* * *

Rachel hit the ground hard. She rolled onto her back, breathing heavily, and looked blankly into the sky.

Keel stopped beside her with hands on his hips as he got his breath. She'd ripped the knees of her tights and he imagined her wrists ached from where they'd taken the force of impact, but she seemed okay otherwise. Another rocket soared over the garden and exploded. He watched the colours shimmer over her face like water. She looked at him and he saw the terror in her eyes.

"You shouldn't have run," he said.

"Please don't hurt me. I haven't done anything to you."

She flinched as he squatted beside her. "I don't intend to hurt you. I just want to get back what's mine."

"But I've never met you." Panic made her voice rise.

He shushed her and looked up at the building. The windows he could see were all in darkness. The house next door was all but invisible through the trees.

"We met briefly on the stairwell at the Newborough Centre today."

She frowned. "I don't…"

"It doesn't matter. Can you stand?"

"What?"

"Did you break anything when you fell?"

Her expression became indignant. "I didn't fall, you tripped me."

"I stopped you from running away. Now keep your voice down and get to your feet."

She didn't move. "And what if I don't keep my voice down?"

He leaned forward. "Then I become unpleasant."

* * *

Rachel's indignation withered.

The man stood up and offered her his hand but she ignored him. She rotated her wrists which had jarred badly when she landed, but nothing felt broken. She rolled onto her stomach and got to her hands and knees.

"Come on," said the man and grabbed her arm.

"Keep your hands off me," she shouted and tried to shake his grip off.

"Keep your voice down," he hissed.

"Or what?" Her fear felt tangible like a heavy coat and she knew it would cloud her decisions and slow her down. He had the upper hand and she needed to turn it around.

"I told you before. Now get up."

"Let me go then."

He stepped back and she got slowly to her feet. Her arms ached but everything else felt as well as it could. She took a deep breath and held it before letting it out slowly as she looked around. Another rocket soared overhead and exploded over the house. The bang echoed across the garden.

"Let's go," he said and grabbed her elbow.

"Let me go," she shouted.

A window opened somewhere. "Hey you, you want to knock it off?"

Rachel recognised the voice and looked up. Moonlight glinted off glass.

"Mr Fekkesh?"

Her neighbour, so friendly when they met on the stairs, didn't seem to hear.

"First with the bloody fireworks, now with all the talking. Go to bed. People have to work in the morning."

"Mr Fekkesh, it's Rachel Turner. Please call the police."

He didn't seem to hear her.

"Stop with the noise or I'll come down there and sort you out myself."

The window banged shut and the man leaned close to her. "Do that again and I'll break your jaw."

She had no doubt he would. He yanked her arm and pulled her to the corner of the building. His grip was unbreakable and he moved so fast she struggled so as not to stumble.

As another rocket soared over them, Rachel tried to think back to place this man at the Newborough Centre.

She couldn't do it. How could she possibly have something he wanted back if she'd never seen him before? And what would he do when he realised he'd got the wrong person? She had to get away somehow.

The man stopped and they both looked towards the corner.

Someone stood in the shadows.

# Chapter 12

When the rocket exploded and briefly coloured the world red, Jack got a quick glimpse of the man's face. He also saw the terror in Rachel's.

"Let her go," Jack said and palmed his car key so the metal shaft stuck between his fingers.

"Who're you?" the man asked. He sounded calm and that scared Jack.

"I'm her friend. I have her house keys."

"That's nice for you. I need her to help me, then you can help her. So just turn around and walk away."

"Jack," Rachel said helplessly.

"I don't think so," Jack said.

The man stepped onto the grass and seemed to regard Jack, but with the shadows it was difficult to tell.

"Ah," he said. "The old key between the fingers job, eh? Have you ever hit someone like that before?"

How did it come to this? Jack wondered. How could this evening, which had turned out so nicely, now be reduced to standing in a moonlit garden with a stranger threatening him? The injustice aggrieved him and his temper started to fray through his panic.

"Leave her alone," he said, trying hard to keep his voice steady.

"Why? Are you planning to fight me?"

"If I have to."

The man laughed and came closer. "Get out of my way."

Jack moved almost without thinking and quickly covered the two paces between them. He dipped his shoulder meaning to bury it in the man's midriff but the man moved enough so the blow glanced off. He brought his hand down sharply on Jack's shoulder.

* * *

Rachel pulled back as the man moved and his grip loosened. As he chopped at Jack, his fingers came free completely and Rachel broke away.

She kicked the back of his left knee as hard as she could. The man grunted and sagged towards her. Rachel swung her leg again and aimed for his balls but the kick glanced off his inner thigh instead. The man grunted again. Rachel pulled Jack to his feet.

"Come on," she said and they ran towards the car park.

* * *

Keel bit down quickly on his frustration before anger could take hold. He'd let his guard down by not expecting some kind of tag-team manoeuvre, but he could still wrestle back control. Thankfully, Rachel's blow had only taken him by surprise and not damaged his knee, but his thigh smarted.

He stalked after them and by the time he reached the corner they were in the car park area and heading towards the road.

A car approached and a pale Fiat 500 came into sight within a moment. Munro was behind the wheel and she slewed across the pavement and onto the driveway. The tyres fought for grip on the gravel.

Rachel pulled the stranger back towards the house out of the way.

The Fiat slid into a parked car with a heavy thud and came away at an angle. The front end dropped out of sight and there was a dull bang. The back end settled at a forty-five-degree angle. Munro opened the door and scrambled out quickly.

Keel raised his hand and Munro nodded to him then looked at Rachel and ran for her. Keel ran too.

Munro caught Rachel and the stranger at the tree line and grabbed Rachel's upper arm. She warded off the stranger with an outstretched hand. Rachel tried to prise Munro's fingers away and complained loudly as did the man.

"Well caught, Munro," Keel said when he reached them.

The stranger turned and glared at him.

"What the hell is going on here?" He looked between Keel and Munro and the concern and worry were clear on his face.

Keel summed him up in an instant – a good person caught in a bad situation – and decided to play on it.

"We are conducting enquiries," Keel said briskly. The man looked at him and frowned. "We've had reports of a disturbance."

Another rocket exploded overhead.

* * *

Panic rippled through Rachel as she struggled against the woman the man called Munro.

"That's not what he said before," she told Jack.

"What?" Jack looked from her to the man and back again.

"He said I had something he wanted." Rachel tried to wrench her arm free. "Can you ask your friend to let me go?"

The man shook his head. "We have to be careful of violence," he said. "Your friend has already come at me with a key and you're the only person here resisting."

Rachel's head was spinning as the nightmare unravelled before her. "What are you talking about?"

Nothing made sense anymore.

"I came at you because you were attacking Rachel," Jack said with force.

"Hardly."

Rachel grimaced as Munro dug her fingers harder into the flesh around her elbow.

"You don't need to hold onto me that tight."

"Then stop squirming," Munro said.

Jack squared up to the man. "You're not the police."

The man didn't flinch. "I think you'll find we are."

Jack tilted his head as if aware something wasn't quite right but not able to exactly put his finger on it.

"Then show me your ID."

Rachel saw the man and Munro exchange a glance and took her chance to pull free. Jack shoved Munro's shoulder hard and she cried out in surprise and staggered back before falling down a slight incline into the trees.

Rachel grabbed Jack's hand. "Come on. We're going."

Munro had fallen into the vee of a split trunk and couldn't seem to get out. She glared at them both with murder in her eyes.

Rachel allowed Jack to pull her onto the pavement and she ran across the road with him towards his car.

# Chapter 13

Jack let go of Rachel's hand and she ran around the front of the car as he unlocked it. They opened their doors together and he got in as quickly as he could, convinced he could hear footsteps behind him.

He slammed the door. Once Rachel was safely in, he locked the car and took a deep, shaky breath.

"Jesus," she said.

"What the hell was all that?" he demanded and turned the engine on. "What have you got me mixed up in?"

She turned angrily to face him. "Me? It's got nothing to do with me."

Astounded, he glared at her. "How can you say that? He knew who you were."

She shook her head. "I don't know him. He said we'd met and I had something he wanted back."

"How does that even make sense?"

She looked towards the road then back at him.

"It doesn't," she said quietly.

Neither the injured tone of her voice or her downcast expression suggested she was lying.

"I swear, Jack, I didn't get you into anything deliberately. On Tilly's life."

He bit his lip as his anger seeped away. "I'm sorry."

"Don't be. I can see how this must seem."

"Are you okay?"

"I've been better," she said grimly. "But what about you? He hit you."

"Not hard," he said and pulled away from the kerb. "So who is he? And where did that Munro woman come from?"

"I don't know," Rachel said and her voice cracked.

* * *

Keel watched the Insignia go as he helped pull Munro from the tree.

"The fucker pushed me," she said, her face like thunder.

"It's an occupational hazard."

"You're not helping." She put a hand to her throat then looked at the ground.

"Are you hurt?"

70

She shook her head briskly and knelt down.

"My necklace," she said.

"What?"

She held out her palm so he could see. "This is all I have left from my gran. She brought me up and taught me everything and that fucker snapped the chain."

"We don't have time for this, Munro," he said and walked towards the pavement.

"We will though," she said as she followed him. She carefully put the necklace in her jacket pocket and zipped it away.

"I had her, Keel, but he took advantage when I looked away."

Keel held up his hand. He needed to quell her anger. "They're not away yet."

She stalked towards the Range Rover. "I fucked up."

"We both did," he said calmly. "They took us by surprise."

She considered him for a moment then shook her head. "Whoever the fuck he is, when we catch up with Rachel, I'm going to kill him."

Keel unlocked the Range Rover and watched the Insignia as it turned out of Moore Avenue.

"He won't get far. I got his registration."

* * *

Rachel hadn't managed to clip in her seatbelt and the alarm rang. She looked more panicked so Jack slowed and reached across to help her slot it home.

"Thanks. Sorry I'm a mess."

"We both are," he said as headlights flared in the rear-view mirror. He felt an icy trail run down his back and gripped the steering wheel harder. "Where's the police station?"

"Should we call them first?"

"Shit." Why hadn't he thought of that? "Ring and tell them everything."

She reached into her bag and groaned. "Oh no, I don't have my phone."

"Where is it?"

"I think Tilly's got it."

"Use mine," he said and handed it to her. A junction was coming up. "Which way?"

"Take a right. We have to go into the one-way system."

He glanced at the rear-view mirror and felt dread settle heavily on his chest. The headlights were closer now.

Rachel dialled a number and held the phone to her ear.

"Yes," she said after a moment. "Police, please." She paused. "Hadlington," she said then paused for longer this time. "Hello?" She held the phone in front of her then turned to him. "For fuck's sake, Jack." Anger made her voice rise. "The battery's dead. Have you got a charger?"

"Not in the car."

"For Christ's sake. Why would you carry around a phone that's about to die?"

Her hysterical tone grated on him. "Because I didn't know this would happen tonight," he said through gritted teeth. "The only person I call is Luisa and I rang before I went to the party so I didn't think I'd need it again."

"Not much bloody help to us now."

"No," he said curtly. Now wasn't the time to get into an argument. He made the turn and took a deep breath. "Look, I didn't think. I'm sorry."

Rachel leaned her head against the rest.

"It's not your fault," she said. "I'm sorry."

She turned the phone in her hand then put it into the tray under the stereo. He watched her and saw her head snap sideways as she looked in the mirror.

"That car?" she said.

"It's been behind us for a while."

"Is it them?"

"I don't see how," he said. "She must have wrecked the Fiat in the car park."

"He must have come in another car." She let out a cry of frustrated anguish. "Why would they follow us?"

Jack didn't reply. They were coming up to a junction with three distinctly marked lanes. "Which way?"

"Right lane. I can't think of any shortcuts to get there quicker."

Traffic lights glowed red. No cars were waiting to move but others crossed the junction.

"What happens if we go left?"

"You join up with the A14."

"I have to follow the system then?"

"Uh-huh," she said. "And I should have said it earlier but thanks for coming back and helping me."

"I found your keys."

"You could have still walked away and not got involved."

"How could I have lived with that?" He couldn't think of what else to say. "I still don't understand any of this."

"Or me, but he knew my name. I mean, I'm an office clerk. I don't do things that make people try and grab me. I'm just a thirty-four-year-old divorced single mum."

Jack checked the rear-view mirror as he braked for the junction. The car was close enough he could see it was a Range Rover and it moved to the right and ran along the middle of the road. It drew alongside and Jack gripped the wheel. He glanced at Rachel who stared through his window.

"What are they doing?" she asked.

Jack's lips suddenly felt dry. He licked them.

"They're trying to stop us turning right."

# Chapter 14

The Range Rover twitched, and Jack instinctively jerked the steering wheel to the left. The move took them into the middle lane and the other car edged forward to slot itself into the right lane just before they reached the traffic island.

"Shit," said Jack and braked for the lights.

Something tapped the window, startling him. He looked to see Munro holding what looked like a crossbow bolt. She flicked it with her fingers so it bounced off the glass. Something shimmered on the back of her hand.

She mimed winding the window down and Jack shook his head. Her expression soured and she bared her teeth as she mimed again.

"What do I do?"

Panic made his head swim and he could feel heat in his throat and chest.

"I can't think straight," Rachel said and hugged her arms. "I'm so bloody scared."

Jack leaned forward and saw CCTV cameras above the traffic lights. Might that deter them?

He wound the window down an inch or so and Rachel stared at him, open-mouthed.

"What're you–?"

"I don't know," he said.

"Hey," said Munro. She smiled and flicked the bolt again and he realised the shimmering on her hand was scar tissue.

"Thank you, Jack. It's so much easier to talk with the window down."

Jack looked at her. Had she really called him by name?

"You took off at some speed back there," Munro said. "When you shoved me into that tree you broke my necklace." She let the silence run for several seconds. "That necklace meant a lot to me and I'm not likely to forget what you did."

"Oh," he said.

"So why did you run off?"

"Because we didn't know what was happening."

She shook her head as if he'd said something foolish.

"So what brings you out this evening then? Are you and Rachel dating?"

"I don't think that's any of your business," he said, not dropping his gaze. If he showed he was intimidated he was done.

"How would your wife feel about it?"

The question was like being punched in the throat and it took Jack a moment to properly draw breath.

"What?"

"I asked about Luisa, your wife. How would she feel about you dating Rachel?"

"Hey, we're not–" said Rachel.

Jack put his hand on her arm.

"How do you know my name, and my wife's?" he asked, fighting to keep his voice level.

"It's my job." Munro leaned her elbow on the windowsill. "I'm curious now why you'd protect Rachel if you're not dating her."

"Because it's the right thing to do."

"Ah, you're a Good Samaritan, is that it? Well I'll level with you, Jack. We need to speak to Rachel but she's in your car."

His heart thumped so loudly he was convinced everyone in Hadlington would be able to hear it.

"And until you tell us how you know us, that's where she'll stay."

He put the car into gear as carefully as he could, not wanting to make any noise or let Munro see his movement.

"What're you doing?" hissed Rachel.

"Trust me," he whispered.

"Hey," Munro called and tapped the crossbow bolt against his door frame.

Jack put his foot down and hoped there were no cars coming. The tyres fought for grip and squealed on the tarmac. The juddering sensation seemed synchronised to his heartbeat.

"What're you doing?" asked Rachel, clutching his arm.

"Getting a head start."

The driver of the Range Rover had good reflexes and accelerated a beat or so after Jack but the power of that car kept it level and Jack quickly realised he couldn't outrun him to turn right.

"Fuck," he muttered.

Rachel grabbed the edge of her seat. "Jack! The barrier!"

The Range Rover didn't give an inch and held a course straight towards the barriers at the next traffic island. Jack swerved left at the last moment and went into a skid. The Range Rover mounted the kerb and hit the barrier with a bang. Jack fought to steer through the skid and the tyres finally gripped the road making the car lurch. He glanced into the rear-view mirror as he put his foot down and saw the Range Rover reverse away from the wrecked barrier.

Rachel turned and peered between the gap in the seats. "He's coming."

"Where does this lead?"

"To the A14, like I told you."

"Can we get back into Hadlington from another junction and go to the police station?"

"Yes."

He passed a side road and saw a narrow channel with cars parked either side.

"I could go up one of them and try to lose him."

Even as he said it he knew it was a bad idea. He wouldn't be able to drive quickly and if anyone stepped out, he'd hit them.

"Forget it," he said before she could speak.

Jack glanced at her. In the darkness, her face looked calm and attentive, but in the quick washes of orange he saw the fear and a sense of dislocation. She looked how he felt.

"I'm more scared than I've ever been," she said. "This doesn't happen to people like me – it happens in films and on TV."

He couldn't offer any comfort so he kept quiet.

"I mean," she said with an expansive gesture with her hands, "what could they possibly want with me? Or you? How do they know us?"

"None of it makes sense."

She shook her head and made a frustrated sound deep in her throat. Jack's mind tumbled with thoughts. What could Munro and the man possibly want? Worse, what would they do to get what they wanted? The violence at the house could have been bad luck, but now he knew it was premeditated and the level of it had escalated from a fight to being chased on open roads. At these speeds, the weight advantage of the Range Rover trumped all.

"What happens if they do something stupid like run us off the road?" she asked.

"They won't," he lied, scared that she was thinking along the same lines as him.

"No," she said and he couldn't tell if she believed him or was buying into his charade. "Why would they? I've read too many horror stories in the papers."

"You and me both," he said and glanced in the rear-view mirror.

The Range Rover was getting closer, its headlights dazzling. He adjusted the mirror to push the glare against the ceiling and pulled into the centre of the road to stop them overtaking.

He drove as fast as he dared. The shops they passed were brightly lit but closed. He didn't see any speed or CCTV cameras and road signs flashed by too quickly to read, not that he had any idea of where he was. Anxiety seemed to creep up his neck, threatening to swamp him. He tried to shake it away and rubbed his eyes.

"We're in trouble, aren't we?" Rachel asked quietly.

The road curved and he tightened his grip, hoping the wheels held the tarmac.

"I think so," he said.

The road took a slight incline and then he was almost on top of a wide roundabout that spanned the A14 dual carriageway.

"First turn," said Rachel.

He managed to steer into it and follow the slip road down. No headlights showed in his rear-view mirror. He accelerated and tried to build a gap between the two cars as he joined the brightly lit carriageway.

"How far to the next junction?" he asked.

"Not far."

Headlights flashed in a staccato blur between the safety barrier uprights as a lorry passed on the other side of the road.

The lights made him feel worse because he realised how alone they were now. In the artificial orange glow with nothing but fencing and industrial units on his left and trees on his right, Jack felt as if he'd wandered into an alien landscape.

He checked the rear-view mirror but saw nothing behind him.

# Chapter 15

"They're not coming?"

Rachel's disbelief mirrored Jack's own. He took a deep breath and let it out slowly but only relaxed his grip on the steering wheel when the slip road disappeared from sight.

"That's it?" she asked.

"Looks like it," he said and an accumulation of emotion hit him. His eyes watered and he palmed away a tear with a trembling hand.

The car seemed to eat up the tarmac. They went under a footbridge with graffiti sprayed on the panels and passed an industrial yard with several high cranes standing to attention in the darkness.

"Are you okay?" Rachel asked.

"No," he said and tried to laugh. It wasn't a pleasant sound. "You?"

"So-so," she said and touched her index fingers under her eyes. "I thought we were seriously in trouble when they pulled around us."

"Yeah."

He wanted to stop the car and get out to breathe the night air in deeply and get rid of the pent-up anxiety he'd accumulated that made his body feel too small to hold it. He rubbed his neck and tried to ease out the kinks already feeling knotty under the skin.

"I don't know how you did it," said Rachel and rubbed her face. "If I was driving, we'd have been in a ditch by now."

"You'd have been fine. Now let's get back to Hadlington and get this sorted out."

"I wonder why they'd just give up?" she asked. "After everything at the house and what Munro said?" She bit at the corner of a thumbnail. "Do you think the police'll do anything? There must be CCTV in the town centre surely?"

He shrugged. "It's hard to tell. I don't think I even saw their number plate."

"I got a good look," she said.

Jack checked the rear-view mirror. A barely discernible shape in the gloom seemed to move across the carriageway before vanishing. He blinked and looked again. The road seemed empty.

"My eyes are so tired," he said.

"Not surprised," she said. Her voice was soft. "You must be knackered."

"I feel like I'm seeing things."

As if in sympathy she rubbed her own eyes. "Like what?"

How could he explain it? "Nothing. I think I'm just going a bit mad."

"After the night we've had, I wouldn't be surprised."

Jack checked the mirror again and saw the same movement. Could it be a car driving without lights?

"I think there is something there behind us."

"Where?" Rachel craned around in her seat. "What?"

"Some way back there's a shape in the darkness."

"I can't…" She squinted. "Oh shit. What is it?"

Neither spoke for a few moments until a streetlight caught the shape.

"It's them," she gasped.

Fear rattled through him like pins and needles. If the Range Rover was coming without lights, then they intended to finish whatever it was they'd set out to do. Jack saw Rachel's panicked expression but tried to shut it away and thought of the slip road he desperately wanted to see.

The Range Rover's headlights burst into blinding life and Jack blanched at the glare. He touched the brake pedal but the Range Rover maintained the same distance. The driver clearly had professional-level reflexes and if that were true, why would he want Rachel and how did he know Jack and Luisa?

* * *

Rachel felt like panic was pushing her down in the seat. She glanced at Jack. He was steering with his left hand while his right pressed against his neck and shoulder.

"Are you okay?" she asked.

"Just tense," he said, pressing hard enough to grimace.

She rubbed at her own neck. Tension knotted at the base of it.

"What do they want with you, Rachel?"

"I honestly don't know."

She'd wracked her brains for an answer since the conversation at the traffic lights, but she'd told Jack the truth – she didn't have enemies. The only people in her life were either old friends or work colleagues. She couldn't remember hurting anyone, hadn't been hurt – except where that comment could be prefixed with "Glen aside…" – and there seemed no reason at all for anyone to want her so badly they'd grab her or chase her.

She watched the Range Rover sweep into the fast lane. Tears prickled her eyes and dread clenched her stomach muscles.

"Do you think they'll try and keep us on the road?" she asked.

"Maybe."

"Have you got enough fuel?"

"I've got plenty but it depends on how far they want us to go."

She shook her head. "If we break down…"

"Don't think about that. How far is it to the next junction?"

"Another few miles."

"Is there anything on the way? A lay-by or a petrol station or something?"

"There's a garage but it has a really short slipway."

"How short?"

"Enough that cars sometimes don't make the turn in time."

"That's it," he said. "I have a plan."

"What do you mean?"

"We're calling into the garage."

# Chapter 16

Rachel watched as the Range Rover kept tight to the central reservation. A string of lights appeared across the other carriageway and ran parallel to the road.

"Train," she said even though she didn't know whether Jack had noticed the lights or not.

She needed to say something to make herself feel part of the real world and not slip into some kind of conspiracy theory. Nothing about the last half hour made sense but she knew she had to keep her wits about her. If either of them broke down now all was lost.

Jack's face was set in grim determination as the Range Rover pulled level with them. Rachel saw, through the trees, the welcoming blueish glow of the petrol station.

"There it is," she said and he put his foot down. "What do we do if this doesn't work?"

"Then we're in trouble," he said and offered her a tight smile.

"Not the most reassuring answer."

He gave a joyless chuckle and she smiled.

"It'll work," she said.

The Range Rover drew ahead but kept to its lane. Jack edged over so he straddled the white lines. The petrol station slip road seemed to race towards them and the cat's eyes glowed green.

"Shit, it is short," he said.

A hundred yards or so along the slip road was a low sloping wall painted white with chevrons pointing towards the forecourt. From her vantage point and at this speed, the turn seemed impossibly tight to Rachel.

"It's not enough, is it?" she asked. She thought it looked almost suicidal but kept that thought to herself.

Jack glanced at her. "You ready?"

"No," she said with a small smile.

"No," he said and matched her smile. "Me either."

The slip road seemed to shrink the closer to it they got. There surely wasn't enough room.

Rachel braced her legs into the footwell and gripped the edges of her seat tightly.

\* \* \*

Jack tensed his arms and stamped on the brakes. The wheels locked for a moment before ABS kicked in. His heart pounded as he steered onto the slip road and pulled on the handbrake. The car slewed and he steered into it. Rachel shouted something he couldn't understand through the sudden static fuzz in his ears. He released both brakes as the car came out of the skid then cadence braked to avoid the ABS.

"Jack!"

He heard her this time as the static faded into his heartbeat.

He pushed the brakes harder and the tyres squealed and juddered. The wall still seemed to be coming too fast but he thought now they might make it. At the last moment he turned the wheel hard and the tyres protested as they drove onto the deserted forecourt. Breathing a heavy sigh of relief, he steered the car easily between the petrol pumps.

The pumps were doubled up over three islands and a roadway separated the forecourt from the red brick shop building. White lights set into the forecourt canopy lit the area like a summer's day. A handful of display bins stood against the front wall, all of them padlocked shut. Half a dozen parking spaces were marked in front of the building but all were empty. The shop windows glowed with light and someone moved inside.

Jack parked across several spaces near the main doors and unclipped his seatbelt before stopping. Rachel looked at him, startled.

"What're you doing?" she asked as she reached for her own seatbelt clip.

"I'm going to use the phone. You stay here."

"What? Are you mad?"

He put his hand over hers so she couldn't release the belt.

"I'll leave the engine running, so you stay in the car. They'll probably come back but it's going to take them a while to turn."

"Why can't I come?"

"You'll be safer in the car, Rachel. I'll ring the police."

Jack opened his door and listened. He heard his own engine idling, the buzz of the lights and the occasional chirp of a bird but no other traffic noise. The air stank of hot brakes.

He glanced at her as he got out and she nodded once. "Be quick."

"I will. Lock the doors behind me."

He closed the door and the locks thudded into place. He walked around the back of the car to the double doors but they didn't move. He stepped back and raised a hand towards the monitor but still nothing happened.

"Night pay only, mate," said a voice that echoed across the forecourt. He looked around until movement in the shop caught his eye. The person he'd spotted earlier was a thin-faced man in his late twenties or early thirties with dark eyes and hair the colour of dirty dishwater. His too-big uniform made him look like a scarecrow. He talked into a desk-mounted microphone as he filled the cigarette rack.

Jack rushed towards the night pay window. "I need to use your phone."

The cashier didn't turn to look at him. "You haven't got any fuel."

"I don't need any, I just need to use your phone."

The cashier glanced over his shoulder and looked like he wanted to be anywhere other than here.

"Why?"

Jack took a deep breath to calm himself. He couldn't afford to piss the bloke off now.

"It's an emergency."

The cashier laughed bitterly. "Always is," he said and turned his attention back to the cigarettes.

"Please," Jack said and struggled to keep his voice level.

"You got a mobile?"

"I have but the battery died."

"My heart bleeds."

Jack bit his lip. "Please, mate, it's an emergency."

The cashier put a carton of cigarettes on the counter and sighed heavily. "Is she in labour?" he asked and flicked his head towards the car.

"No. What're you talking about?"

"Unless any close family members are in trouble, there's no chance on earth you're coming in here to use my phone. I've already been turned over once this year and it's not happening again."

"Honestly, I just want to use your phone. My friend and I are being pursued."

The cashier raised his eyebrows. "Well that's new."

"We are, by a couple in a Range Rover. They tried to run us off the road and I need to call the police."

The cashier looked astonished. "Fuck me sideways," he said. "So you're in trouble with some nutters and you bring them here to me. Well thanks very much, that's all I need."

"So call the police. That'd make us both happy."

The cashier sneered. "Do you know how long it'll take them to turn up if they realise Lois isn't doing the night shift?" He shrugged. "Any idea, mate?"

"How could I?" Jack asked. "Are you really not going to help me?" He couldn't believe it.

The cashier picked up the cigarette carton. "If I let you in and you rob me, I haven't got a leg to stand on. And if you are telling the truth, which I seriously doubt, then you won't be here tomorrow night, but I will and if those people in the Range Rover get all pissed off then they'll know where I am."

"They won't be interested in you," said Jack but he could see it was a lost cause. "If you won't let me then please, at least, slide your phone through the drawer so I can use it."

"Just piss off, you dickhead."

Jack felt nauseous and leaned on the drawer casing. As he let his head drop he heard an engine from behind the shop. The sound came closer.

"Shit."

The cashier turned. "You still there?"

"Yes," said Jack and felt his panic rise. "They're coming."

The cashier looked up at something on the wall and blanched. "Shit. They're coming down the off-ramp."

"I know, I can hear them," Jack said. "They're coming for me and my friend and you're here too."

"Good job I'm locked in tight as a nut then, eh?"

Jack felt his anger build and glanced towards the Insignia. Rachel raised her eyebrows in query at him then she seemed to notice something behind him. Her hands flew to her mouth.

He turned to see the nose of the Range Rover come smoothly into view like the snout of a shark.

# Chapter 17

Grit creaked under the heavy tyres as the Range Rover pulled to a stop in front of the Insignia. The driver's window wound down halfway.

"Get back in your car."

Jack was so scared he felt faint and braced himself against the drawer as saliva filled his mouth. He spat it out. Blood roared in his ears.

Nobody spoke for a few moments. The Range Rover engine idled. From somewhere came the faint rattle of a train on tracks.

"Don't try my patience, Jack."

Jack looked into the shop. The cashier had moved to the far end of his counter but was watching him.

"Please let me in," Jack said.

The cashier shook his head.

The driver's window wound all the way down and the man put his elbow on the sill and leaned out. He wore dark glasses and cast a glance over Jack's shoulder.

"Get back in your car. I won't ask again."

Jack looked behind him to see what had drawn the man's attention. A chain-link fence enclosed the forecourt perimeter and beyond it were darkened industrial units. When Jack looked up to the roof he saw three cameras over the door. Had the driver been looking at them?

The driver gunned the engine and the Range Rover jumped forward. It hit the Insignia just off the front bumper and Rachel's mouth opened in a scream Jack couldn't hear.

Jack stepped away from the night pay window. "You hit my fucking car."

"With Rachel inside, don't forget," said the driver calmly.

That pulled Jack back instantly. The potential damage to his car paled to insignificance if Rachel was in danger.

"Get back on the road, Jack."

"You've had your fun. Now leave us alone."

The Range Rover reversed a few feet then leapt forward and caught the nearside front panel of the Insignia. The dull thud of the impact didn't drown out Rachel's scream this time.

"Last chance," the driver called.

Jack looked towards the cashier who wore a shocked expression as he edged back into the shadows. "You're a fucking arsehole," Jack shouted at him.

Rachel beckoned him into the car.

Jack stepped off the kerb and left the relative safety of the building to cross the parking spaces. His heart pounded with every step and every part of his body felt tense.

He kept his face towards the Range Rover as he walked and knew if it came forward suddenly now, he wouldn't stand a chance. The driver and passenger sat without moving behind the darkened glass.

Jack reached his door and breathed a quick sigh of relief. He opened it and got in and Rachel offered him a weak smile.

The tenseness left him and he felt sick again. Cold sweat beaded his forehead and upper lip.

"Thank God," she said and leaned over to cup his cheek. "I thought you were in trouble then."

"Me too." He put his hand over hers. "I shouldn't have left you. I didn't realise they'd ram the car."

"How could you have known?" There was strength in her voice now as if the incident had somehow instilled a confidence in her. Or maybe it was just bravado. "So what now?"

"We go back on the road." He gestured towards the cameras. "He had sunglasses on like he wanted to avoid the CCTV."

"If that's right then perhaps we could play that to our advantage."

"How?"

"The self-defence classes I told you about are run by a woman called Kim who always tells us to go for the most simple option. 'KISS', she calls it – 'Keep It Simple, Stupid'. If the Range Rover wants to avoid CCTV then let's take him to where there's CCTV all over the place."

"Back into town?" he asked, not entirely convinced. He shook out his hands, trying to get some energy back into himself.

"Why not? We'd already said about going off at the next exit so let's do it."

He still didn't know if it was confidence or bravado but Jack liked it. Her positivity countered his increasingly negative thoughts and what if she was right? Maybe the driver hadn't shunted the Insignia into the wall or tried to run Jack down because that would have taken them into full view of the cameras. They needed to keep their heads now and he needed to follow her attitude.

"I like your plan," he said and put the car into gear.

As he edged forward slightly, the Range Rover reversed. It pulled sharply to the right and stopped. Munro watched them impassively through her opened window as she rolled the crossbow bolt along the fingers of her left hand.

Jack drove past the Range Rover and she gave a jaunty little wave.

"I really don't like her," said Rachel.

Jack didn't reply as he drove around the building.

"Here they come," she said.

He checked the rear-view mirror as they drove onto the A14. The Range Rover pulled onto the carriageway and moved into the overtaking lane but stayed back a couple of car lengths.

"Looks like he doesn't want to get caught out like last time," Rachel said. "You know, I'd love to have seen their reactions when you pulled in."

\* \* \*

Munro watched the Insignia and rolled the crossbow bolt over her fingers in an effort to keep calm. She wanted to make a good impression and she knew one of Keel's pet hates was allowing anger to overcome rational thought. Most of the time she could balance it, but Jack Martin, the shit, had really got under her skin. Partly because he was an unexpected wrinkle adding time and hassle to the job, but mostly because he'd shoved her. Getting into scrapes was an accepted part of the job but she almost always dictated the terms and he'd caught her off-balance. He'd beaten her. And she hated that because it hurt far more than the branches had.

"What do you see as the likeliest outcome here?" Keel asked.

He looked composed; like a man out for a quiet drive in the country. He'd almost lost his temper when Jack pulled into the services but quickly slammed a lid on it and came up with the perfect solution – he simply drove to the exit slip road and headed back.

"Rachel knows the area and we can now assume, since Jack used the petrol station, they don't have access to a phone. I think they'll try and get off the A14 at the next junction to head back into Hadlington for the police station."

He nodded and tapped his left thumb on the steering wheel to a beat only he could hear. "So which exit will they take?"

"The first we'll come to is a couple of miles away."

"What's on it?"

She closed her eyes to better picture it.

"Five exits in total – Hadlington first and Marham third though it's closed for roadworks. Then there's the golf course and a farm beyond it."

"Okay," he said and thought for a moment. "Can you get hold of your crew again?"

Munro looked at the dashboard clock and saw it was half past midnight. "You think we'll need them?"

"At some point we're going to stop Rachel and Jack, but if they're in an open environment I don't know the area well enough to be able to contain them. Back-up would be a good idea."

"Agreed," she said.

"Have them head to the junction and wait for further instruction."

Munro took out her phone and placed the call.

* * *

The road curved to the left. "This is our junction," Rachel said.

Jack checked his mirror. The Range Rover was in the overtaking lane a couple of car lengths back and the driver was obviously taking care not to get caught out again. But would he try to keep them on the A14?

He felt weighed down with dread from the constant presence of this fucking Range Rover. Other than handing Rachel over, he couldn't see how this situation could possibly end up other than badly.

Yard markers for the junction appeared and, at the last moment, Jack pulled onto the slip road. The Range Rover followed smoothly and moved onto the narrow hard shoulder as they passed the sign stating the first exit was for Hadlington Central. The Range Rover pulled alongside.

"Shit," said Rachel. "They're going to stop us taking the exit, aren't they?"

"Looks like it. Hold tight."

He twitched the wheel to the left but the Range Rover didn't give the slightest ground. He twitched it again even though the other car was so close, but the Range Rover didn't move.

"We're too small," he said and hit the steering wheel hard. "He's not scared of us."

They were running out of slip road. The Range Rover jerked up and down and he guessed the wheels were running on bare earth at the edge of the hard shoulder.

"He's not going to give us any room," said Rachel. She didn't sound confident anymore.

"What's the road to Marham like?"

"Single carriageway." Tears glistened on her eyelids. "I'm scared, Jack."

"Me too," he said. "We need a plan to get us out of this."

"Yeah." She nodded and a tear ran down her cheek. She swiped it away angrily with her palm.

"How many exits are there?"

She told him the layout.

"How about we make him think we're heading for Hadlington but keep going for Marham?"

They drove onto the roundabout and the Range Rover blocked the Hadlington turn so Jack twitched his wheel slightly. As the Range Rover pulled forward Jack braked. The other driver did the same and Jack accelerated past the A14 exit driving in the middle of the road. A quick glance in the side mirror showed the Range Rover twenty yards behind.

"We did it," he said, amazed it'd worked.

"Oh no," said Rachel, voice full of disbelief. Plastic barriers with flashing lights sealed off the Marham exit. Diversion signs pointed further around the roundabout. "Shit."

The Range Rover was right behind them now and easily outpaced the Insignia. At best, Jack might get back to the A14 exit without incident but if it was a straight race, they didn't stand a chance.

The decision wasn't his to make as the Range Rover shunted them on the offside. The dull thud of collision made him yell with surprise. Rachel screamed. Munro glared at Jack through her open window and pointed towards the next exit.

"What's up here?" he said.

"A golf course and Fowler's Farm."

The Range Rover shunted them again and Jack steered into the exit. The streetlights stopped after the first bend and the roads were now cast a pale blue with the moonlight. The full beams lit a narrow road bordered by thick hedges on both sides.

The Range Rover tucked behind them and seemed to fill the rear-view mirror.

Between gaps in the hedge, he saw a darkened building in the middle of a field. Moments later they passed the golf course entrance where a lit sign informed him it didn't open until eight am.

"There's no one here," he said.

"Did you expect there to be?"

"Not really," he said and shook his head. "What about this Fowler's Farm. Is it big?"

"No idea."

"Okay." His mind was racing so fast he couldn't gather his thoughts to focus on a plan. "Where does the road go after the farm?"

"Nowhere," Rachel said grimly. "It's a dead end."

# Chapter 18

Pippa went into the cafeteria for her last break. The long and low-ceilinged room was almost empty, with only a couple of tables out of the dozen or more occupied. Most of the shift, it seemed, were still out on calls. She looked around but couldn't see anyone she knew so she got a cup of coffee from the vending machine and sat down. Her stomach rumbled even though she still didn't have her appetite back from finding Mrs Gilbert in the Newborough Centre. As it was there were only a couple of sandwiches left in the dispenser and neither of them looked particularly appetising.

She took a sip of the coffee and winced at the taste then she looked out the window. The sky seemed clear now with most of the fireworks long since finished. She'd listened in on other calls during the night, including what appeared to be a car chase through downtown Hadlington caught on CCTV, as she spent most of the shift working at her desk.

The family liaison officer reported back after seeing an understandably distraught Mr Gilbert. As far as her husband knew, Barbara hadn't shown any suicidal tendencies and wasn't prone to depression. Her only stress, he believed, came from the data company she worked for being absorbed into another, though she hadn't discussed anything specific with him. Neither the police nor Chris Wood's security team had made any progress on identifying the mystery woman who'd entered the stairwell.

Pippa turned as the cafeteria door clattered open. She hoped it would be Maley coming in to update her but instead saw her friend and fellow officer Rosie. Rosie scanned the room and when she saw Pippa she raised her hand and made a gesture for a drink. Pippa held up her cup and Rosie nodded. She got her own coffee then sat across from Pippa.

"What a night," Rosie said, blowing her fringe up. "I've only just got in from patrol."

"Anything exciting?"

"Not really. It was mostly idiots trying to act cool with explosives though we did nick a couple of little shits trying to start a fire down by the canal."

Pippa shook her head. Nothing she ever heard about shifts on Bonfire Night made her feel any more inclined to enjoy it.

"What about you? Weren't you on the jumper?"

"Maley and me were first on the scene."

"Ouch." Rosie grimaced like she'd smelled something terrible. "How was it?"

"I've had better starts to a shift."

"They're never good." Rosie sipped her coffee, pulled a face and put the cup down. "I thought about you earlier, actually. Have you moved in with Richard yet?"

Pippa shook her head. It was a conversation she and Richard, her boyfriend, had been having for a while now. He was a paramedic over at Marham and didn't want to move even though her flat was bigger and she was happily settled in Hadlington.

"No. We're still talking it through."

"You need to talk it through quicker," Rosie said. "Take it from me. So are you still living on Lamont Street?"

Pippa sat forward, intrigued. "I am. Why?"

"There was a thing up there," Rosie said. "I didn't attend myself but Julia did and she told me all about it." Rosie seemed pleased to be able to pass on the gossip. "It was a noise complaint that started out as fireworks but then switched into something else. First reports were a domestic, but it was all outside in the gardens of a premises on Moore Avenue. That's just a couple of streets over from you, isn't it?"

"It is." She knew the street because when she looked after her nephew he loved to call into the little swing park they had there. "So how did the call turn out?"

"Not sure, because it got weirder. When the Battenburg turned up they found a wrecked car in the driveway which wasn't registered to anyone living anywhere near the house. It had apparently been driven in at speed and had fallen partway over a low wall."

"That's odd."

"I know." Rosie tried another sip of her coffee and winced again. "It's the full moon," she said. "It drives people crazy."

# Chapter 19

The narrow road wound up a gentle hill and while its twists and turns kept Jack's speed down, it also meant the Range Rover couldn't pass. Rachel caught glimpses of the fields surrounding them through gaps in the thick hedges that lined the road. Gateways flashed by on both sides.

A sign, half hidden by hedgerow, flashed out of the darkness. It declared 'Fowler's Field' as a 'prestigious and exclusive development of five-bedroom executive homes', due for completion within a couple of months.

"I thought you said it was Fowler's Farm?" Jack said.

"Field probably sounds better to property developers."

"We might be able to find somewhere to hide if it's a building site."

"It has to be better than being out here."

She checked her side mirror. The Range Rover had dropped back far enough to be out of sight around a curve though its headlights were clearly visible over the hedgerow.

"Can you see the farm from the A14?" he asked.

"You see the main house but, you know, I've never looked specifically. It's just something that's there. Why? What are you thinking?"

He glanced quickly at her then back at the road. She could see the intense concentration in his expression as he gripped the wheel.

"I'm just thinking that if we get trapped up there…" he said.

"Which we will."

"Then perhaps we can do something to draw attention to ourselves."

"What? Like set fire to something?"

"Why not? If it's a farm there might be some old barns there."

"You're mad," she said, but as she thought about it the idea made some sense to her. "But it could work."

"Do you smoke?"

"No. Do you?"

He shook his head.

"Well there's a flaw," she said.

His lips briefly twitched into a smile. "Okay, but if there's a building site we might find some equipment we can use. And perhaps someone's monitoring the CCTV, because we must have left a trail on that."

"You'd hope," she said and hadn't anticipated it sounding so negative.

A sense of defeat seemed to settle over them and she could feel the despair leeching into her. She tried to shake the sensation off but it was getting harder to picture the night ending well and she felt overwhelmed by it all.

"Does anyone live here?" he asked after a while.

"I don't think so and even if they did, do we really want to drag them into this?"

He took a deep breath and licked his lips. "No."

"Me either." She touched the back of his hand. "I'd be scared to."

"Scared?"

Now she'd exposed her terror she felt a little lighter as if it could be examined now. "I'll be honest, Jack, I'm fucking terrified." Her eyes watered and she felt a lump gathering in her throat. "I don't want to drag anybody else into it but I'd be willing to involve absolutely anyone if it meant we could get away and I can see Tilly again."

"You will."

"How?" She knew he was probably just trying to protect her but she'd now passed the point of ignoring the obvious. "This is a dead end, Jack. The only way back is down the road and we don't know how far those twats in the Range Rover are willing to go. We're both in trouble here."

"I know," he said. Although he didn't meet her gaze his expression told her everything.

Now this can of worms had been opened she could feel its negative energy drawing her in and she needed to stop that as quickly as possible. "We can't give up though, Jack. If we do, it means I might never see Tilly again." She had to talk around the lump in her throat. "And you won't see Luisa."

He glanced at her and light caught the tears in his eyes.

"I'm not ready for that," she said. "Are you?"

"No, I'm not."

"Then let's not give up."

\* \* \*

"You're sure there's no access road leading away from here?" asked Keel.

"Nope, nothing at all." Munro shook her head firmly. "This is it."

"Excellent." He eased up on the accelerator and allowed the Insignia to pull out of sight. "Do you trust your crew?"

"Yes, but not as much as I trust myself." She looked at him. "Or you."

He nodded though she barely caught the movement as his gaze remained fixed on the road.

"That's not what I asked," he said. "Will they follow orders? Rachel and Jack are civilians but we're backing them into a corner and people react differently."

"I've worked with a couple of them in the past and never had any issues. They're operators, they know the score and I trust Carlisle."

He glanced at her then back to the road. "Fine. Get them up to the farm."

She felt a sharp thrill that he trusted her to bring in back-up and made the call. It answered after two rings.

"Carlisle."

"Where are you?"

"On the A14 coming towards the junction. Where did you want us?"

"Fowler's Farm."

"Got it, see you there in about five minutes."

* * *

A large farmhouse rose above the hedges at the top of the hill. Dark against the sky, its windows reflected the full moon. Two large barns stood behind it and beyond, almost lost in the gloom, poles reached out of the ground like grasping hands. Next to them stood several large shapes that might have been diggers and other mechanical equipment.

"I'm not even sure anyone's living there or if it's all part of the building site," Rachel said.

"We need to figure out our plan," Jack said.

"Yes." Rachel worried at her thumbnail again. "Because very soon we're going to run out of road."

"Have you been up here before?"

"No. Glen did a gig once at the golf club but I've never been further than that."

"What kind of farm was it?"

"I think it was a piggery. At least, it certainly used to smell like it in the summer."

"You said the road ends up there so there must be some kind of gate or turnaround, from when the farmer used it or the builders are now."

"So what are you thinking?"

"Not much, just that we basically stop near the gate then hide out somewhere. Perhaps in one of the barns?"

"And what then? Do we wait for them to come in and try to find us?"

"Yes. Then we sneak past them and drive back into Hadlington."

She raised her eyebrows. "You make it sound so simple."

"I think the sneaking back to the car bit might be the hardest."

"Precisely. We're not the A-Team, you know."

Her reference surprised a laugh out of him. "It's a shit plan, isn't it?"

"Not so long as they follow us," she said.

Talking through it seemed to be having a similar positive effect on Rachel and she sounded brighter and more alert.

"The farm covers a wide area and that's a lot of ground for two people to cover," she said. "If they split up to investigate then we have a better chance of getting back to the car and away."

The plan made sense to him even though it had holes in it wide enough to drive the Range Rover through. What if their assailants didn't get out of the car or had somehow blocked the lane further down? No, he decided. That kind of sour thought would just pull everything down around their ears. He kept quiet about his worries because he didn't want to dent Rachel's enthusiasm. Keeping up their energy now would be half the battle won.

They passed a wooden gate barring access to a small path through the hedge that led to the house.

The road ended in a large turning circle where a dry-stone wall separated the tarmac from the fields. A five-bar metal gate was set into it.

"Shit." He was going too fast and had to brake sharply. The car came to a halt with his side against the wall. "Are you okay?"

"Fine," she said and quickly unclipped her seatbelt. She got out.

Jack watched the Range Rover headlights through her window as he unclipped his own seatbelt. He opened the door and heard a dog barking wildly. It sounded like it was coming from somewhere behind the house.

"I hope Cujo's locked up."

Rachel stood by the boot and nodded nervously. "It doesn't sound like it's getting closer so perhaps it's chained up."

He got out. "I think it'd be best to keep away from it though. Let's go the other way."

She grabbed his hand and they rushed to the metal gate. A heavy and padlocked chain fastened it to a post.

"Climb over," he said. The engine note of the Range Rover was getting louder and closer.

He followed her over the gate. It creaked and rocked slightly but held steady. The dog launched into more frenzied barking but didn't seem to be coming towards them.

On this side of the gate, a narrow lip of concrete gave way to a wide cattle grid. The field beyond was enclosed by a dry-stone wall and deep ruts had been carved into the earth, some of them partially filled with hardcore.

"Now what?" Rachel asked. She looked towards the lane with wide eyes.

Jack took a steadying breath to compose himself. Out here the moon seemed impossibly bright and lit everything with a pale blue glow. The poles he'd seen earlier were scaffolding on three houses under various stages of construction about a hundred yards away. The ruts were part of a makeshift track that led to them. The one furthest to the left had been built to the first floor while the middle plot was little more than a concrete footprint. The nearest shell had brickwork that stood perhaps two or three feet high. The barns stood across from them and formed a barrier between the new builds and the farmhouse.

"We'll hide in that first house," he said. "Give ourselves a bit of time to get our bearings."

"Okay," she said. "Mind your ankles."

Holding hands to keep each other steady, they crossed the cattle grid together as the Range Rover got louder.

## Chapter 20

The ruts were deeper than Rachel had expected and pools of water in the bases reflected the moon in an oily glaze. She jumped over a couple and then they ran across the uneven ground towards the nearest plot. Jack kept a tight grip on her hand and his presence reassured her.

"Crouch behind the walls," he said.

It didn't look like there'd be anything much to hide behind but it had to be better than standing in the middle of a moonlit field where they'd be clearly visible.

She glanced back as the Range Rover headlights washed through the gate and across the cattle grid. The sound of the engine competed with her ragged breathing, the rush of blood in her ears and the barking dog. She looked back at the nascent house and wondered if they would reach it before the car stopped. She put on a burst of speed and Jack matched her pace and then they reached the plot.

She ran through the partial doorway and slid on the smooth concrete floor for a moment before catching some grip and twisting herself around. Jack slid past her and she felt his hands on her hips pushing her down towards the wall. She put her arms out to cushion the impact and dropped to her knees. Jack thumped into the bricks beside her and rocked back on his haunches.

She leaned in close to him. "You okay?" she asked breathlessly.

He held his right shoulder and was clearly in pain. "I think so."

The rush of adrenaline over, she now felt pain flare across her left knee. When she checked, she saw her tights had been ripped further and a fresh smear of blood showed. She told herself it was just surface damage but had to grit her teeth when she put her knee back on the concrete.

The engine stopped and doors opened and slammed shut. She leaned slightly to her left and held the bricks with her fingertips as she peeked around them.

Munro stood by the gate talking on a phone. The man was by Jack's car and she said something to him. Their words drifted on the night air in fragments but weren't quite loud enough for Rachel to understand.

* * *

Keel leaned on the gate and looked into the field.

His late mentor Llewellyn had once told him a full moon 'is your best friend or your worst enemy'. Tonight it was the former. The clear sky held a few wisps of cloud and the moon lit the field past the three house shells. Anyone moving out there would be immediately obvious.

He rubbed his chin and turned in a slow circle taking everything in. There appeared to be no breaks or gateways in the dry-stone wall, which made it unlikely they'd gone over that way. To his right were two old barns. The big house was unlit and the windows were bare of curtains. A small, enclosed garden stood between the house and the lane. From somewhere behind the house a dog barked as if trying to wake the neighbourhood, but nobody had come out to check on the disturbance.

"Where are you, Rachel?" he said quietly. They might have a lead of thirty seconds so could have probably covered a hundred yards or so.

In his experience, when people were frightened they resorted to the tactics of five-year-olds playing a game of hide-and-seek. The building plots made the most sense to check – they were a simple choice and an easy enough distance for them to cover. He couldn't see the barn doors from here, which made them unlikely, and the dog would be making even more noise if they'd hidden near the house.

Munro finished her call. "They're almost here," she said. "So what's the plan?"

He leaned on the gate. "I think they're in the house shells. When your crew arrives, we'll disperse them to force our friends out to us."

Munro nodded as she surveyed the field herself, paying particular attention to the building plots.

"You think they'll come out?"

"What's the alternative? At the moment they assume it's a level playing field with two against two. When your crew arrives, their odds diminish rapidly."

"And they get scared."

"True. But never assume scared means weak."

She nodded and smiled. "Of course."

"When people become frightened and desperate, rational thought will disappear. Whatever we think they'll do, they probably won't."

Munro reached into her backpack. "So we need to think through every eventuality?"

"Precisely."

She shrugged off her backpack and knelt down to unzip it. She took out a crossbow pistol with reverence and a handful of bolts she put into her pocket. She cocked the pistol and loaded a bolt as she stood up.

"One eventuality taken care of," she said and shot the Insignia's rear offside tyre. She walked to the front of the car, reloaded and re-cocked the crossbow, and shot out the front nearside tyre.

* * *

"What was that noise?"

The first bang had taken Rachel by surprise and she watched Munro walk along Jack's car before the second bang came.

"I think it's to do with your car."

"Shit. Do you think they've punctured the tyres?"

It felt like she'd been punctured too. If he was right then they couldn't get away even if they got past the Range Rover.

"Shit."

She sat back against the wall with her knees to her chest.

"You're injured?" He was looking at her ripped tights.

"I skinned my knees. It's worse than it looks. Tilly went through a period of coming home from school almost every day with holes in the knees of her tights and never complained." She wanted to complain though. Skinned knees might not have been fatal but they were bloody painful. "What do we do if they've punctured the tyres?"

"We have to think of something else. Is there another town nearby if we go over the field?"

"Not really. I think the closest village is at least a mile away."

"Is there a footpath to it?"

"I have no idea but I don't want to be standing out in full view of everyone." An idea struck her. "You said before that you run across country. Why don't you go?"

"What?"

"Let's face it, Jack, it's me they're after. You could get away. I'll head for the house and you go across the field."

He looked offended. "Are you mad?"

"No, I'm trying to be fair."

"You're not being fair, you're insane. They know my name and both our lives are at risk so let's get out of it together."

She felt so grateful she wanted to cry.

"Okay," he said. "If they start a search then they're probably going to look here first. If we head towards the house we might keep a step ahead."

Rachel wiped her eyes. "And the house might have a phone."

"Yes."

She glanced around the wall. The first barn might have been fifty yards away. It looked like an oversized garage with brick walls and a corrugated metal roof. Two windows reflected moonlight. An old plough had been left to rot equidistant between them.

"Could we make that gap?" she asked, not at all convinced.

"We might reach that plough without being seen, but beyond that would leave us open."

"We don't have much choice, do we?"

"No," he said and she felt his shrug. "I don't think so."

The noise of an engine drifted across the field. "Can you hear that?" she asked.

"Maybe it's the people from the house coming home?"

"Could be. And it might mean those arseholes are distracted."

"Good thinking." He pushed himself onto his knees and worked his way past her to the end of the wall. "I'll go first, okay?"

"I'll be right behind you."

She got gingerly to her knees and bit her lip as her skin grazed the concrete.

He peered around the wall then ran and quickly covered the area between the concrete and plough. He skidded to a halt behind it and raised a thumb to her.

Rachel didn't look towards the gate in case her courage deserted her and she just ran. She watched the ground as treacherous little indentations jarred her back and thicker tufts of scrubby grass knocked her balance. She tried to keep a good pace and pumped her arms but her mind was full of how exposed she must be in the moonlight.

Then she was dropping behind Jack. Nobody shouted. He grabbed her arm and shook it.

"You did it!"

She took a moment to get her breath then looked over to the barn. The distance seemed less than what she'd just run but she thought they'd be visible from the gate for a good five seconds at the very least.

"The car's almost here," he said.

She hoped it wasn't the people from the farmhouse. Nobody deserved to come home to this kind of nightmare.

"As soon as we see the lights in the turnaround we'll run."

"Agreed."

As they waited, Rachel's heart beat ever faster until it felt like it would burst out of her chest. Then the field and cattle grid lit up.

"Go," she said and Jack did.

# Chapter 21

Keel looked away from the glare of headlights to maintain his night vision.

When the car stopped and the headlights were off, he turned and folded his arms to regard the people carrier. The side door opened and a tall thin man got out. He gave Munro a quick mock salute.

"This is Carlisle," she said.

Carlisle pulled off his leather glove and held out his hand. Keel shook it.

"Pleased to meet you, Mr Keel," said Carlisle. "It's an honour to work with you."

Keel appraised the man quickly. He wore black shoes, dark trousers and a shiny black bomber jacket.

"Good to meet you too."

"I'll introduce the team."

Carlisle turned towards the people carrier, held his gloveless hand up and made a circular motion. Keel bit his lip so as not to smile. Carlisle clearly liked the theatrical.

Two people got out of the vehicle and stood in front of it. Keel waited for more but that appeared to be it.

"So," he said. "Did you want to introduce me to Take That?"

Carlisle looked at him and frowned. "Eh, Mr Keel?"

"Your team," said Keel. Carlisle and his colleagues were all dressed the same. "Are you all bouncers by any chance?"

"That's right, how did you know?"

"Just a guess."

Carlisle looked momentarily confused.

"Okay," he said, recovering quickly. "This is Stephens."

Stephens was broad and blond and well over six foot tall. When he grinned at Keel, he showed plenty of teeth.

"He's good at close quarters work," said Carlisle.

"I try to take people down before they even realise the fight's on," Stephens said seriously.

Keel nodded as Carlisle said, "And this is Hatcher."

Much shorter than Stephens and very slim, the brunette woman exchanged a nod with Keel. She wore a thin backpack, similar to Munro's, over her right shoulder. Hatcher nodded at Munro, who smiled warmly at her.

"Good to see you again," Hatcher said.

"And you," said Munro.

"Thank you for that," Keel said. "Okay, you lot need to listen because I don't like talking and I don't like repeating myself."

Nobody spoke. Hatcher rubbed her hands together.

"We are after two people, Rachel Turner and Jack Martin. You already know what Rachel looks like. We don't have a picture of Jack but if you find a man up here who's not me, Carlisle or Stephens, then you can safely bet it'll be him."

Carlisle snorted out a laugh.

"We need them both rounding up but Rachel especially. Restrain her by whatever means necessary but do not, I repeat do not, excessively harm her. She needs to be fully lucid and if anyone incapacitates her, I will do the same to them."

"What about Jack Martin?" asked Stephens.

"Same rules," said Munro quickly, "but Jack is mine."

"Are we clear?" Keel asked.

The team nodded their assent.

"Munro and I haven't left the turnaround here," he said. "We don't know if anyone is in residence at the farm but we assume not. That will need to be checked."

"There's a dog somewhere," said Hatcher. "It's getting on my nerves."

"Whoever finds the dog should deal with it as they see fit," Keel said. "Rachel and Jack had a head start of maybe twenty seconds. It's my guess they've run towards the building plots." He turned to Carlisle. "My suggestion would be to fan out across the field then work your way back."

"Agreed." Carlisle nodded. He took two small two-tone handsets out of his jacket and handed one to Munro and another to Keel. "Now we're all on the same tech," he said.

* * *

Rachel reached the edge of the barn. Jack, who had let her go by then, peered around towards the gate. She put her hands on her knees and got her breath back.

"What's going on?"

"It's a people carrier," he said. "Three people have got out."

"Are they the people from the farmhouse?"

"I doubt it. They're all talking like they know one another."

"How does that make sense? Unless the Range Rover driver is very charming."

Jack checked his watch. "It's one in the morning, he'd have to be pretty fucking charming not to at least get a 'what the hell are you doing here?' shouted at him."

"Unless…" she said and let the sentence taper away because it was surely better not to give voice to the horrible thought she'd just had.

"What?" he asked after a few moments.

"Unless they do know each other."

He snapped his head round to regard her with wide eyes.

"How could they know each other?" In the dim light she saw realisation spread over his face. "Unless they've come to help?"

Her stomach rolled. "What did I do, Jack? What does he want?"

"I don't know. I still can't work out how he knows me or Luisa."

She licked her lips, her mouth suddenly dry. "What can I do? Should I speak to him?"

"No. He's chased us through town, risked our lives and his and now he's got his mates up here to hunt us. That's not someone who wants to talk rationally."

The sound of voices drifted to her and she leaned out past Jack. "Oh shit, there were three people in that car."

"Three?"

"Uh-huh, so now we have five people against us."

"Fuck," he hissed.

She put her head in her hands. Terror and anxiety fought for dominance and she wanted to shake them both away because now she needed to be rational and not fall apart.

"I'm so scared," he said quietly. "I haven't been this scared since..." He stopped and looked at Rachel and she held the gaze until he glanced away. "I can barely breathe."

"Or me, but we have to pull ourselves together. If we crumble they've got us." She patted his back. "I need to get away from this. I need to get home."

"So what do we do? I don't suppose you've got time to teach me anything from your self-defence classes?"

She smiled, more at the futility in his voice than the attempt at humour.

"Just the KISS thing Kim tells us – keep it simple, stupid. Go for the face, eyes, nose, throat, the soft bit of cheek. If you have a chance, go for the liver or kidneys or, failing that, kick them between the legs."

"I thought as much." He looked towards the other barn and the house beyond it. "We should go."

She gave him a look and he nodded.

"There might be a phone in the house so we can call the police," he said. "It's our only chance."

The house seemed so far away and she felt the terror burn in her chest. What if one of them hit a divot and sprained their ankle or worse? They couldn't hide here forever but surely that'd be better than writhing in agony, visible to everyone?

"Okay," she said, "let's go."

"Are you sure?" The moonlight cast half his face in shadow.

"No, because the gap's huge, but we need to get to the phone."

Jack looked around the corner. "They're still talking. I'll go first and if they see me, just stay put. That way they won't know where you are."

"No," she said, aghast. "I couldn't do that."

"Then we go together," he said, grabbed her wrist and pulled.

They ran, both crouched low, and the ground passed in a blur with tufts of grass casting shadows that might have been hollows. She avoided as many as she could and didn't twist her ankle in any she hit. The second barn seemed like a mile away and it felt like they were on a treadmill, running fast but standing still.

\* \* \*

"I want you, Hatcher, to head up to the building plots," said Carlisle. "Start at the furthest and work back but be alert as there's plenty of places to hide."

She nodded.

"Stephens, you head for the house and mind that dog."

"Or muzzle the fucking thing," muttered Hatcher.

Carlisle turned to Keel. "Are you okay with that?"

Keel nodded and climbed onto the gate. "Rachel!" he called, cupping his mouth. "Jack!"

The only response was a faint echo of his own voice.

"I know you can hear me and I need you to understand we have you trapped. If you give yourselves up, we'll head back into Hadlington and all will be well. If you don't then my colleagues will flush you out and that won't be pleasant. They will enjoy it but I seriously doubt you will."

Nobody replied. The dog kept barking.

"Okay," he said to Carlisle. "Away you go."

Munro smiled and seemed happy as if she'd been given licence to exact her revenge on Jack.

Hatcher vaulted the gate and skipped across the cattle grid. Stephens jogged around the people carrier and down the road to the gate before his progress was swallowed from sight by a hedge.

* * *

Still scared after Keel's speech, Rachel took a moment to try and figure out their next move. The barn marked the furthest edge of a courtyard enclosed by another dry-stone wall. The two-storey farmhouse they'd seen from the lane marked the other edge. It had a wide chimney breast on this side and two windows upstairs, two downstairs. None appeared to have curtains.

Trees behind the house hid from view whatever lay beyond including the dog. There were no cars in the courtyard.

"It's very open between us and the house," she said.

"So why not let's just go in the back?" Jack said.

"Good idea."

Heart thumping, she held his hand as they left the relative safety of the barn. The courtyard was paved with slabs that looked old and uneven but felt smooth.

They ran at an angle towards the back of the house and all she heard were their footsteps and the rushing of her blood.

She slipped into the shadows beyond the corner of the house. The tree line was perhaps ten or twelve feet back and a paved walkway led further down the hill.

The Range Rover driver shouted again and his voice echoed. Rachel risked a look and saw a dark-haired person vault the gate and run into the field. Two other people came through the gate from the road.

She thought quickly. The person in the field would discover they weren't there and come back this way to join the other two. Either way, they were very soon going to have company.

"Let's get inside," she said.


# Chapter 22


Rachel looked through the window into a kitchen. Another window looked out over the courtyard and moonlight flooded through it. The room had modern appliances and an island with pots and pans hanging above it. A dark wood dining table with four chairs around it stood near the door. It looked like her idea of a dream kitchen but everything seemed a little off somehow.

She moved along to Jack who stood by the back door. "It's locked."

"Could we smash the glass and break in?"

"I suppose so," he said. "It's not something I've ever tried." He looked around and picked up half a brick near the tree line.

"It'll be double-glazed."

"So where do I hit it?"

She shrugged. "I've never tried it either, Jack. Just whack it."

"What about the noise?"

"They know we're here," she said but looked around anyway in case someone was trying to creep up on them.

Jack raised the brick and she turned her face away. He hit the glass panel so hard the brick almost came out of his grasp as it bounced off with a dull thud. He tried three times before it finally cracked and the fourth attempt put the brick cleanly through.

"Jesus," he muttered. "I didn't expect it to be so difficult."

Rachel reached carefully through the gap and her fingers groped below the door handle until she felt something rattle.

"The keys are in the door," she said and quickly unlocked it.

She slipped her hand out and opened the door. Jack followed her in and closed it behind him.

Crouching, they duckwalked into the kitchen. Rachel went towards the courtyard window and Jack went left. She reached the sink and pulled open the wide drawer next to it. She reached in and her fingers danced through emptiness. She tried the next drawer and found it empty.

"There's nothing here," Jack whispered loudly.

"It's a fucking show home, isn't it? They've just modernised the old farmhouse."

He beckoned for her to join him by the island. "What now?" he asked.

"Same as before; we try and find a phone. They might have a sales desk or something in here."

"Okay. If we split up, we can do it quicker."

"I'll go upstairs," she said and got to her knees but winced as her wounds came into contact with the cold tiles. She quickly made her way through to the hall but the thick carpet there was worse. The staircase was to her left and two doors opened to the right. After the newel post the hall opened into a broad square with a wide front door set off to the left. To the right of it was another door marked 'Toilet'.

She looked up the wide staircase.

"Take it easy," Jack whispered.

Rachel held up her thumb over her shoulder then went up the stairs on her hands and knees.

\* \* \*

Jack remained downstairs and opened the first door off the hallway into what looked like the living room.

There were two bare windows. One overlooked the courtyard while the other showed the front garden and lane.

He took some steady deep breaths as he looked around. The windows let in plenty of moonlight and he saw a sofa, a coffee table and a low cupboard filled with books. A wide naked fireplace stood between the windows and a very big TV was mounted to the wall above it.

Jack crawled across the room and knelt beside the fireplace. He gently raised himself enough to see through the window. Munro and the driver of the Range Rover stood by the gate.

He turned to face the room and saw, by the other door, an occasional table with a lamp and telephone on it.

"Yes," he hissed.

He crawled to it. The handset felt too light as he picked it up and he realised it was hollow.

"Shit."

He dropped the toy handset and opened the second door. He couldn't see or hear Rachel. Another door was set into the wall on his right and he crawled to it but stopped when he heard a noise from the kitchen.

He glanced left, eyes wide, a cold sweat on his forehead.

The back door opened.

\* \* \*

When Rachel reached the top of the stairs she squatted below the wide window which looked out over the trees and let in a slant of moonlight. Four doors opened off the landing, two to her right and two across the front of the house.

She moved to the first door and opened it slowly. Nobody came for her. She leaned against the jamb to look in and saw a bedroom that was as much a showroom as the kitchen. There was no phone.

The second room was the same.

"Bollocks," she muttered and then heard the back door open.

She felt the shock of it in her chest and pains jabbed her arms and fingers. She held her breath and focussed her very being on listening.

Glass crunched.

"This is Stephens," a man said, his voice low. "There was a broken window on the back door so I'm just going to check it out."

Rachel could hear Stephen's progress through the kitchen as glass crunched on the tiles. He came into the hall and while the thick carpet swallowed the sound of his feet she heard a swish of fabric, like he was wearing something nylon. As the swish moved she tried to place him in the hall and gauge his progress. He breathed quickly through his mouth. She heard a door open and then the newcomer was quiet.

Where the hell was Jack?

\* \* \*

Jack listened in darkness so complete that his eyes struggled to make out any details at all.

Hiding in the small windowless toilet had been a mistake. He'd panicked when he heard Stephens come in the back door and should have gone into the lounge. To make matters worse, the handle hadn't been fitted properly and came away in his hand when he shut the door. He'd tried to grab the barrel but it dropped out into the hall. A quick search of the room had yielded nothing he could use as either a weapon or to help him get out.

He was trapped and a cold sweat coated his forehead as he listened to Stephens get closer. The man went into the lounge and came back out again and Jack knew he was done for then. The terror was almost dreamlike in its intensity and made him feel sick.

If Stephens opened the door then Jack might have a slight element of surprise but the man must have been expecting to find him. What could Jack do then? He might get a chance to swing a punch but that was about it.

* * *

Rachel's fingers clawed on the wallpaper and her back ached from being so ramrod straight. Her chest hurt from holding her breath and she released it slowly, blowing quietly towards the ceiling.

Another door opened and she heard the swish again and tried to place it. It sounded almost like a bomber jacket. Sweat beaded in Rachel's hairline.

"Downstairs seems clear," Stephens said quietly. "I'll try upstairs."

Panic hit Rachel and popped in front of her eyes like flashbulbs. She slipped into the nearest bedroom and closed the door almost shut, leaving herself just the smallest of cracks to see through.

Stephens came up the stairs slowly. As his head cleared the line of the landing it brought her fear to a peak but also humanised him. He wasn't a monster now she could see him; he was just a man who could – in theory – be dealt with.

Keep it simple, stupid, she thought.

He might be able to hurt her or ward off her blows without breaking a sweat, but she wouldn't make it easy for him.

Rachel stepped back from the door and looked slowly around the room, thinking about the mantra from her self-defence class. Anything could be a weapon and she needed to defend herself now. She quickly checked the items she could see on the shelf unit and desk but everything was fake and would crumple as soon as she tried to use it. She picked up a can of deodorant and realised it was real. A quick shake confirmed it was full.

She heard a handle turn and rushed back to the gap to see him go into the first bedroom. He wasn't in there long and as he came back onto the landing, she realised the swishing noise came from his bomber jacket.

He came towards the door and she stepped back to give herself some space. When he opened it, he seemed to fill the gap and moonlight picked out details of his face. She saw him jump a little when he caught sight of her and then he grinned and his teeth flashed in the light.

"Well," he said. "Little pig, little pig…"

Her breath caught and it felt like all the air had been squeezed from her lungs. This was it. This was just the situation she'd been going to Kim's self-defence classes for. She tried to push the terror back and force herself to breathe. She could do this. Stephens looked big and he was frightening but she had to treat him like one of her fellow classmates who'd volunteered to be the aggressor.

"Keep back," she said and her voice cracked.

Stephens laughed sourly. "Has that ever worked?"

"Leave me alone," she said louder and held up the deodorant can. "Stay there."

Still laughing, he stepped into the room. "You'll have to do better than that, love."

She stood her ground and watched him. He was broad like he worked out a lot, and she remembered Kim telling them that sometimes people who built muscle didn't always pay as much attention to cardio work at the gym as they should. If you could keep them moving it might be to your advantage.

"Why are you doing this?" she asked and took a step back.

He matched her move. "Who cares?"

"Me."

He came at her and she side-stepped so he lurched towards the window. He tried again but she simply stepped away and he bounced off the wall coming straight back to her. She ducked away from him and edged towards the door, keeping the distance between them the same as before.

Stephens wasn't grinning now.

"Think you're clever, do you? I eat people like you for breakfast."

She laughed at that and his face flashed with anger.

"What the fuck?"

She decided she had nothing to lose. "Do you always talk in clichés?"

He looked surprised. "You…" He didn't finish and rushed at her again.

She went to the right and ducked down. His grasping fingers didn't even graze her skin.

Stephens planted his foot to stop his momentum and whirled around. Rachel moved towards the desk.

"You're not that clever," he said but his breathing seemed heavier.

"I don't have to be."

"You won't get past me. And even if you do there are others outside."

As she backed towards the desk he came again. She ducked under the span of his hand and came up quickly letting her left hand go with the momentum. It slapped hard into his face.

He yelled with surprise and rubbed his eye as she moved across the room. The door was now behind her and she could see in his expression he knew he'd been played with. Anger pulled his lips tight and narrowed his eyes. He looked like he wanted to kill her.

* * *

The commotion upstairs sounded loud in the enclosed space of the bathroom and Jack knew Rachel was in trouble. He quickly checked around the toilet again in case he'd missed anything before but still came up with nothing.

How could this be? They'd come so far and now she really needed his help and he was trapped in the toilet like a fucking idiot while she battled with some thug upstairs.

He tried pushing the door then slammed one of the panels with the heel of his hand. It didn't have an effect but gave off a hollow ring.

Jack stopped. It was a modern door which meant it was probably just panelling over a simple structure. If he could find the weak spot, he could perhaps smash through and who cared how much noise he made because the enemy was already in the building.

He sat on the toilet and kicked out.

* * *

Rachel backed onto the landing and heard a thud from downstairs. Stephens grinned at her.

"Sounds like your friend has found one of mine," he said.

"Why don't you let us go?"

He shook his head and his fringe flopped on his forehead.

Rachel could feel the tension starting to overwhelm her and shook her head to try and clear it. Stephens took a step towards her and she moved back, trying to keep away from the banister in case he tried to tip her over it.

He took another big step and closed the gap enough to grab her left shoulders. His fingers dug in as he pulled her off balance. He wrapped his arms around her and laced his fingers over her breasts then yanked her back hard against his chest. She could barely move.

He dragged her towards the banister then stopped outside the bedroom.

"Shall we have some fun?" he asked. His mouth was close to her ear and his breath felt warm on her neck.

She felt a surge of outraged energy because she hadn't endured everything tonight just for this lump to assault her. She kicked back with her heel and he groaned in pain. She kicked twice more then dragged her heel down his shin. He pushed her forwards and she let herself drop. He moved his hands to try and get a better grip and she spun out of his grasp, brought the deodorant can up and sprayed it into his face.

Stephens screamed and moved backwards, shielding his eyes with his left hand and swatting at her with his right. Rachel went with him and the can ran out as he reached the top of the stairs. She threw it at him and it bounced off his forehead with a clank.

He stumbled and grabbed for the banister but missed and Rachel saw what would happen a moment before it did.

His hand grasped thin air and his foot went over the first riser and he pitched forward. He landed with a sickening crack that stopped his screams and heavy breathing instantly. He fell to the bottom in a jumble of limbs.

\* \* \*

The toilet door splintered and Jack pulled it open as Stephens landed in a heap at the bottom of the stairs.

"Rachel?" He could hear her gasping breath but she didn't respond right away. "Rachel? Are you okay?"

"No." A pause. "Is he…"

Jack didn't have to look too hard at the angle of the man's neck to know Stephens was dead. "Yes," he said.

She came downstairs and held the banister tightly, her attention focussed on the body.

"He fell," she said haltingly. "He tried to hurt me and I sprayed deodorant in his eyes. I didn't think this would happen." Her voice hitched. "He fell, I didn't mean to hurt him."

Jack helped her down the last few stairs then hugged her hard. "You did the right thing. He would have hurt you."

"Yes," she said, her voice muffled against his coat.

Jack saw something glow in Stephens' inner pocket and carefully released himself from Rachel. He squatted next to the body and pulled the object out. He thought at first he'd found a mobile phone but instead it was some kind of radio handset.

"I feel sick," Rachel said.

"I know." He stood up and put the radio in his pocket.

"What have I done?"

"What needed to be done," he said. "Come on."

Hand in hand, they walked to the dark kitchen. Jack opened the back door and, after a quick glance to make sure no one was about, Rachel stepped out into the night.

# Chapter 23

By the time Pippa drove home, most of Hadlington appeared to have gone to sleep.

There were no revellers left in the street and the fireworks had long since stopped exploding overhead where the moon glowed bright.

Her shift had run over slightly and the pressure of it still weighed heavily on her. Suicide, especially at this time of the year, wasn't uncommon and she'd been taught coping mechanisms as part of the job but it never got easier. It was worse when they had to knock with the news and she didn't envy the family liaison officer in this case dealing with loved ones and close friends.

She yawned as traffic lights stopped her at an empty junction. Early morning finishes generally didn't bother

her though the timings often played havoc with her private life. Often times, the drive home through empty streets did her the world of good in allowing her mind to unwind.

Hopefully that would be the case this morning even though she couldn't quite rid herself of the image of Barbara Gilbert hanging in the stairwell. Even so, she was looking forward to getting home and having a quick shower before driving over to her boyfriend Richard's place in Marham. They'd arranged it last weekend when she still had hopes of getting this shift off, and decided not to cancel when she couldn't. He'd be asleep when she got there but she always enjoyed waking up next to him.

The song on the radio ended and Pippa tuned out the DJ's unfunny commentary as her mind wandered to what Rosie had said in the canteen about the incident near her home. She decided to take a slight detour because it wouldn't take more than five minutes to drive past at this hour of the morning.

Moore Avenue was a pleasant walk from Lamont Street. She and her nephew had only been at the park a few weeks back. The building behind it was being slowly dismantled and her nephew loved to see the workmen hammering away and dropping bricks down the chutes.

She turned into the road. Her headlights illuminated the Battenburg sticker pattern on the patrol car parked over the driveway of a big house set back from the road. Pippa pulled up beside it. The wrecked car was a Fiat 500 and it stood at a forty-five-degree angle between two properties. The front end was hidden by bushes and the bodywork had a few dents.

An officer appeared from the offside of the vehicle and startled her. As he turned, it was clear she'd startled him too so she waved and wound down the window. He came around the back of the Fiat and she recognised him.

"Evening, Des," she said. They'd met as probationers and struck up an easy, casual friendship that still endured.

Des had a large sticker in his hands. As he walked down the driveway Pippa got out of her car and crossed the road to join him.

"What're you doing here, you plonk?" he asked.

She grinned at him. "Off shift," she said. "And it's nice to see you too."

He gave a thin-lipped humourless smile. "I'm tired, cold and bored. Don't be driving past now to take the piss."

"As if I'd do that."

"Yeah," he muttered, "as if. So what're you here for? Not to help me out, I suppose?"

"Help you to put stickers on an abandoned car? Hardly, Des. That's the kind of job they give to probies."

He offered another thin-lipped smile and walked back up to the car. "There's never one around when you need one, judging by tonight. So what're you here for?"

"Rubbernecking," she said and followed him up the driveway. "I live a couple of streets over and thought I'd check it out."

"Not much to see. Couple of noise complaints for some fireworks let off over the back, and then raised voices and a possible altercation in the garden. Then another complaint later on about this abandoned car."

"All good fun, eh?"

"It's the full moon, I'm telling you." He wiped the rear windscreen of the Fiat with a cloth and checked the writing on the front of the sticker. He started to unpeel it and checked the writing again. "How did it go with your jumper?"

"We've had nothing through yet."

He put the sticker onto the rear windscreen and peeled the remainder of the backing away. "Gruesome?"

"Aren't they always?"

"Uh-huh." He folded the backing and slipped it into one of the pockets on his stab vest. "Now I'm going to clock out and bugger off home."

She nodded towards the Fiat. "You stuck it on the wrong way up."

"What?" His startled look made her smile as she turned and walked down the driveway.

"The sticker's upside down."

"Very funny," he said in a tone which suggested he found it anything but.

It made her laugh.

# Chapter 24

Keel rubbed his gloved hands together. Munro stood beside the Range Rover, deep in thought as she rubbed a cloth over the large crossbow she'd taken from the boot and assembled. Moonlight glinted off the crafted piece.

She smiled when she noticed him watching her.

"This is the hunter," she said. "It belongs out here in all this space. The pistol's only good for close-up work."

"Let's hope you don't need to use it."

"I'll shoot to wound, I'm a professional."

He knew she used the cleaning as a meditative act to keep her mind occupied. Carlisle, on the other hand, didn't have anything to occupy him and his constant pacing from the people carrier to the Range Rover was starting to get annoying.

Keel glanced at his watch. The crew had been gone a little more than ten minutes and he'd expected to have heard something by now but he knew time could be elastic in the middle of the night in a place you didn't know and the minutes stretched like one of Dali's watches.

The Google map of the area showed a line of trees running from the house onto a wide field. A railway line cut across this and ran down to the A14 and followed the line of the carriageway. On the other side of the railway was a dense wood. If Rachel and Jack made it there then the hunt would be more difficult, so it was important to flush them out quickly.

All three radio handsets bleeped and Carlisle answered his.

"All three plots clear," said Hatcher. "Both barns are locked tight, so I'll come in."

Carlisle glanced towards the farmhouse and worried the inside of his cheek. He looked at Keel.

"I've got a bad feeling," he said.

Keel leaned against the Range Rover and folded his arms. "About the farmhouse?"

Carlisle nodded. "Stephens should have cleared it by now."

* * *

Rachel's adrenaline rush faded and she felt suddenly woozy. Her legs got heavy and she toppled sideways as her horizon shifted.

"Oh," she gasped.

Jack was holding her hand and managed to keep her upright for long enough to lean her against the wall.

"You alright?" he said.

She saw it hit him too then. His expression went slack and he sat down heavily opposite her.

"Jesus," he muttered. "The adrenaline's worn off."

"I feel fucking awful," she muttered, and the fatigue was only part of it. "He wanted to hurt me, Jack. It was scary."

"There was nothing else you could do."

She massaged her neck with a hand that didn't feel properly hers. Pins and needles raced through her fingers.

"I killed him," she said and her voice cracked. She took a deep breath and let it out shakily.

"It's not that simple," he said.

She looked at her fingers as she flicked them to try and clear the pins and needles. Was he right and, even if he was, could she possibly believe him?

"What happened?"

"He came at me. He wasn't interested in anything I said and was going to do stuff to me before he dragged me out."

Her voice shook again and she took another deep breath, letting it out slowly as she fought back tears. She didn't want to give Stephens the satisfaction even in death.

"I defended myself and he fell."

"You see, it wasn't your fault."

"Except I sprayed the deodorant and blinded him and that's why he fell. I killed him."

"I think falling down the stairs did that."

She shook her head briskly. "Don't joke."

"I won't so long as you don't beat yourself up about it. He was here to get us so it's not your fault, it's the twats in the Range Rover who set him onto us. He's collateral damage to them."

"Do you think?" She wanted to believe him because she could feel the guilt starting to press down on her.

"Of course, we didn't ask for any of this."

"But we must have, somehow." She shook her head. "I feel like shit."

"I can only imagine. But nothing could justify what they're doing so we need to keep going and tell somebody and get some help."

"Yeah."

"And keep moving before someone else tries to hurt us."

"Yes," she said. From this vantage point she could see a compound through gaps in the trees. It contained a long static caravan, a small digger and two mopeds, and was enclosed with a chain-link fence. A large tower stood in one corner with a feeble spotlight mounted on it. A big

Alsatian came out from behind the caravan with its head lowered and prowled to the other end of its domain.

"What are you looking at?"

"That compound. The caravan might be a site office for this place so maybe it's got a phone. If not, the A14 is down the field from there so we could try and get back to civilisation that way."

He shifted around so he could see the compound. "Why don't we try it?"

"How do we deal with the dog?"

"We'll figure something out when we get there." He struggled to his feet. "Can you stand?"

* * *

Munro's mind worked as she cleaned the crossbow flight groove. While she respected Keel and understood his explanation of why anger played no part in their job, she couldn't square it with her desire to make Jack Martin pay for breaking her necklace and shoving her into that tree. Part of it was wounded pride that Keel saw her moment of weakness, but mostly it was because she owed Jack some payback.

The ongoing conversation between Keel and Carlisle snagged her attention and she walked over to them.

"Trouble?" she asked.

Carlisle pursed his lips and lifted a shoulder in a shrug. "I wouldn't have thought so."

"Are you sure?" Now wasn't the time to fuck around. She'd suggested the crew and it would reflect on her if Keel wasn't impressed, and Munro definitely didn't want that.

"I'll try them again." He held his radio up and indicated a button to Keel and Munro. "Silent alarm," he said. "You use it to summon assistance and it vibrates slightly without making it a sound. Two taps is the call-in code."

He pressed the button and the unit vibrated for a second a few moments later.

"That's Hatcher," he said looking at the screen.

They waited and Carlisle tried it again but there was no response.

"Something's wrong," Munro said though it made no sense to her how two civilians could best Stephens.

Carlisle nodded. "I'm going to check," he said.

* * *

Rachel stopped at the edge of the house and peered cautiously around the corner.

No one was there. From here she could see down the hill across a wide field bordered by a narrow line of trees. The lights of Hadlington and the A14 were barely visible through the branches.

"It's clear," she said.

Jack patted between her shoulder blades gently. "Come on then."

A narrow gravel path ran at an angle from the house through the trees. As they started walking something buzzed in Jack's pocket and he made a startled sound.

"What was that?" she asked.

He let go of her hand and took the handset out of his pocket. The glow of the screen lit his face and he held the unit up and squinted before handing it to her.

"Haven't got my glasses," he said sheepishly.

The pale blue screen had three app buttons on it and she didn't recognise any of them. The handset vibrated and she almost dropped it in surprise. One app icon flashed.

"Call-in," she told him. "Maybe they're making sure their thug's okay?"

"Well, they're in for a surprise." He smiled grimly as she handed it back to him. He put it in his pocket.

They followed the path through the trees which were only four or five deep, and out onto a wide gravelled area that was deeply rutted in places. The compound faced them and the dog had noticed them. As big an Alsatian as she'd ever seen, it was painfully scrawny and growled as it stared through the fence.

"We can't go in there with that thing," she said.

"No."

The dog began barking ferociously.

"He's going to give us away," she fretted.

Jack turned as if checking for another route and gasped. He pulled her arm.

"What're you doing?" she demanded.

"Look behind you."

Rachel turned to see a man running towards them along the side of the house. The sight would have been frightening at any time but now she had to bite her lip to stop screaming.

"Shit," Jack said.

He grabbed her hand and pulled her with him as he ran across the gravel. The dog went wild and threw itself at the fence which bowed with every impact. Rachel glanced over her shoulder not knowing whether to be more frightened of the wraith chasing them or the dog with saliva coming off his muzzle in ropes.

Jack was pulling her towards the compound and terror swamped her. She shook her head to try and clear it. He'd clearly gone mad because the dog would surely tear them to pieces.

"Only option," he said, breathing hard. He stopped a few feet from the compound gate. "Look, it's not locked. The padlock's only slipped through the hasp."

"What?" She could barely hear this close to the barking. "Are you insane?"

He shook his head. "We'll check the phone then steal one of those mopeds and ride down the field."

"They have a Range Rover."

"He hasn't brought it off-road yet, has he? I had a moped in my sixth form days, if they're on foot we can make time on them."

"What about the fucking dog?"

He glanced behind him and she did the same. The man had almost reached the gravel path now and she could see he wore a bomber jacket and dark trousers like Stephens had.

"We're going to open the gate," Jack said.

* * *

Munro had watched Carlisle go with a sinking feeling.

"He shouldn't have done that, should he?"

Keel didn't say anything and that didn't inspire any confidence.

"He's not usually like that. I got him involved because he's normally level-headed."

"He's not used to being on the back foot."

"Are you saying Rachel's better than his team and us?"

"Not necessarily, but she's besting us. Take a look around. This place is isolated. With a twenty second head start they found a hiding place we didn't discover and we're one operative down."

"You surely don't think they're professionals like us?"

He shook his head. "Not at all, but maybe this isn't going to be the walk in the park we expected and Carlisle might regret charging in."

* * *

"Open it how?" Rachel asked.

Jack looked at the gate. His plan was stupid and dangerous but it might just work. "I need you to trust me." He almost had to shout to be heard.

"Okay," she said after a moment.

Jack glanced over his shoulder at the running man who was only two hundred or so yards away then walked closer to the gate. Rachel followed a pace or two behind. Jack pulled on the padlock. The dog jumped at him and the chain-link bowed.

His heart pounded in his ears louder than the dog's barking.

"Stand by the gate," he told Rachel. "Far enough back so the dog can't reach you."

She looked like it was the last thing she wanted to do, but once she'd checked the progress of the man racing towards them, she did as he asked. The dog, if anything, got more frantic.

Jack grabbed the padlock and pulled it out of the hasp. The Alsatian crouched and he saw its muscles bunch as it prepared to leap. He pressed Rachel against the fence and pinned her to it with his body. He yanked the gate and tucked himself behind it.

The gate swung open and the dog leapt through the gap. Jack pulled the gate against the fence and effectively imprisoned him and Rachel.

The dog landed and didn't look at them instead focussing on the man who'd now stopped running on the gravel. He looked terrified and his chest heaved as he held out his hands in a calming gesture. The dog growled and its hackles rose.

The man turned and ran but the Alsatian covered the distance between them in an instant and leapt onto his back. The man fell forward into the trees.

Rachel squeezed Jack's hand tightly and he swallowed back bile as the screams started. Is this how she'd felt in the house? That hadn't been her fault, and this wasn't his doing but at the very least he'd been the architect of the destruction.

He felt ill as if something in him had changed – not broken exactly but certainly chipped. His conscience maybe?

"Hey!" The voice came to him from away. "Hey, Jack!"

He shook his head and the night swam back into focus. He heard the dog and the man screaming and other noises he didn't want to identify. His stomached rolled.

"Hey!" Rachel shouted at him.

"I'm here," he said but his voice sounded clogged.

"Good," said Rachel and nudged her backside against his thigh.

He let go of the chain-link and she pushed the gate open.

"We have to get into the compound," she said.

She manhandled him through the gate, pulled it shut and dropped the latch.

The screams stopped.

# Chapter 25

Munro snapped her attention towards the farmhouse as a scream erupted.

"Could be them," she said.

Hatcher appeared at the gate and vaulted it easily. Another scream rolled to them.

"Is that Carlisle?" Munro asked.

"Could it be the bloke we're after?" Hatcher asked.

"Unlikely," said Keel. "I only heard a male voice. Jack and Rachel wouldn't split up so we'd hear both of them scream."

"How did they beat him too?" Munro asked.

It felt like her world had shifted and she didn't like it. She needed to regain control before events spiralled too far out of it.

"Maybe they didn't," Keel said calmly. "We need to understand the situation."

"I'll go," Munro said.

He nodded. "Take Hatcher and follow Carlisle's route. Stay alert though and don't forget we need Rachel alive."

"Agreed." If Jack had caused Carlisle to scream though, the man wouldn't see out the night.

"Munro," Keel said, his voice steely.

"I've got it," she said and they exchanged terse glances as she walked away.

* * *

Rachel crossed the uneven ground of the compound feeling horribly exposed and was relieved to get to the caravan.

It was propped up on bricks and a small wooden staircase led to the narrow door in the middle of the body. Two windows were covered by pale threadbare curtains.

"I'll check for a phone," she said. He looked at her blankly. "You check the mopeds."

"Yes," he said absently. "I will."

She touched his arm. "It can't be helped," she said. "It's not your fault."

He gave her a wan smile. "I remember saying the same to you."

"Still true," she said and tested the wooden steps which were made from an old pallet. They held her weight. She tried the door. It opened easily and she went into the gloomy interior. She felt for the light switch then closed the door before she turned it on.

The caravan was an office. A metal desk sat under the window opposite, and papers covered the top almost completely. She couldn't see a phone. A low sofa that looked filthy in the poor light sat under the bay window at the far end and a cardboard box full of hard hats sat on top of it. There was no other furniture or storage.

It didn't take long to check the desk drawers and sift through the papers to find there was no phone.

"Shit."

She hoped Jack managed to get one of the mopeds working.

* * *

The screaming stopped before Munro reached the house.

135

She kept her finger tight against the trigger of the crossbow with a bolt loaded and ready to fire. She looked around cautiously.

"Take it easy," she whispered. "Those fuckers seem to be indestructible."

"I'm right behind you," Hatcher whispered back.

They walked the length of the house slowly and Munro stopped at the corner and rested her shoulder again the brickwork.

"Count of three," Munro whispered and Hatcher nodded.

Munro counted then moved and crouched low with the crossbow at her shoulder. A quick look left and right revealed a paved path behind the house and a line of trees that masked a compound.

She heard a snuffling noise but couldn't identify it. Munro gestured to Hatcher and they moved to the trees together. The noise seemed louder here. She followed a gravel path through the trees and stopped with her crossbow trained on what she could see but not quite believe.

An Alsatian regarded her coolly with a blood-coated snout. It bared its teeth and growled low in its throat. Munro looked at its prey and took in the bomber jacket and dark trousers. A bloody left hand was missing half a finger.

Hatcher gagged. "Fucking dog," she hissed.

The Alsatian's ears pricked and it growled louder.

"Motherfucker," Munro said and aimed down the crossbow sights.

The dog snarled and leapt towards her but she threw herself sideways into Hatcher who managed to keep them both upright. Munro watched the dog land and turn before moving further into the trees. She tracked the animal and squeezed the trigger with a gentle motion.

She thought, for a moment, the bolt would miss but it speared the Alsatian's upper thigh. The dog squealed and stumbled. It howled and got slowly to its feet. It had hobbled away through the trees before she could re-cock the crossbow.

"Fuck," said Hatcher. "I knew we should have shut the fucking thing up the minute we got here." She gagged. "Oh, there's so much blood."

Munro pulled Hatcher roughly out of the way and knelt beside Carlisle's head. Blood covered his face and a flap of skin hung loose from his right temple.

"Carlisle?" She cleared her throat. "Carlisle?" she said again but louder this time.

His eyes fluttered open, bright spots in the dark mess. "Munro?" He coughed blood onto his chin.

Munro felt her eyes water. How could this have happened?

"Things…" He grimaced and coughed again. She wanted to wipe the blood from his lips but didn't know where to start. "Haven't gone so well."

"Could be better," she said and pulled out her phone. She rang Keel and he answered immediately. "We've got a situation," she said.

"Us or the targets?"

"Carlisle got taken down by the dog."

"Is it bad?"

Munro looked at her friend's mangled hand and the growing blood puddle under his head. "Yes, he needs lifting."

Keel took a moment to reply. "I'll get it sorted. Where are you?"

She gave the location. "There's a lot of blood and his forehead is split. He needs picking up quickly."

"I'll sort it. What about Stephens?"

"Nothing yet."

"Okay. Someone has let the dog out because it wasn't running loose when we got here. What can you see from where you are?"

"There's some kind of compound."

"Check it out."

"I will." She paused and willed her voice to sound professional. "You'll get him out, won't you?"

"Trust me," said Keel and broke the connection.

"What now?" asked Hatcher.

Munro stood up and rolled her head until she heard tendons creak. Anger burned through her like lava and she found it hard to ignore.

"I'm counting Jack responsible for this," she said. "And I intend to take him out with as much pain as I can muster." She cocked the bow. "We're going to check the compound. They won't have got far."

* * *

Rachel headed out of the caravan carefully. The compound gate swung open but nobody came towards it and she couldn't see any sign of the dog either. Jack was bent over one of the mopeds and the other was laid on its side.

She ran towards him and he looked up briefly, looking terrified, before giving her a little wave. He stood up as she reached him.

"Do they work?" she asked.

"That one's knackered," he said and gestured to the one on its side. "This one looks okay. I think we can use it."

"Come on then," she said with a glance towards the trees.

She couldn't see or hear anyone but felt like they were being watched. Jack wheeled the moped towards the compound gate and she walked alongside him.

"Have you ridden one recently?"

"Not since my late teens," he said. "At least a decade, I'd say. And rarely off-road."

"Great, so what could go wrong?"

* * *

Keel got into the Range Rover.

He had to make a six-point turn because of Carlisle's bad parking and took a final look at the farmhouse as he gunned the engine and drove rapidly down the hill. He wanted to make sure he was in position to mop things up in case there were further issues. Carlisle's amateurish team hadn't helped any of them.

# Chapter 26

It was hard work pushing the moped over the uneven gravel and by the time they were out of the compound Rachel's breath was burning in her throat.

At last they were through the gate.

"Get on," he said as he jumped astride.

The two-tone moped had a pale step-through that might have once been white. He sat on the front of the seat but still the back of the bike sagged. It looked dangerously unsafe but she got on anyway and felt it shift beneath her.

"Put your arms around me," he said.

"I remember," she said.

It had been a long time since she'd last been on the back of a moped but some things you don't forget.

She heard a click and an electric whine. Something caught her eye in the trees and she glanced over but the shadows hid whatever had been there. The whine became a rumble and the bike vibrated as the engine started. Jack stuck his thumb up over his shoulder.

"Success!" he called.

"Then go," she said and watched the trees.

Munro stepped out of the shadow carrying what looked like a gun. No, not a gun but...

"Shit." She tapped Jack hard on the shoulder. "Munro's got a fucking crossbow!"

The moped wobbled and Rachel gripped him tighter as he popped the clutch. The whole bike seemed to vibrate and Jack seemed to struggle to keep it upright. Munro slowly raised the crossbow. Fear raced through Rachel, and she felt sick as she leaned into Jack.

"You have to go!" she shouted.

Something hit the front wheel.

Jack leaned forward as the moped bumped up onto grass. Rachel watched Munro walk across the gravel and raise the crossbow once more.

"She's firing again."

Jack steered left then banked to the right. Rachel felt an impact below her but Jack didn't react and nothing seemed to change. Another glance back saw Munro reloading but the gap between them was growing as the moped picked up speed. Jack kept up his evasive course but something now ticked on the tyre like an out-of-control metronome.

"Hold tight," Jack called over his shoulder. "There's a ridge ahead."

Rachel glanced back. Munro had faded into the gloom and the compound was a silhouette against the sky.

The moped took the ridge and the underside scraped along the ground as they thudded over it. They now faced a long, wide field. The line of trees to her right became a small wood while Hadlington and the promise of safety spread out before her. On the left she could see railway tracks and a dark wood beyond them.

Jack seemed to aim towards the railway as the bike rattled and bounced over the uneven ground. Rachel tried to tighten her grip but her palms were clammy.

She felt another impact in the bodywork and Jack wrestled to keep the bike upright. Rachel put her foot down on instinct and it caught on the grass, almost whipping her off.

\* \* \*

Jack felt the impact and pulled the hand and foot brakes as the field sloped away. The back end fishtailed so he quickly released the foot brake and continued on.

"Did I hit something?" he called over his shoulder.

Rachel shifted in her seat. "I don't think so."

The way the bike was riding it felt like he'd blown the rear tyre. Perhaps Munro – who was clearly some kind of psychopath – had shot at them again.

The front wheel hit a divot and the shock jarred his shoulders but he kept accelerating. If he could keep the moped under control, it might not get them all the way to the A14 but would give them a decent lead nonetheless.

Woods spread out to his right and he thought they might give good cover in this limited light but he also knew they were bloody dangerous. He'd done a night run through woods in Bristol a year or two back and the instructor sounded like someone from a werewolf film as he warned them over and again to stay on the path. One of the party took a shortcut and took precisely eight strides before his right foot caught in a tangle of root. Jack could still hear the man's agonising cry as his ankle snapped neatly in two.

No, the woods were the last resort.

A series of ruts appeared out of the gloom and he knew the moped wouldn't be able to take them.

"Hang on tight," he shouted and she did.

He managed to avoid them even though the sagging back end slewed drunkenly for a moment or two and he pointed the bike towards the railway lines to his left.

* * *

Munro's anger burned in the base of her throat.

That fucker Jack had done it again, but each time he got away it just added more fuel to the fire. Even thinking about Carlisle made her feel sick. She'd liked him a lot and they'd worked well together in the past – done more than work together on occasion – and seeing him brought down like that made her rage.

"Now what?" asked Hatcher.

Munro couldn't see them but the sound of that stupid moped engine gave her a constant update as to their location.

"We catch them."

"But they're on wheels."

"They have to head for the railway lines to get down to the road." She took out a new bolt, stroking the flight lightly before locking it into place and cocking the bow. "We'll cut across the ridge here and join the railway line at the top of the hill."

"I'm looking forward to getting my hands on those two."

"We both are."

\* \* \*

Jack struggled to keep the moped upright as he steered as best he could around the hummocks and holes that kept appearing out of the gloom. The back end was slewing as if it was running without a tyre and Rachel's arms were clamped resolutely around his waist.

He'd risked a glance back for Munro but couldn't see her anywhere. He wasn't sure how much of a head start this reckless ride would give them but it had to be something. They would probably have to abandon the moped at the fence by the railway line, but if they could then follow it down, at least they'd know they were heading in the right direction.

The handlebars jumped in his grip and he heard a bang. There was a brief, horrible sensation of falling and then the moped was dropping. The footrest dug into the ground and jerked the machine to an abrupt stop. Jack fell away from it, rolled and quickly got to his knees. He looked for Rachel and saw she was lying on her side staring at the sky.

"Rachel," he called. His arm ached and he stood up carefully in case anything was sprained or broken. Nothing appeared to be so he jogged to her and knelt beside her head. She was breathing heavily. "It's me, are you okay?"

She looked at him. "I think so. We came off a bit quickly there."

"Yeah, sorry about that. Can you stand up?"

"I can try."

She let Jack help her up and he held her arm until she shook him off and rubbed the back of her head briskly.

"I'm okay," she said, in a tone that didn't invite contradiction. "How are you?"

Jack could feel himself coming out of the shock but his breathing was steady. "I've been better."


## Chapter 27


The field angled up sharply before the ridge which was stark against the sky.

"If Munro wanted to spot us," Rachel said, "she'd be able to see the whole field from up there."

She couldn't see anyone but that didn't mean no one was there and hiding from view.

"Oh shit," Jack said.

She glanced at him but he was looking up the field and she looked back, following his pointing finger. Something tightened in her chest. A dog prowled the ridge as it kept pace with them. It was impossible to identify from this distance but could have been the one from the compound.

"That's all we need," she said.

"It might be another dog," he said but sounded unconvinced. "Is it limping?"

"I can't tell but bearing in mind how bad-tempered it was before, I hope it doesn't come down here."

"Perhaps it can't see us."

"That's unlikely."

She looked down the field and tried to get her bearings. The woods beyond the railway lines seemed denser and dark now and she couldn't remember seeing them from the road.

"I was going to follow the railway down," Jack said. "Do you think that's the best idea?"

"It has to be. The tracks run parallel to the A14 then go under it at some point to get to the station so if we follow them, we should get back into town. Then we can find a phone box or flag down a taxi."

He looked at his watch. "It's past two on a school night, I can't see many taxis running at this hour."

"Well whatever we do, we need to get out of sight. If Munro's up there, we must stand out like a sore thumb in the moonlight."

"I think if we get to the railway, we can hide in the shadows of the trees." He stopped. "Wait, can you hear that?"

"What?" All the sounds Rachel could hear were so dislocated – the call of a bird or animal from the wood along with the occasional rush of tyres from the A14 – she'd almost stopped hearing them.

"It sounds like a train."

"At this time of night?"

"Could be a goods train," he said.

"Do you think we could get the driver's attention?"

"Wouldn't hurt to try, would it?"

\* \* \*

Hatcher grabbed Munro's arm and dug her nails into the soft underside.

"What the…?"

"Fucking dog's back," Hatcher muttered, and Munro followed her line of sight.

The Alsatian came along the ridge towards them with its head low as it favoured its rear left leg. Munro checked the crossbow was cocked and held the weapon low. The dog looked down the field then back to them.

"What's it doing?" Hatcher hissed.

"I don't know."

"Kill the fucking thing."

Munro glanced at her. "It's on the edge so anyone down the field will see it. If our fugitives are keeping their eyes peeled, we'll give away our position if the dog goes down."

"But it mauled Carlisle."

Munro closed her eyes and saw the ruin of him. "I know."

"If you don't kill it now, promise me we'll finish the job when we've delivered those two idiots."

"Agreed."

The Alsatian maintained its distance and kept a wary eye on them as it went by. It paused at the end of the ridge where the ground dropped away. As it shifted position, Munro saw the bolt buried deep in its right thigh and felt a small flash of satisfaction that she'd at least been able to avenge Carlisle, however slightly. The dog stepped over the edge, obviously following some kind of path. Once it was out of sight, Munro relaxed her trigger finger.

"Come on," she said and started to the ridge. "Let's see what's going on."

She knelt down five or six feet from the edge of the ridge and crawled to the lip.

"What're you doing?" Hatcher asked.

Munro bit her lip, frustrated her friend wasn't quicker on the uptake.

"If they're down there and we appear against the sky, they'll see us."

"Right." Hatcher got to her knees as well.

Munro peered down into the field and felt a sudden wave of anger as she saw Rachel and Jack walking towards the railway lines. They were like the proverbial bad pennies, and she would enjoy ensuring at least one of them never turned up again.

The moped lay in a heap several feet behind them and they no doubt planned to follow the railway line into Hadlington.

Munro heard a rumble and it took her a moment to place the sound.

"Is that a train?"

Hatcher checked her watch. "Mail train," she said. "I've heard it a few times coming off shift at Cinderella's on a Friday night."

Munro looked back at her targets. "If we've heard it, they have."

"So? The driver's hardly going to stop and pick them up, is he?"

"No, but they might get his attention."

She got up onto her right knee and braced her elbow against it as she sighted down the crossbow.

"I thought we weren't supposed to harm them."

"No, we're not supposed to kill them."

* * *

The railway lines were about a hundred yards or so away now.

"If needs be, we could go into the woods," Rachel said.

"We could but it'd be dangerous. I've done some orienteering night trials through woods, but you need to keep to the trails or you're asking for trouble."

"What kind of trouble?"

"Sprained ankles at best and fractures at worst."

"Ouch." A shiver of revulsion ran through her lower back.

"On the other hand, Munro probably doesn't know the woods any better than we do. If we go far enough in to drop out of sight we could then hide."

He stopped and touched her arm. When she looked at him his face seemed more animated than it had in a while.

"Actually, think about it. If they know we're in there and come blundering in after us and step on a root or walk into a branch, we could get away."

It almost made sense. "But how would we see those things?"

He didn't get a chance to answer and screamed as his left leg went out from under him. He landed heavily on his back and rolled into his front. Startled, she knelt beside him. His face was contorted with pain and his eyes were screwed shut. Moonlight reflected off the tears on his cheeks.

"What is it?"

"My leg," he gasped.

"What did you do?" Had he twisted his ankle? She checked his leg and saw the flight at the end of the crossbow bolt buried in his trousers. "Oh my God."

Gritting his teeth, he reached for the back of his knee, gripping it tightly. "What is it?"

She thought of the projectile that had hit the moped and shredded the tyre.

"Rachel." He was crying now. "It burns."

She looked towards the ridge and saw someone silhouetted there as they held what looked like a rifle against the body.

"Munro shot you."

* * *

"Nice shot," said Hatcher.

Munro stood up as she watched Rachel kneel beside Jack. When the woman looked up, Munro resisted the urge to raise her hand in greeting.

147

"That'll slow the fucker down," she said and Hatcher laughed. "He won't be able to outrun us on the hill now so they'll hide in the wood. I'll go down the field, you head across to the left and into the trees and we'll cut them off."

She reloaded the crossbow and cocked it.

"They won't get away this time."

# Chapter 28

Jack felt cold sweat on his head and back but his right calf was on fire.

He gripped his knee with both hands and gingerly lifted his leg so he could see clearly. The flight of the bolt poked through a bloodstained hole in his trousers but looked loose and he realised it must have grazed him deeply rather than penetrated the skin.

"Shit," he said through gritted teeth.

Rachel put her hand on the back of his head as if she didn't know where best to touch him. "It's not sticking in you."

"I noticed," he muttered, not unkindly. "But please don't touch it."

"I wasn't going to," she said and he could hear the panic in her voice. "What can I do?"

"How bad is it?"

"Well, on the plus side, it would've been worse if she'd shot either of us in the head or chest."

She surprised a chuckle out of him.

"You're not helping," he said.

"And I can't," she said with a smile, "if you don't let me look."

"But it hurts."

"It will because it's a crossbow bolt."

"It feels like it."

"You're worse than Tilly."

"When did you last shoot her with a crossbow?" he demanded and that made her laugh.

"Let me see," she insisted.

He lowered his leg and pushed himself up onto all fours. The burning sensation intensified with each movement.

"Okay," he said.

"Right, what I'll do is tell you before…"

Sharp and intense pain flared through his lower legs. Tears sprang to his eyes.

"What did you do?" he said.

"I went before I said I would but I've moved your trousers now."

He let his head drop and focussed on the sound of the train as he tried to block out the pressure of Rachel's cool fingers on him. The bolt pressed hard against his skin a couple of times and he bit his lip hard enough to taste blood.

"It's made a mess and I can't see properly but I think it skimmed your calf. The bolt's free, your trousers were holding it in." Fresh pain coursed up his leg. "There, it's away. I just wish I could see how far it had dug in." She touched his arm. "Oh shit. Will this never end?"

"What's up?"

"We've got to go. Munro's coming."

* * *

Munro felt the disappointment keenly as Jack stood up, though his agonised cries had warmed her.

Hatcher had followed the dog off the ridge and found a narrow trail that switched back to the railway cutting. Munro went after her and kept watching the activity in the field.

Rachel bent over Jack and did something to his leg that was lost to the gloom but Munro didn't care. If he was injured, they would be seriously slowed down and the thought of making his life painful gave her a twinge of delight.

Munro had covered half the distance between the ridge and them before Rachel turned and saw her. She helped Jack to his feet and the cry of pain he gave as he started to walk made Munro smile.

\* \* \*

With Rachel supporting him they made slow but steady progress to the railway lines.

The train was out of sight but the rails sang with its progress. Munro didn't seem to be in any kind of hurry but even in her agitated state Rachel could see their options were limited. The wound on his calf had almost incapacitated Jack and it was unlikely they could stick to their original plan and outrun anyone. Munro could now pick them off at her leisure.

"We can't do this," Jack said. "I'm slowing you down."

She struggled to stay upright against his weight but wasn't going to give up.

"You are," she said. His surprised laugh quickly died but made her feel better briefly. "I still think we should go into the woods."

"But she'll catch us."

Rachel could feel her strength draining and knew they had to stop somewhere and try to hide. The railway line was a few yards away now and a plan began to form itself in her mind. If it came off, it might just give them a little bit of breathing space.

"Let's try and head over the rails," she said.

He went without question but stumbled and pulled on her shoulder. A pain shot across her lower back and she groaned.

"Sorry," he said.

She glanced over her shoulder and saw Munro was even closer.

"Just keep going," she said and leaned to her left in an effort to try and keep them both upright.

A waist-high fence cut off the railway lines from the field and the woods beyond looked even more dense than before, with trees fading into black after the first three or four rows. A narrow stretch, covered with what looked like bramble, lay before it. She didn't know if Jack would be able to negotiate it but they didn't have a choice.

A flash of light from the top of the hill caught her eye. "Here comes the train."

She hefted Jack up as best she could and took longer strides, pulling him along. "We won't make it," he said.

"We will, we just have to get over the rails."

They reached the fence and she half helped and half shoved him over. He cried out as he landed. She pulled herself over and risked a glance over her shoulder. Munro had picked up her pace.

The tracks lay in the middle of a gravel bed supported by concrete sleepers. The gravel shifted as they walked and made them stumble. Her shoulder burned and lower back smarted. Her legs felt like lead but adrenaline pushed her on.

"Stop or I'll shoot!"

A cone of light from the train lit the field. Rachel looked at Munro for a moment then got a better grip on Jack's arm.

"Come on," she shouted.

The rails sang and this close she could feel the heavy vibrations of the train through the soles of her feet and in her belly. The light seemed to be coming towards them frighteningly fast as they reached the narrow strip of gravel between the tracks.

Munro reached the fence. "I could shoot you in the head from here," she shouted but made no move to do so.

Rachel pulled Jack over the second set of tracks. She could now see a drop past the edge of the gravel.

"What now?" Jack shouted.

The train thundered past in a whirlwind of noise and hot air. She and Jack held each other tightly as they backed away from the rails and the slipstream threatened to knock them over. The rolling stock blocked out everything but the sky.

"It's a goods train!" she shouted.

This suited her plan perfectly and would give them even more time, perhaps two or three minutes, before Munro could get across the lines.

She stopped at the edge of the sleeper and looked down at the bramble. The drop might have been five feet or more; it was impossible to tell.

"Over we go," she said.

"You're kidding?"

A narrow gully ran below and continued down the hill. Moonlight reflected off patches of water. Rachel sat on the sleeper and realised it was part of a bridge.

She lowered herself and turned to face Jack as her feet sought something solid to connect with. Her upper arms burned with the effort and she couldn't find anything to stand on but couldn't stay there forever. Hoping for the best, she let go. The drop was only a few feet and she landed in water no deeper than a puddle. When she looked up at him the moon gave Jack a halo.

"It's nothing," she said, raising her voice over the sound of the goods carriages. "Lower yourself down and I'll catch you."

"Just don't touch my leg."

"I won't."

He pushed himself backwards over the edge and as his legs dangled, she saw the smear on the back of his trouser leg was bigger than before. She reached up and grabbed his belt.

"Let go!" she called and he did. He landed next to her and grunted with the pain. "Are you okay?"

"Not even slightly."

The bridge was a brick wall with two outlet channels set into it – one covered with a mesh grill, the other open. Thin ribbons of water trickled out of both although neither were wide enough to climb into. The bridge spanned a shallow valley with inclines up both sides of the wall to the railway lines. They could easily walk up them but would be clearly visible to Munro.

Rachel turned to survey the valley. Thick bramble covered the ground up to the tree line and she felt a rush of panic but tried to shake it away. She'd led them down here and had to get them out before the train went by and Munro was standing up there looking down on them.

She kicked at a bit of bramble and a branch popped up over the leaf cover in front of her. She squatted down and saw a couple of wide ditches running up to the trees. The branches overhead were surprisingly thick and covered with vicious-looking thorns but had a good two or three feet of clearance.

"I think we can go through," she said and felt a charge of adrenaline.

When she stood up he was looking off to the left.

"Look," he said. "There's a light." She followed his gaze and saw a vague glow through the trees. "It could mean somewhere with electric and maybe a phone."

"We could get there through the wood," she said. "I think I've found a way."

She pulled him down to squat beside her. The water was cold on her hands and legs. Could she do this? She took a deep breath and then, on all fours, crawled under the canopy of bramble.

# Chapter 29

Munro wasn't surprised to find Rachel and Jack gone when the train finally passed. The bitch had clearly planned this when she stood between the tracks and somehow guessed Munro wouldn't shoot her.

Munro climbed over the fence and crossed the rails. Now she could hear water and leaned over to see the gully. A light caught her eye off to the left. Had Rachel seen that and perhaps decided to head there? It seemed more likely than them trying to fight through this mass of bramble.

She took out the handset. "Hatcher?"

"Got them?" Hatcher responded with an almost childlike sense of excitement.

"No, the train blocked me off. Where are you?"

"In the trees at the top of the field."

"I think they're heading into the woods so cut down from where you are towards me. And if you see any lights, check it out."

"I saw something earlier."

"It might be nothing but with the luck those two are having, I wouldn't assume anything."

"Got you."

"I'll meet you in the woods."

\* \* \*

The ditch was some kind of run-off channel that narrowed the further Rachel crawled into it, and as the bramble cover lowered it pulled at her clothes. She felt crowded and her breathing got quick and shallow. She had to fight the urge to stand up and be done with it and bit her lip to keep her focus.

The radio handset beeped and they listened in to the conversation between Munro and Hatcher.

"She doesn't know where we are," Jack said.

"But we don't know where Hatcher is."

The ceiling of branches grew denser and the thorns seemed to get larger, some now as big as her thumbnail. Something squeaked and moved through the bramble ahead and she shivered. The motion rocked her entire body.

The channel seemed to have turned into a ditch with loose earth walls a foot or so deep. Panic fogged her and painted the banks steeper as it forced the breath from her lungs. She imagined a dozen creatures with too many teeth and legs waiting to drop into her hair or run across her face. She tried but couldn't see past her fears, and the sensation of being trapped slowed her movements.

"Keep going," hissed Jack and she realised she'd stopped.

"I can't."

"Why? What's happened?"

"I'm stuck." She tried to take a deep breath but couldn't and that just set fresh panic coursing through her.

"With the thorns?"

She shook her head, unable to move anything else. "No, with me. I'm scared, Jack, and I'm stuck."

The walls edged closer and darkness wrapped around her head like a cold and itchy blanket. Her chest felt like a huge weight was pressing on it.

"Are you bogged down?"

"No. I just can't move."

He touched the back of her ankle and made her jump. "Are you claustrophobic?"

"I didn't think so."

He patted her ankle. "Luisa got that a lot. It doesn't feel like it but the best thing you can do is keep moving. Look forward and start crawling."

"Easy for you to say," she muttered. What would she do if the sides caved in and buried her?

"I know, I'm sorry. I'm trying to help."

The panic was dancing through her. "It's not working."

"Listen, Rachel. Whatever this channel's designed for, it goes up to the tree line. You saw that. We must be halfway there by now."

She could see it in her mind's eye and knew he was right but it didn't help her.

"If we get to the trees, Rachel," he said with a calmness she couldn't imagine, "we can hide. If we stay here in this water we'll freeze."

A rat came through a gap in the branches to her right. Moonlight caught its eyes and whiskers as it stared at her.

"No," she said and felt her panic escalate. "No, no, no."

The rat watched her and wiped its left ear.

"Piss off," she said sharply at it.

The rat dropped onto the incline and slid on the loose earth. Rachel could see that it might land between her hands and knees and it was enough to get her moving again.

"Nice work," said Jack.

She kept moving and concentrated hard on a small gap in the bramble ahead. A couple of times she put her hands into something soft but fought the urge to vomit.

* * *

Munro lowered herself off the bridge and dropped into the shallow water in the gully. She activated the torch app on her phone and checked the wall and both outlet pipes. The eyes of something glowed back at her from the larger one and startled her before the animal scuttled back up the pipe.

"Shit."

Surely they couldn't have gone through that bramble without getting torn to shreds? Munro made her way up the slope back to the lines. There was no one further down the hill.

Where could they be?

* * *

Rachel tried to zone out and keep crawling and she soon left the awful ditch and bramble behind. Blinking in the moonlight and feeling a huge sense of relief, she could see she was now on a flat piece of land with ferns moving gently above her head. She moved to one side and lay on her elbows and stared at the sky.

Jack came out of the ditch slowly and winced as he settled next to her. He offered a tight smile and moonlight painted streaks on his cheek. When he took a deep breath it sounded jittery.

"How're you feeling?" he said.

"Better, I think. And thank you for what you said."

"I didn't say much."

"It was enough. How're you?"

"Having the best night ever," he said grimly. "It looks like the tree line is about twenty feet away."

"What if Munro's watching? She might see us running."

"If we keep low all this bracken should cover us, and once we're in the trees we'll be all but invisible to anyone in the field."

She nodded, but with Munro watching, that twenty feet would feel more like two hundred.

* * *

Hatcher had quickly found the light source but it was just a beaten-up solar lantern in an old empty shack near the railway line. Nobody had been there in a while judging by the dust thick on the wooden floor.

Now she followed a narrow path between the trees that towered over her and cut out the moonlight so she could barely see in front of her. The torch on her phone would have been ideal but Carlisle had demanded they surrender all mobiles on the way over to make sure they were all on the same comms.

She saw Munro on some kind of bridge structure and they exchanged a wave. She'd long admired Munro and enjoyed working with her and wanted to do more of it. Maybe tonight's job would be enough to get her invited to another – a bigger one perhaps, more high profile. Anything that got her out of Hadlington would be good.

Something moved in the trees to her left and Hatcher realised she had nothing to defend herself with. She backed up the trail and searched in the undergrowth until she found a thick branch as long as her arm. She slashed it through the air like a sword a couple of times to assess its weight, and it felt heavy and reassuringly solid.

The thing moved again.

She growled and it took flight noisily.

* * *

Jack peered through the fern leaves towards the bridge but couldn't see Munro. He worried she might have come into the woods from further down the hill but had no way of knowing unless they ran into each other. And he wouldn't be able to do much running.

His leg ached with a deep throb across his calf that burned every time he moved and he wondered how clean the wound was. What if some of the cloth from his chinos was embedded in it? Or dirt from the run-off channel? It didn't pay to think like that; he needed to be more positive.

"We should go," he whispered.

Rachel jumped and he wondered where her thoughts had wandered to.

"Now?"

"Uh-huh," he said and carefully moved into a squatting position, horribly conscious of his head pushing up the fern leaves.

Rachel held out her hand and he took it. They both stood slowly. No one moved in the field beyond, and no one shouted from the woods.

"Aim for the horse chestnut tree," he said. "Keep as straight a line as you can and keep going even if I drop back."

"What?"

"Seriously, Rachel, just keep going."

"But I…" She paused. "Okay," she said.

Rachel covered the uneven distance quickly and Jack managed to keep up with her. They plunged into the darkness of the tree line and he had to stop in case he ran into a tree or tripped on a root.

"I'm here," Rachel said.

He couldn't see her until she reached out a hand which he took gratefully. He leaned against the trunk and lowered himself slowly to his knees.

"Are you okay?"

"I'm drained."

"Me too." She knelt in front of him. "There's some kind of dip over here that's covered with pine needles and leaves. We could rest for a bit and get our bearings."

She helped him up and they moved around the trunk to a shallow depression that stretched six or seven feet and spanned a couple of feet across.

"If we stay low we might even be invisible from the path."

"I like that."

They laid on their bellies, their heads a few inches apart.

"Snug," he said.

"I'm pretending we're glamping."

# Chapter 30

Munro's phone vibrated and she pulled it out of her pocket.

"Hello, Keel."

"What's the situation?"

"They've gone to ground in the woods. Hatcher's in there after them and I'm watching from the railway lines."

He cleared his throat, as if to calm himself. "Everything suggests they're regular citizens so how have they managed to evade your crew so easily?"

"I don't know." She felt a failure not being able to respond. "I shot Jack in the calf though which should slow them down."

"Well done but we need to speed this process up. Get Hatcher to sweep them towards you."

"I will but she's hindered because it's so dark in the trees."

"They can't see any more than you can. Keep me updated."

* * *

Rachel shifted her legs in an effort to find a more comfortable position but that just reminded her how full her bladder was. She ignored it and hoped the sensation would pass.

The woods settled around them and the creatures they'd frightened into silence found their voices again. Things moved softly in the undergrowth and she hoped they weren't rats. The memory of that one in the ditch made her shiver.

"You alright?"

"Yes," she whispered. "Just thinking stuff through. I'm so sorry I got you into all this."

He shook his head. His face was a pale circle in the gloom.

"It's not your fault. They know both of us though I'm buggered if I can figure out why."

"Are we going to get out of this?"

"I hope so." He shrugged and sounded a long way from hopeful.

She suddenly needed to know. Left to her own devices she'd easily imagine the worst – worrying seemed to be her default position these days – but right now she didn't need that. She needed to believe they could make it into town, call the police, and see Tilly again. Thinking about her daughter made her eyes water.

"Please tell me we can."

He touched the back of her hand softly. "We can."

"No," she said and tears prickled her eyes. "I mean it. I need to know things won't end here in this wood."

He rubbed his thumb gently over her knuckles. "We'll get out. They don't know where we are and if they come lumbering through in the dark they'll get hurt. Someone'll come up here in the morning for the building site and they won't try anything then."

She watched his face as they lapsed into silence. The pressure on her bladder felt painful now and she knew the sensation wouldn't go away.

"You know..." he started.

She waited for him to continue but he didn't. "What?"

"This is going to sound weird," he said and sighed. "But even though tonight's been shit and terrifying and fucking painful, I'm glad you were here with me."

"Could have been worse, you mean?" His sentiment brightened her. "I know what you mean. This is the worst night of my life but you're the first bloke I'm not related to I've spent this much time with in ages."

"Don't you go on dates?"

"How could any compare to this excitement?"

He exhaled a small laugh. "That aside."

"A lot of men are put off by Tilly. Well not by her personally because she's lovely, but the thought of her. Dating's a scary thing now and I'm out of practise."

"I can't imagine."

"You don't want to." She laughed quietly. "Stick with Luisa and tell her from me she's a lucky woman. You're a good man, Jack Martin."

"I have my moments."

She felt another twinge from her bladder and glanced around the depression trying to figure out the logistics.

"And now, to add indignity to injury, I have to go to the loo."

"Ah."

"One of the joys of motherhood is I'm not always in command of my bladder."

"You don't have to explain. I could do with going too."

"We don't have too many options here. I'm used to not peeing in peace but it's one thing to go in front of a kid who won't leave you alone..." She let the sentence go.

"I promise not to look. Not that I could see anything..."

"I'm sorry, it's this weird thing I have. I never even peed in front of Glen."

"I understand." He got to his hands and knees and grimaced as he moved his leg. "You go left, I'll go to the right. Don't go too far though, okay?"

She patted his fingers and slowly got to her hands and knees. The pine needles pressed into her knees as she edged back.

The woods had gone quiet again. She walked a dozen paces along the path and stopped beside a big tree. However she did this, she was going to feel horribly exposed but her bladder wouldn't hold out forever.

She crouched behind a tree, pulled her tights and knickers down and rucked her dress up and relieved herself.

* * *

Hatcher's stick caught a tree and, tucked under her arm like a jousting pole, it jarred against her shoulder.

"Fucker," she muttered and felt her anger flare.

She was annoyed at herself for not catching the quarry and more so at them for managing to evade Munro and the rest of the crew.

She rubbed her shoulder so briskly it hurt and took a moment. Munro had often told her not to let anger cloud her judgement and it seemed like great advice so she took some deep breaths and calmed herself.

Hatcher repositioned the stick and started through the trees again. She put her foot on what looked like a stone but it shifted out from under her and turned her ankle. A sharp pain ran up her leg that was strong enough to bring tears to her eyes. Cursing Rachel and Jack, she breathed deeply again until the wave of nausea had passed then tested her weight on her leg. Her ankle throbbed but held her.

"Stupid fucking woods."

* * *

Jack was already back when Rachel crawled through the bracken. Easing past his legs she looked at the dark stain around the hole in his trousers.

"Did you want me to have a look at your leg?"

"Not really."

"I'll be careful," she insisted.

Shifting around so her body didn't block the moonlight she pulled his trouser leg up. He made a hissing sound but didn't say anything.

The wound was midway up his calf and looked like the bolt had skimmed across the muscles. It had left a deep welt that must have hurt like a bastard. The edges of it looked raw.

"We really should clean it up."

"Not much chance of that here."

"We can make do," she said. "Give me your belt. Have you got a handkerchief?"

He moved so he could get the handkerchief out of his pocket and then unthreaded his belt and handed it to her. She put the cloth gently over the wound and kept going even when he blew air through his teeth in pain, then slipped the belt around to keep it on.

"That'll do until we get back," she said

"Thank you."

She rested her head on her arm. He smiled and touched her cheek lightly. She wanted to close her eyes and rest, to take comfort in his proximity and realised she felt safer at this moment than she had in a while.

# Chapter 31

Jack watched Rachel's eyes flicker closed. He thought about waking her then decided it wouldn't hurt for her to have a quick nap. He'd stay alert. They were safe enough here and unless Hatcher was as light on her feet as a dancer, he'd hear her long before she saw them.

The radio vibrated and danced lightly on the ground. Rachel's eyes snapped open and bored into his.

"Someone'll hear," she said with a tight voice. "Shut it off."

"I don't know…" He squinted at the screen but couldn't see any of the three buttons clearly. The vibration panicked him and he pressed the middle button. The radio went silent.

"That was close," he said.

* * *

Munro frowned at her handset.

Hatcher checked in and then, thirty seconds later, Stephens did.

She pressed the alert button again. Hatcher responded immediately but Stephens didn't. Munro counted to thirty then pressed it again.

* * *

The radio vibrated again, startling Jack. He dropped the handset and Rachel picked it up.

"It's Munro," she said. "There're three buttons lit - 'comms', 'alert' and 'off'. It must be some kind of call and response for the idiots."

The radio vibrated again and he pushed her hand against the carpet of pine needles to try and deaden the sound.

"Which one's the off? I haven't got my glasses on."

"The one on the left."

"Shit." He closed his eyes with a dawning sense of dread.

"Which one did you press before?"

"The middle one. I couldn't see." He shook his head. "I've really fucked up."

"Maybe not. Perhaps they didn't notice…"

The radio vibrated again. "Hello, Jack."

Rachel dropped it like it had burned her. "What do we do?"

The sense of defeat felt like a lead weight in his belly. "I don't know."

"Interesting situation we find ourselves in, Jack, isn't it?" Munro asked.

Jack let his head drop and his forehead touched the ground. Rachel put her hand on the back of his neck.

"We have to ignore her," she said.

"Come on, Jack," Munro said. "It's rude to ignore people."

"We should switch it off," he said. "Or throw it away."

"But if she and Hatcher talk this at least gives us an idea of where they both are."

Something cracked in the undergrowth behind them and he looked at Rachel. Her eyes were wide.

"Is it Hatcher?" she mouthed.

He thought the heavy steps sounded more like a deer and there was a swish of undergrowth as the creature cut a swathe through the wood. He heard a snuffling breath as the thing moved by them and off further into the trees.

"So what do you think Luisa would say, Jack?"

"Ignore her," said Rachel. The light from the screen lit her face.

"I'm going to."

"I mean," Munro continued. "It's very early in the morning and there you are in the woods with that bike."

"Did she just call me a bike?" Rachel asked, struggling to keep her voice low. "Fucking bitch."

"What would Luisa say?" He could almost hear the spite in Munro's voice. "How are you going to explain away being with that slag?"

Rachel reached for his hand and he gripped hers tightly.

"Is that your thing, being kinky outdoors? Did it put Luisa off?"

Rachel frowned. He shook his head.

"Am I getting warm? Are you with Rachel because she'll do anything for anyone who buys her a bottle of vodka?"

He didn't think Rachel's eyes could open wider but she proved him wrong.

"It destroyed her marriage you know."

Rachel closed her eyes and he squeezed her fingers.

"Whatever gets you off, eh? There's nothing wrong with liking a bit of cheap dirt. Did you ever take it home with you?"

He felt the anger growing as tears pricked his eyes before rolling down his cheeks.

"When you were in bed with Luisa, did you tell her the truth? Did you like to look into her eyes and see how much it hurt her?"

"It's okay," said Rachel. She hadn't opened her eyes and hadn't seen him crying.

"Could you see the pain in her eyes, Jack?"

The anger boiled over and he grabbed the radio. Startled, Rachel opened her eyes and he saw the confusion in her face.

"Was there a lot of pain, Jack? Did she cry? Did you?"

Rachel tried to pull the radio away from him. "What're you doing?" she hissed. "She's winding you up. Let's turn it off."

Munro continued relentlessly. "You can tell me, Jack, we're all friends here. Was her pain constant? Did you wish it would go away so you didn't have to look at it?"

He jabbed at the 'comms' button. "Fuck off, you miserable bitch."

"Jack!" Rachel pulled the radio away and quickly pressed the 'off' button, but not before he heard Munro laughing.

* * *

Hatcher had been listening to the radio as she moved carefully through the trees to make sure she didn't turn her ankle again. She couldn't work out Munro's strategy until Jack responded.

She heard him in stereo and the real-life version was somewhere in front of her.

The radio went quiet and the screen faded. The handset vibrated and she clicked to respond.

"Did you hear that?" Munro asked.

"Uh-huh, he's ahead of me."

"Good. Flush them out towards the railway line. I'll pick them off from there."

"Did you have an affair?"

"No." Jack shook his head. "She died, Rachel."

"Died?"

The revelation caught her by surprise and she didn't understand. They'd talked about Luisa; he said he only used his phone to call home and had done so earlier this evening.

"I don't–"

"Cancer," he said. "Super fucking aggressive and she didn't stand a chance. Came on a few months ago and chewed her up then spat her out. It was the most awful thing I've ever experienced."

"I'm so sorry."

He pursed his lips and it was the look of a man who'd heard the same sentiment a thousand times before and never taken comfort from it.

"This is why I was scared before that they knew enough about me to know about her."

"Why didn't you tell me?"

"Because I didn't need to and you wouldn't believe how wonderful it feels to deny it's true."

She saw the sadness in the turned-down corners of his mouth. "How long ago?" she asked softly.

"Forty-three days."

"Oh Jack, I'm…"

"No, please don't say it. I already know." He palmed away the tears roughly. "It'll get better, they say; it'll pass or time's a great healer. I've heard it all from the nurses and friends and people I don't even recognise in the street."

She looked at him with sympathy and that almost felt worse than her struggling to know what to say.

"I'm sorry, that was rude. I don't mean to be but, you know, it's fucking raw."

"Are you seeing anyone about it?"

"Like what, an expert in how to raise the dead?"

"That's not what I meant."

"I know."

"But you said you'd spoken to her and that's why your phone was dead."

"It is why it was dead. I ring home every morning and every night because she recorded our voicemail message and that's the only recording I have of her."

"Oh Jack," she said and cupped his cheek.

Something cracked loudly behind them and to the right and Hatcher cried out in pain.

"She must have heard me when I shouted," he said.

Rachel got to her hands and knees. "We need to get moving."

# Chapter 32

Hatcher had tried to pay attention to the terrain but the hole was hidden by leaves and her left leg dropped six inches into it; her forward momentum wrenched her knee enough that something snapped.

She cried out in pain and her mouth filled with bile. Pain raced up and down her leg and cold sweat coated her face.

"Fuck," she muttered. She wanted to scream but knew that Jack and Rachel had probably already heard her and didn't want to give away her position any further.

She tried to stand up using the stick for support and it held. She took a step and put her left foot gently on the ground. Moving didn't hurt but planting her foot did. The pain that radiated from her kneecap was so intense she actually saw colours in the darkness and thought she was going to faint for a moment. Her stomach rolled and her mouth filled with foul-tasting saliva.

"Shit."

Hatcher balanced on her right leg as she tried to figure out her next move. If she called Munro they would hear, but if she didn't and they ran she could never keep up with them. Maybe the best plan would be to keep moving so they wouldn't know how hurt she was.

There was movement in the undergrowth, and she was instantly alert even above the pain. Had this pair of apparent weekend Rambos somehow outflanked her? She raised the stick and braced it against her side. If they came through at her, she'd jab at least one of them even as she shouted for Munro.

Another movement. Why didn't they just come through? Were they watching her and just waiting until her attention was drawn back to her broken knee? She wanted to scream at them, to bring them out and get this thing over with.

The dog jumped through the bracken and landed heavily on the path in front of her. Its head was down as it regarded her with its teeth bared and it growled deeply. Her breath caught as if a weight was pressing on her chest.

She waved the stick at it and the Alsatian took a cautious step back. Its eyes never left her and she saw the crossbow bolt was still in its right thigh.

"Get away," she commanded and waved the stick again. The dog didn't move. "Go on, fuck off."

Hatcher hopped forward and grabbed a tree for support. There were sticks and pebbles at its base and she scooped a handful up. Fresh pain rinsed through her leg and made tears run down her cheeks.

She threw a pebble at it as hard as she could and it caught the animal mid-flank. The next missed and disappeared into the undergrowth. The third caught the dog's snout and made it howl and step back.

"I said fuck off," she shouted and went to throw another stone.

The dog leapt for her and she tried to turn away. It landed on her back and she threw out her arms to break her fall. Her bad leg twisted under her and she screamed then the dog's jaws clamped on her neck.

* * *

Munro stopped pacing when she heard Hatcher shout. She couldn't see any movement but brought up the crossbow just in case.

Another shout was more clearly defined with Hatcher telling someone to "fuck off". Surely Jack and Rachel hadn't overpowered her? The thought of him causing more hurt ran a cold ripple across Munro's belly. His life wouldn't be worth living.

The dog howled and a scream erupted. It echoed out of the trees.

"No, no, no."

She scanned the tree line through the crossbow sights but still couldn't see anything. The screams stopped and were replaced by sounds of struggle. Munro closed her eyes and saw Carlisle and all the blood and his missing finger. She swallowed bile.

"I am going to kill you, Jack," she said quietly.

* * *

Rachel's heart began to hammer in her chest when she heard Hatcher shout. Had the woman seen them? Was she calling in the rest of them?

The next shout sounded like "fuck off" and then Rachel heard the dog growl.

"Oh shit," she said. "The dog's found her."

Jack got to his knees slowly. "Sounds like it."

She heard the sound of a struggle and then Hatcher's scream echoed through the trees. Rachel's arms dimpled with goosebumps.

Jack grabbed her hand.

"You have to go," he said.

"Yes," she said, before she realised he hadn't said 'we'. "What do you mean?"

"You need to get down to the A14, find a phone and call the police."

This was all wrong. His words fluttered around her head like restless butterflies.

"*We* need to," she corrected him.

"No." He squeezed her hand. "I'll slow you down. You can make it much quicker on your own."

"But…"

"But nothing. You head down the hill and I'll make my way up to that light we saw through the trees."

"We don't even know what it is."

"It'll be some kind of shed or cabin. But it's got electricity and it'll have a phone."

"That's bollocks and you know it."

He gave an exasperated sigh.

"Fuck off," she said. "Don't treat me like this."

"Like what? I'm trying to do what's best for both of us. I've been shot and my leg is fucking killing me, and I'm not even sure I could walk very far let alone run if I have to. You can, Rachel, and with Tilly you have something to lose. I'll slow you down."

"You won't."

Her vision swam and she knew he was right even though she didn't want to admit it. He held her shoulders.

"If the dog's had Hatcher, then it could just be there's only Munro and Keel left. She's on the bridge and we don't know where he is but the odds would balance. If I can draw her away by going up to that light we saw then all the better. If I find a phone we're sorted. You get back into town and find a phone box and tell the police everything."

She glared at him.

"Rachel, please, we haven't got time for this."

"You're a fucking arsehole."

He smiled thinly. "I know."

# Chapter 33

After a much-needed shower that helped her to unwind from the shift, Pippa drove out towards the A14. As she passed the police station the fuel light came on, but rather than head for the 24-hour Tesco she decided to call into the first services on the dual carriageway. She knew one of the attendants who worked the night shift, and he often got her a free coffee when she picked up fuel.

She wouldn't tell Richard, her boyfriend, she'd been running on fumes again because he'd have just laughed. He often did when she told him how close she was to running out, unless he was in the car too, in which case he'd have been annoyed. Richard liked to plan everything to the nth degree and knew exactly how things should go. He was her exact opposite, as it happened. She had to work to strict routines and procedures at work so in her own time she preferred to make things up as she went along. This same attitude had driven her dad nuts when she was a teen while her mum always said 'nobody died' as if that made Pippa's late or non-appearance acceptable. She treated fuel the same way – until the lights flashed at her, she carried on regardless.

The news update came on the local radio station. The report about Barbara Gilbert hadn't been updated since the early evening.

A chime sounded to warn her that even the fuel fumes were just about finished when Pippa saw the blue glow of the petrol station through the trees. She indicated and pulled off the carriageway then drove onto the forecourt and stopped at the outermost pump. She got out and waved towards the shop even though she couldn't see the attendant and filled her car with petrol. When she finished, she locked the car and walked towards the night pay window. Her friend Alan appeared from the shadows and gave her a wave.

"Evening, Pippa," he said when she reached him. She'd never heard his voice without the slight mechanical echo of the intercom.

"Evening, Alan. How're things?"

It was impossible to tell by looking at him. He had deep-set eyes and a grey pallor, and his overall appearance wasn't helped by an oversized uniform that flapped around him.

"Not bad."

He rang up her fuel and she paid for it. He put a steaming cup of coffee into the tray and slid it through to her. She took the cup out carefully.

"You're a star," she said. "What do I owe you for this?"

"Nothing, same as always." He gave her a shy smile. "Just make sure you keep coming back."

"I will." She lifted the lid and inhaled the steam deeply. "Lovely."

"How's your shift been?" he asked. "Busy, I should imagine, with Bonfire Night and a full moon."

"I've had better. How about yours?"

He leaned on the counter so his face was close to the glass. "Pretty good, no bikers tonight."

"Always a bonus."

He nodded. "Did have one weird thing though. A bloke came in and wanted to use the phone then he got all edgy when I said no."

Intrigued, she sipped her coffee and waited for him to continue.

"And then – get this – just after he'd come in, this bloody Range Rover comes slinking around. It'd come down the exit slip road. How insane is that?"

"Ridiculous. So did they know each other?"

"The bloke who wanted the phone seemed shit scared when he saw it."

Pippa felt the little hairs on her arms stand up. "Scared?"

"Yeah and then it got really weird. The bloke went back to his car but the Range Rover drove into it – on purpose, I mean. Nudged the car hard enough to make it rock. The bloke had a passenger, a woman and she was in the car when it happened."

As Alan had said, it seemed weird and something nagged at the back of her mind. There was something earlier in the shift about a car chase through town and she tried to remember the details of the vehicles.

"What happened after that?"

Her concern seemed to throw him slightly as if he hadn't expected her to take him seriously.

"He drove off and the Range Rover followed him."

"Did you report it?"

The corners of his mouth turned down. "Wasn't much else to report, to be honest, other than what I've just told you. Did I do the wrong thing?"

"Probably," she said. "Sounds iffy enough to have let us know about it anyway." She jabbed her thumb toward the CCTV camera. "Did you get it all?"

Alan held his finger up like he was one step ahead. "Already checked," he said. "When I watched it back the Range Rover didn't appear at all. It was like the driver knew how much the lens could see."

"As if the Range Rover wanted to keep out of view?"

"Yeah. Weird, eh?"

"Very weird," she agreed. It could be something or nothing. "Just in case something comes up later, what colour was the Range Rover?"

"Black," he said. "And the bloke's Insignia was blue."

"Thanks." She lifted the coffee cup in a toast to him. "I'll see you soon, Alan. Thanks for the drink."

"Drive safe, Pippa."

# Chapter 34

Munro watched the woods and hoped to see Hatcher come through the trees and wave as she made her way down to wherever Jack and Rachel were hiding. She hadn't heard any more screams and the dog had stopped barking.

Her phone vibrated. She took it out of her pocket and debated switching it off even though she knew he'd keep trying.

"Hello, Keel."

"It's not getting any warmer down here, Munro. What's going on?"

"They're still in the wood." She heard him sigh and felt a jolt of embarrassment that she'd disappointed him again. "But I'll get them."

"Where's Hatcher?"

Something caught in Munro's throat. "She's in the wood too. I think the dog might have got her."

Another sigh, louder this time. "For fuck's sake, Munro. I'm coming up."

"No, don't, I'll get them to you."

"We don't have all night, you know that. People are starting to worry."

She felt flustered and hated herself for the weakness. "I understand. I'll contain the situation."

He broke the connection without replying and she put the phone in her pocket as shame burned through her. This had to end now.

\* \* \*

Rachel carefully made her way along the narrow trail until she reached a particularly large tree. She stopped and leaned around the trunk and saw Munro on the bridge. She'd expected to feel scared but, instead, it was anger that stabbed at her rather than fear. She was frightened of what Munro might be capable of but she was angry the woman had put her into this situation and separated her from Tilly as well as badly hurting Jack. As much as she wanted to confront Munro, Rachel knew the best way she could beat her now was by getting back to town and reporting everything.

Rachel kept the tree between her and Munro then followed the trail as it ran parallel to the railway lines for a couple of hundred yards. Through the trees she could see the lights of the A14 and Hadlington and, for the first time in a while, felt a surge of confidence.

* * *

Munro kept watching the trees for signs of movement until at last she spotted something. She dropped to one knee, raised the crossbow and looked through its sights.

She held her breath and waited.

A bird called.

There it was again – a shift in a shadow. A small burst of colour quickly swallowed by the darkness. Munro felt the familiar thrill of anticipation she got with a sense of impending violence.

The third time she saw the movement she knew it was someone hopping as they worked their way through the trees.

She smiled as she watched Jack make his slow progress.

* * *

Jack smelled Hatcher before he saw her.

He gagged and grabbed a tree in support. Hopping up the hill had sapped his energy and this ghastly sight took the rest of it. The air around the small clearing felt heavy with the scent of copper and something meaty. The smell of shit was all pervading.

Hatcher lay on her front, toes together and heels apart, her upper body hidden under some ferns. Something dark spread between her legs.

Jack gagged again and his eyes watered as he quickly made his way across the clearing.

* * *

It took Rachel a few minutes to pluck up the courage to leave the relative safety of the trees for the exposure of the railway tracks, but she couldn't see any sign of Munro and knew if she didn't move then, she never would.

It was an anti-climax. She didn't hear Munro shout and didn't hear pursuing footsteps and, even better, didn't feel a crossbow bolt come at her. Fatigue hit her and she wanted to curl up in a ball and sleep, to wish all this away and go back to the party and never leave.

"No," she whispered and the sound of her voice grounded her in reality. She repeated the word to reassure herself and started walking.

Soon, the tree line curved to the left. Off to the right she could just make out the lane Jack had driven them up. Ahead, a thick line of bushes formed a natural border between the A14 and the lower part of the field that seemed to be some kind of flood plain. It was flat and dotted with bodies of water that reflected moonlight. A bridge spanned what looked like a narrow river.

It took a moment for her to realise someone was standing on it.

* * *

Jack was exhausted by the time he reached the edge of the woods. His hair was damp and his shirt stuck to his back. His good leg felt like he'd run a marathon on it and his injured one was aching badly again.

A road of pale gravel led towards the field and the cabin was on the other side of it. Up close it seemed little more than an oversized decrepit shed. Planks – some broken but all of them looking worse for wear – made up the walls, and in the one window on this side was a solar lantern.

Jack rubbed his right thigh vigorously to get the blood pumping and crossed the road. Heavy tyres had packed the gravel tightly but even so he almost turned his ankle within four or five hops. Despite this, he gritted his teeth and covered the distance faster than he'd expected.

He leaned against the planking and gave himself a minute to get his breath back and rest his leg before edging to the corner. He peered around cautiously but saw no one and moved carefully along the front elevation to an ill-fitting door secured with a padlock. He rattled it against the hasp then put his shoulder to the door. It took three goes before the wood split under the onslaught. He pulled the hasp away and the door swung wide.

The spartan interior stank of decay, piss and sweat. A table made from old pallets stood in one corner and a sleeping bag had been laid out in another. An upright paraffin heater was under the window with a battered box of matches on top of it.

The shed clearly had no electricity or phone. He'd come on a fool's errand.

\* \* \*

The person on the bridge moved towards her and panic wrapped around Rachel's lungs and squeezed out her breath. She looked around wildly. Could she outrun someone on this uneven ground and where would she go? Heading back the way she'd come surely meant the threat of Munro and her crossbow.

She watched the person walk briskly up the field. Determined not to simply give up, Rachel decided to head towards the lane, but it was only moments later when someone called her name. She turned slowly as the driver of the Range Rover stopped four or five paces in front of her.

"Good morning, Rachel," he said and came closer.

"I suppose you're Keel?"

"Well done," he said and touched her elbow. "I need you to come with me."

She shook his grip off. "And what if I don't?" she asked with as much insolence as she could muster.

"I think you might."

"Well you thought wrong."

"Rachel," he said calmly. "We have your daughter."

# Chapter 35

Jack found a metal container under the table with 'Valor' printed up the side of it. He unscrewed the cap but didn't need to put the container near his face to smell the paraffin.

The paraffin heater stood perhaps two feet tall and was heavily dented. He shook the matchbox and opened it. Inside were two or three dozen live heads.

Jack felt a surge of triumph and the makings of a plan. If he doused the sleeping bag with paraffin and lit it up, it might make a tidy little bonfire to draw some attention from the town.

As he hopped towards the sleeping bag he felt, rather than saw, someone move into the doorway. Startled, he fell against the back wall next to the pallet table.

"Found you," Munro said.

* * *

Keel's words winded her.

"What?" she asked, all trace of insolence now gone from her voice.

"We have Tilly."

Rage overcame reason and she went for him. He backed away and put his hands up to ward her off. She aimed for his eyes and screamed so loudly she thought her throat would rupture. He batted away one hand and she saw an opening and drove her thumb into the soft of his cheek. She felt his teeth and pushed harder; her nail sank into the flesh.

Keel grunted in pain and knocked her hands away. He made fists but his posture exposed his cheek and she went for the same place. A ribbon of blood ran down to his jawline.

She went with him as he pulled away. When he grabbed her hand she pinched his cheek savagely. He cried out and grabbed her hair. He yanked her head back and it felt like boiling water had been poured on her scalp. She screamed and tried to keep up the pressure of the pinch even as she felt her hair being pulled out.

She kicked him just above the ankle. He hopped out of the way and pulled her to one side. Tears blurred her vision. He raised his fist high to the left and brought it down in a scything movement.

The back of his hand clattered against her jaw. Everything dimmed for a moment then her ears filled with a horrible static. If he hadn't kept hold of her hair she'd have fallen. Her legs gave way and more pain seared across her scalp.

"Enough," he shouted and sounded like he was on the other side of the field.

The sky shifted colour and the static crackled. She held her hands up in surrender and he pulled her upright by the hair then let go. She staggered back but kept to her feet and didn't take her eyes off him.

He said something but the static tore away most of the words.

"I can't hear," she said.

He rubbed his cheek. She looked at her thumb and saw blood under the nail.

\* \* \*

Keel looked at his blood-smeared fingers and shook his head. He'd allowed an amateur to cause him damage and now had to control his sense of failure and anger to stop it eating him up.

"I understand why you did that," he said and brushed her hair out of his fingers. "But if you do it again, Rachel, you're going to get very hurt. Do you understand?"

She nodded and he could see most of her fight had gone.

"What have you done to Tilly?" she asked in a soft voice.

"You'll find out."

He could see the defeat in her eyes. "Please," she said and tears spilled down her cheeks. "Don't hurt her."

"I won't – as long as you co-operate." It was a lie but she wasn't to know that.

"Of course I'll co-operate," she said with a spike of anger. "She's six years old."

"I know," he said.

It was another lie. Until Wilson rang him fifteen minutes ago, Keel hadn't realised kidnapping was part of the deal. Professionally it wasn't a bad idea, but given the choice he'd have traced the girl and kept her in sight. Collateral damage from an act like this would be far-reaching and it would have been better agreed upfront. It could certainly have avoided a lot of the trouble this evening. Not that the evening was going to get better. Wilson had stated he was disappointed in the way things were going and had felt the need to get involved personally – something that very rarely happened.

"If you give me what I want then we can avoid any more unpleasantness."

"I don't know what you want," she said and spread her arms wide. "I don't even know you. Nothing has made sense to me tonight since you were at my flat."

"It isn't supposed to," he said briskly. "Now walk," he said and pointed towards the lane.

* * *

Jack held up his hands. "I'm unarmed."

"I don't care." Munro stepped into the room and her boots clomped on the chipboard floor. She looked around the shed. "Not a bad place to end your days, eh?"

His head ached and his stomach rolled. "I don't know what you want."

"I want you," she said with a frightening sense of detachment.

"What have I ever done to you?"

"I told you. You broke my fucking necklace and pushed me into a tree. Then you killed poor Carlisle, and what happened to Hatcher?"

"Who's Carlisle? I didn't kill anyone."

She held up her hand and he stopped talking.

"Somebody let the dog loose."

There was no answer to that. He debated putting the paraffin container down but adjusted his grip on it instead.

Munro kicked at the end of the sleeping bag. Now he could see her crossbow with a bolt loaded and he felt sweat in his hairline.

"What do you want me to do?" he asked.

She shrugged and moved to the window so she could peer out of it.

"You could scream or beg for mercy. Or why don't you call on your dead wife?"

His hackles rose even over the fear but he was determined not to show her it hurt. He had nothing to lose now so why not deny her a thrill?

"You're not even good enough to say her name."

She smiled. "It doesn't matter so long as it pushes your buttons."

"You're a bitch."

"And you're a murdering bastard so I think you win." She nodded towards his leg. "How's the wound?"

He did his best to straighten his leg without wincing.

"Not bad," he said through gritted teeth and enjoyed the flicker of uncertainty that crossed her face. She wasn't sure and he took that as being a positive. She wasn't as cold and calculating as she appeared and he might be able to use that knowledge.

"You're a fucking liar," she sneered.

He pushed away from the wall. "Sorry to disappoint you," he said and limped towards the window.

She mirrored him and took aim with the crossbow. He daren't look at the bolt.

"I could take out your kneecaps and then work my way up."

"You're sick."

He took another step and kept watching Munro. Her finger moved on the trigger-guard and the light caught the back of her hand. He saw the same mark he had when they were in the cars at the start of this nightmare. At the time he'd thought it was scar tissue but now it seemed more like a burn. He gripped the box of matches tighter.

"Maybe your elbow?" she said with a smile. "Doesn't matter to me. I'll make you scream either way."

He jerked the can towards her and the paraffin liquid described a graceful arc that splashed down her left arm. She fired the crossbow but the bolt thumped harmlessly into the wall. He moved forward, gritting his teeth against the pain and threw more paraffin. The front of her jacket glistened with it and there was a dark curve on the floor as if a child had painted a half circle on it.

"No!" she screamed and scrambled back until she hit the pallet table.

He upended the can, not caring if it doused him so long as he got more on her. She screamed again and tried to brush the paraffin off herself. When it was clear she couldn't, she reached for another bolt. He swung the can from side to side to coat three walls, the floor and her. She got a bolt into the flight groove but the spray hit her in the face before she could cock it. She screamed and her left hand clawed at her eyes.

Jack threw the empty can onto the sleeping bag as he backed to the door and took a handful of matches out of the box. "Are you scared?"

She glared at him. Her left eye was only half open. "No."

He backed away another step, his leg burning with pain. White spots burst at the periphery of his vision, and he felt faint.

"That scar on your hand is a burn isn't it?"

Her lips tightened over her teeth. "Fuck you, Jack."

"Are you such a warped bitch because you got burned? When was it? Did it happen when you were a kid?"

She brought the crossbow up. Her left eye still hadn't opened properly. "I'll shoot you."

Jack grabbed several matches and struck them. He looked away from the flare which lit the room and made it look even grubbier. The paraffin patches on the wall and floor glistened.

"I'll drop these."

"No you won't because you're covered too. We'll both go up."

"I'm not scared of dying," he said slowly.

The bolt hit high on his left arm and spun him back. The matches dropped. He took all his weight on his bad leg and reached for the door jamb but missed and fell through.

Munro began a scream that didn't stop.

# Chapter 36

Rachel walked across the uneven field towards a gateway in the stone wall. Keel stayed a couple of paces behind her and didn't say a word.

Every step was agony as she thought of Tilly with strangers. Her stomach churned and she felt sick, her thoughts racing as she tried to figure out how to fix this situation. She couldn't think of anything and in her mind's eye, kept seeing Tilly bundled up in her coat, scarf and gloves as she waved from the back of Naomi's car.

"What did you do to Naomi?"

"She's safe," he said after a brief pause. "They both are. Do as I say and nobody will get hurt." When she stopped at the gate, he said, "Open it."

She unlatched it and he followed her into a narrow lay-by. The Range Rover was a few feet away.

"Get in."

Rachel looked at him and felt her terror mount. Everything life had taught her said this was a bad idea that was only going to get worse. If she got into the car, she wouldn't be able to save Tilly. She shook her head.

"Rachel, get in the car."

"No," she said, her voice so quiet it embarrassed her. "No," she repeated, louder now. "If I get in, I won't get out."

He sighed. "Don't think I'm a reasonable man because you've lasted this long, Rachel." He took a step towards her and she backed away. "I will hurt you if you don't get in. Then I'll go back to my associates who have Tilly."

Her argument deflated as quickly as a punctured balloon, and she backed around to the passenger door without looking away from him. He unlocked the car and waited until she'd got in before climbing in himself. He started the engine.

"A few questions," he said and slipped off the hood of his parka. His salt-and-pepper hair was cut short. "Give me the correct answers and this'll be over much quicker."

She was determined to do whatever was necessary to get Tilly back, but her thoughts were a jumble and her fear made the situation worse.

"I'll do whatever you need me to."

He looked at her but his pale blue eyes didn't give anything away.

"How did you know Barbara Gilbert?"

Rachel drew a blank on the name. She closed her eyes thinking back through previous jobs, college friends, neighbours, mutual friends with Glen, even the women at the deli in town she spoke to at lunchtime. Nothing came to her.

"I don't know her." Tears brimmed in her eyes.

"Maybe you knew her as something else?"

"What?" That didn't even make sense.

"Ignore the name," he said and described a woman who could have been anyone – tall, dark-haired, thin-faced, slim.

Still she drew a blank.

"No." The tears spilled. "I don't know."

His lip pulled into a shrug that kinked his cheek. He took off his glove and reached into a storage box on the centre console for a tissue. He handed it to her and she dabbed her eyes then rubbed her cheeks with the heel of her palms.

"You were at the Newborough Centre this evening."

"Yes," she said, happy to finally understand something. "I'd been to my class."

He waved off her comment. "A woman passed you in the stairwell."

Rachel gripped the tissue and tried to remember the walk from the class. It seemed so long ago. She'd been texting Nat about the party and – yes, a woman had knocked her elbow.

"Yes, that's right. She apologised then you went past me."

Keel nodded.

"You were chasing her."

"I was trying to retrieve something she had which didn't belong to her."

"I don't know her. That was literally the first time I ever saw her."

He looked at her for long enough to make her feel uncomfortable.

"You have nice eyes, Rachel. You can see everything in them."

Dread curdled in her belly and she pressed her lips together.

"You're not lying, are you?"

"No," she said quickly. "Of course I'm not."

He rubbed his thumb and index finger together for a few moments. "I really thought she'd used you to make a switch."

"Switch?"

"She went out of my sight twice – once when she bumped into a man in the car park, then when she ran upstairs and bumped into you. My colleague Munro spoke with the man and he didn't have the item, so we assumed you did."

"But I don't. You just said you believe me. This is all a mistake."

"Were you carrying a handbag or rucksack?"

"My handbag."

"Which is where?"

"In Jack's car."

Keel executed a perfect three-point turn and drove up the hill quickly. He parked in front of the people carrier at the edge of the turnaround across from the Insignia.

"Where is Jack?" she asked.

He got out without answering and walked around to open her door. He gestured for her to get out and she did. The air bit at her cheeks and rapidly cooled the tears clinging to her eyelashes.

His fingers pinched her elbow as he led her to Jack's car.

"Stay there," he said and walked to the dry-stone wall, scanning the ground.

Rachel saw the front tyre was punctured by a crossbow bolt.

Keel came back with a lump of stone and swung it at the Insignia's passenger window. The glass shattered with the second blow and an alarm pierced the night. Keel ignored it as he unlocked the door and opened it. He pulled her handbag out of the footwell.

"Is this yours?" He waited for her to nod. "Is it full of crap?"

"There's all sorts in there, yes."

"Take off your coat."

"Why?"

"Because I'm going to tip it out and won't wait for you to gather everything back up again."

She quickly undid her coat and slipped it off, putting it on the ground as the air bit at her bare arms. He upended the bag and used the torch on his phone to sift through the items. She felt a growing anger watching him paw through her life, especially the items related to Tilly.

"Satisfied?" she asked, annoyed.

He raised his eyebrows. "Hardly. It's not here."

"What isn't? What the fuck are you looking for, Keel?"

"The package Barbara took." He mimed a shape. "It's about so big by so big."

"I don't remember…" And then, suddenly, she did.

In her bag before this nightmare started, she'd seen a brown box she'd assumed was part of Tilly's Little Buddies collection.

"No," she said slowly. "I do."

He looked up. "Where is it?"

"It was in my bag when I went home," she said and explained about the hole and seeing the box.

"So it could have fallen through the hole at any time then? Where have you been?"

"At home, at the party and in Jack's car."

Keel checked inside the car. "It's not there. We'll try your flat first." He gestured at her coat and the contents of her bag. "You've got ten seconds to gather that together or we're leaving it."

Rachel knelt and stones bit into her wounded knees as she put as much of her bag back as she could. The rest she bundled into her coat and tucked under her arm. She stood up and Keel almost dragged her back to the Range Rover and shoved her in.

* * *

Jack sat on the ground and listened to Munro scream. The fire roared and a lick of flame seemed to reach for him and touch his coat sleeve. He slapped at the flames with his hand until he'd doused them and then checked his fingers. There was a curl of burned skin in the centre of his palm and the sight of it nauseated him.

He got to his feet as a train horn sounded off in the distance. He swayed until he got his balance and then he turned to look at the fire. The shed was fully ablaze now with flames curling out the window and door. He could feel the heat on his face.

It seemed as though he'd succeeded in his plan to make a warning sign for Hadlington. He hopped away from the inferno but fell by the railway lines and glanced over his shoulder.

Munro staggered out of the blaze with her face, arms and shoulders on fire. She dropped to the ground and rolled, rubbing her face with her hands. With most of the flames out she managed to pull off her coat and throw it behind her. She collapsed onto her belly and sobbed as she tried to take a breath.

Jack kept moving.

The train sounded nearer. He craned his neck but couldn't see the engine. Would the driver call in if he saw the fire?

He looked over his shoulder and saw Munro get unsteadily to her feet. She staggered towards him quicker than he could crawl. Headlights painted streaks across the field.

Then Munro was standing over him, one foot on either side of his legs. She swayed and something dripped off her face and landed on his cheek. He quickly wiped it away. She smelled like a barbecue.

"Jack," she said and grabbed the bolt in his arm.

He shrieked as she moved it backwards and forwards in his arm. He tried to grab her hand but she swatted him away so he punched the inside of her right knee. She staggered back and pulled the bolt out.

Pain almost overwhelmed him with a white light that filled his head. In silence he blinked and saw nothing. Then the sounds rushed back – the lick of flames, the spit of wood, crying, heavy breathing, the song of the railway tracks. His vision slowly came into focus – the harsh orange blur of the shed and the shifting grey smudge that must be Munro.

Jack struggled to his feet and his focus came back. Munro stood in front of him though they were both unsteady.

"We're going to finish this," she said. Her short hair was rimmed by a nimbus of flame.

She reached for him. The train sounded its horn and she glanced at it. He took advantage of the distraction and threw a punch that connected with her jaw. One of his knuckles popped. Munro stepped back but kept her feet and came at him with her hand raised. He held up his hands in defence and her blow bounced off his arm.

The train came around the corner and its headlight bleached Munro's face. Her face was a dark mess and her left eye was closed. She swung for him again and he managed to hop back so the punch missed him by inches. He brought his right hand up quickly and the top of his fist hit her jaw. She sat down heavily.

"Stay down," he said.

She got slowly to her feet and shook her head. The train made the ground rumble. He hopped back to the rails as Munro reached for him with her arm drawn back for another punch.

# Chapter 37

Pippa came off the A14 at the Marham roundabout with her mind wandering after what Alan had told her.

She knew from on-the-job experience that the dual carriageway occasionally made people irrational, and drivers sometimes got caught up in things they didn't want to just by virtue of overtaking the wrong car. It was possible the vehicles Alan had described were those involved in the chase through Hadlington. Or maybe the man in the Insignia had somehow annoyed the driver of the Range Rover who then exacted his revenge. She didn't blame Alan for refusing to open up the store but did wonder about the repercussions of his actions.

Pippa stopped at the junction. The fatigue of the day nagged at her and made her eyes feel prickly and her neck ache. She tried to massage the knots out before driving onto the roundabout and it was only because she'd tilted her head that she happened to see the flames from the corner of her eye.

Surprised, she looked properly. There seemed to be a fire up on top of the hill where that new housing development was being built over the old farm. The dashboard clock read 3.37. However far behind schedule they might have been, there wouldn't be any builders up there now, so what did that leave? Kids playing around on the machinery? Some merry arsonist trying to burn down the show home or the barns?

She saw the 'Road Closed' signs. She'd completely forgotten about the roadworks, which meant she'd have to go back into Hadlington to catch the B-road to Marham.

The next junction led up to the farm. Should she call it in or go and check on things for herself? If there was a fire, an engine would never get there quickly enough and she was almost on site.

Decision made, she followed the curve of the roundabout into the mouth of the junction. Almost immediately, headlights lit up the hedgerow and a dark Range Rover swept around the corner at speed.

"Surely not," she said and quickly memorised the number plate.

A couple sat in the front seats and a male was driving. The car entered the roundabout and she followed its progress in her rear-view mirror.

Could it be the vehicle from the petrol station? Wasn't it more likely to be a couple having an affair who'd found somewhere quiet to carry on their clandestine meetings? There could be any number of reasons for them to be there, and the flames might be nothing to do with them.

Except, of course, they might.

She flicked on the full beams and put her foot down. As the road wound up the hill, she caught a glimpse of the fire through the hedgerow. It seemed to be right across the field.

Pippa braked sharply at a turning circle by a stone wall. She pulled up beside a people carrier and her headlights lit up a blue Insignia parked in front of a gate. Alan had mentioned an Insignia. She felt a tingle in the base of her neck. This was a dead end and isolated at the best of times. Something felt seriously amiss.

Should she ring control now? Investigating on her own wasn't the best idea but she wouldn't be popular bringing resources up here if she'd got it wrong. She reached under her seat for the jack handle she kept there and got out. The cold air pinched her cheeks.

She buttoned up her duffel coat and took out her phone. She stared at the screen but decided to find out more first before she called it in. She activated the torch app and turned a slow circle to take everything in. The Insignia had a smashed passenger window and a flat front tyre. What looked like a crossbow bolt stuck out of it. The people carrier was empty and locked. A gate to her right led through towards the big show home. A narrow strip of grass cut a path between it and some trees. She stopped at the gate.

"Police!" she shouted. "If there's anyone here, show yourself now."

Her voice was too loud in the still air and the echo of it made her feel uneasy. Something small darting through the hedgerow was the only response.

She remembered something Maley had told her once. 'Go on enough shouts,' he'd said, 'and you'll know instantly if a space is empty of not.' It was an impossible sensation to describe but you could feel it in the air and she felt it now.

"Again," she called and faced the farmhouse. "Show yourself now, this is the police."

Pippa opened the gate and walked carefully along the grass path. She kept her distance from the house and the stone wall in case anyone rushed her. Nobody did but there was an air of trepidation and she found herself gripping the jack handle so tight her knuckles ached.

The smell of the air changed at the edge of the house with a coppery tang she instantly recognised. She made a wide sweep of the ground with her torch and saw a spray of blood on some paving slabs and a puddle of it against a tree trunk.

"What the bloody hell…?"

Enough was enough. Now it was time to call in. With goosebumps speckling her arms she dialled the control room.

"Control room, Jeremy speaking."

She breathed a sigh of relief that it was someone she knew. "It's Pippa Vincent, Jeremy."

"Can't you sleep?"

"It was a long, weird shift. Listen, I need to call something in."

His tone shifted into professional mode. "What's up?"

"I'm at Fowler's Field. I saw a fire from the A14 and decided to investigate."

"Did you call it in when you saw it?"

"No."

"Pippa…" He managed to add syllables to her name.

"I know, I know, but I'm doing it now. I called into the petrol station earlier and the bloke behind the counter told me about two cars in some kind of aggro. I saw the Range Rover on the Marham turn roundabout and now I've found an Insignia near the farmhouse with two flat tyres. I was on my way to take a look at the fire but now I've found blood spatter next to one of the houses."

"Any idea whether it's human or not?"

"No but it's fresh. It all looks a bit suspicious."

"Agreed. I'll get a patrol to swing up there."

"Tell them to cut down the side of the house."

"Keep me posted about the fire."

"If it's just a pile of burning pallets, I'll text."

"You take care, Pip. Don't be a hero."

"I won't. Thanks, mate."

Pippa made her way through some trees onto a gravel plain and tried to get her bearings. The fire was hidden by a compound across from her and she could hear the snap of wood. She moved down the field to get a better view and saw flames coming from a shed beyond the railway lines.

A train horn sounded.

Two figures appeared, dancing or fighting she couldn't tell, silhouetted by the flames.

Pippa ran and her torch painted jagged streaks on the field as she went.

* * *

Munro punched him just above his left eye and Jack saw stars. He staggered back towards the railway line and the pain of putting his weight on his left leg cleared his vision.

She kept coming. Her left eye looked red and swollen and her hair still smoked.

He glanced over his shoulder; the sleepers were about a foot from his heels. He could feel the train in his bones but wouldn't be able to get across the tracks in time even if he wanted to.

Munro glared at him and he could almost feel her anger boring into him. This was his stand, it seemed; this was the end. He had no energy left to fight.

She jumped at him. Jack braced himself but the impact pushed him back and he fell. Munro landed on his chest but her momentum pushed her forward.

Jack gave her a kick as she went over him.

Munro's scream was cut short by a deafening blast of the train horn.

# Chapter 38

Keel drove quickly and didn't speak.

As much as her fear for Tilly made Rachel feel sick, she knew she had to figure out a plan. Kim in the self-defence class had impressed on them time and again the importance of gaining an advantage in any situation and working out the best exit. She was at a loss in the car – there was nothing she could use as a weapon and the idea of taking Keel on as he drove surely bordered on suicide – but there was nothing to lose in trying to ascertain as much as she could about Tilly's situation.

"Is this a big gang then?"

Keel glanced at her. "Gang?"

"Uh-huh. The business at my flat, the twat in the farmhouse, and you and Munro. What did Barbara Gilbert take that's so important you and your gang of bully boys got involved?"

"It's none of your business."

"Are you scared I won't be impressed?"

He smiled. "You're pushing your luck, Rachel."

"How so? You clearly need me."

"You've forgotten we have your daughter?" he asked.

She tried to keep the fear out of her voice. "Not for a second, which is why I asked. How many of you are there?"

He pulled up at a set of traffic lights. Across the way, a bulb outside a Turkish restaurant flickered like a strobe light.

"Enough for what we need."

"How did you find me and know so much about me?"

"You're online, we have people – it's not difficult. You follow someone on CCTV to get their registration number and that gives you their address. Social media does the rest."

She looked at him. "So where are you holding her?"

He shook his head. "You surely don't think I'd fall for that?"

"I'm just thinking out loud."

Her heart hammered against her sternum and her palms were damp with sweat. How far could she push him?

"Well don't."

"Why not? You got to ask loads of questions before. Where is she?"

"I'm not telling you."

"How do I know you're even telling the truth."

"You don't, but you daren't risk it."

"Has she been harmed?"

They stared at one another and she willed herself not to blink. The lights changed and his face went green as he looked towards the windscreen and accelerated away.

\* \* \*

A hundred yards from the railway lines Pippa faltered, not able to comprehend what she'd seen.

The aggressor had stood over the person on the floor and then the train clattered by. Pippa felt, rather than heard, the thud of impact. Something sprayed in the glare of the headlights.

"Oh my God," she shouted.

Pippa stopped at the fence and her legs felt like lead. Had she just seen someone commit suicide? The train seemed to take a long time to go by. When it had, she saw meaty lumps glistening between the sleepers.

She vaulted the fence and rushed across the tracks to the man who lay on his side groaning. He flinched as she knelt beside him and brought up his hand to protect his face.

"It's okay," she said. "I'm a police officer."

The man's hand relaxed and she saw blackened skin and blisters. Blood spattered his face and neck and there was more on his left arm around a hole in his coat.

"Are you really?"

"Yes." She dropped the jack handle. "What's going on here?"

"Too much to explain. How many of you are there?"

"Just me. I came up because of the fire." A hundred questions ran through her mind but where to start? "Who are you?"

"Jack Martin. Who're you?"

"PC Pippa Vincent, Mr Martin."

"Jack."

"You need to tell me what's happened here, Jack."

"I will, just let me get my breath."

"Where do you live?"

"Bristol."

The situation made less sense the more she discovered. "You're a long way from home."

"It's a long story. Where's Munro?"

"Who's Munro?"

"The woman trying to kill me."

"She was hit by the train."

"That's good," he said and his face relaxed.

His response shocked her and she busied herself checking him over. There was a hole in his trousers with blood crusted around it.

"Have you been shot, Jack?"

"Munro shot me twice with her crossbow."

The conversation felt more barbaric with every word he said.

"Is there anyone else here?" she asked.

"A few, I'm not sure. They're all over the place."

Pippa glanced around quickly. "What do you mean?"

"We got attacked in the house and that man died. A man and a woman got attacked by a dog and I think they're dead."

The information was overwhelming.

"Let me call this in and try to make some sense of it all."

"Good luck with that."

* * *

Jack propped himself up on his right elbow to watch the policewoman as she paced back and forth between him and the railway tracks. When the call ended, she came and knelt beside him.

"A patrol car is already en route but they're sending another to do a sweep and I've asked for an ambulance."

"But I'm fine."

"You're not. You've been shot, Jack, and your hands are burned. You've been in the wars."

"I need to check on Rachel. Have you seen her?"

"I don't know who Rachel is."

He tried to get up but Pippa put her hand on his shoulder.

"You need to stay on the ground. You might cause yourself more damage."

He shook his head. "I need to find her."

"You need to tell me about Rachel."

"If they've taken her, I don't have time."

"Who's taken her?"

He took a deep breath and let it out as a sigh. "If I tell you everything, will you help me?"

# Chapter 39

The story he told her didn't make much sense to Pippa, but judging from Jack's pale moonlit expression it didn't to him either.

"I think I saw the Range Rover Keel was driving," she said. "They came out of the lane as I drove in. He was at the wheel and a woman with curly hair was in the front seat."

"That's her." He got unsteadily to his feet.

"What're you doing?"

"Where's your car?" He hopped towards the railway tracks and the pain was visible in his face.

"I can't let you leave, Jack. This is a crime scene and you're a witness."

"This whole place is a crime scene," he said. "We need to help Rachel."

"I didn't see where the car went."

"They went back into Hadlington, I'm sure of it. He was at her flat before, waiting for her. Munro came later and crashed her car."

Pippa felt a little bit more of the story click into place. "What do you mean?"

"She was out of control in a Fiat and ran it over a wall."

"Why didn't you say this before?"

"I can't remember everything," he said and sounded annoyed. "We need to go there."

"Do you know for sure that's where he'll take her?"

He looked over his shoulder. "No, but I'm not doing her any good just lying here."

"Jack, we can't go."

"Then we'll pretend you're rushing me to the hospital and we'll detour a bit."

"I asked for an ambulance."

"You're not helping," he said with exasperation and turned to face her. "Rachel and I have been through hell tonight and we split up to try and draw attention to ourselves. My plan worked but she's not here." Tears rolled down his cheeks. "I can't help her from here."

Her frustration bubbled over. "I understand, but I can't let you leave a crime scene. I can't leave."

It went against everything that had been drummed into her.

"And Rachel might not be alive when we do," he said.

Her first instinct told her he was being melodramatic but something about the way he said it and the imploring way he looked at her made her believe him.

"You're in no fit state to move," she said.

He hopped across the railway lines and she followed him. His foot slipped on one of the sleepers and he almost went over. She grabbed his good arm.

"They tried to stop us getting away, don't you see?"

"Not entirely," she said.

It took them a while to get him over the fence and as they walked, she propped him up. Doubt nagged at her that she was making a terrible mistake abandoning the scene.

"Don't slow down," he said and when he locked eyes with her he seemed to see something. "I know this all sounds mad; it does to me and I'm in the middle of it. You don't know me from Adam but you have to trust I'm telling you the truth."

He stopped and pulled up his trouser leg. His sharp intake of breath let her know how much it hurt.

"I've never seen a crossbow wound before," he said through gritted teeth, "but this is what happened when Munro shot me."

Pippa shifted her torch and winced. She'd never seen a crossbow bolt wound either but this looked nasty.

"Would I do that to myself?" He held up his hands. "You have no reason to trust me but I'm begging you to give me half an hour, at most. Just help me find Rachel."

"Half an hour?"

"That's all we'll need."

\* \* \*

Keel turned into Moore Avenue.

Rachel had been quiet since their staring contest at the traffic lights and he'd been preoccupied thinking about Wilson. What had the old man meant by needing to get involved personally? Was he going to try and babysit the operation? He knew the fuck-up would reflect badly on him and felt a flash of frustration that Munro's team hadn't been anywhere near as good as she'd promised. But Keel had pulled it together in the end – after all, he was heading back to the target's flat with her in the car.

He'd considered updating Wilson on the situation but decided against it. The kidnap issue stuck in his throat. He wasn't squeamish by any stretch of the imagination but he thought the situation had taken a turn for the worse here.

He turned into the driveway for Rachel's building. Munro's Fiat now had a yellow 'Police Aware' sticker across the back windscreen.

"How many spaces do you have?"

"Two," she muttered.

"Where?" he asked and parked where she indicated then switched off the engine. "Have you remembered where the package is?"

"No," she said and opened her door.

He grabbed her wrist and pulled her back. She yelped in surprise.

"Ground rules. No sudden movements or screaming and no coded messages if we see anyone."

"It's almost four o'clock," she said and the resignation in her tone sounded very close to insolence. "Who the fuck are we going to see?"

"You now know the rules, Rachel, and it's up to you what you decide to do."

"Yeah." She wrenched her wrist from his grasp, got out and slammed the door.

* * *

Pippa stopped at some lights and her internal debate about leaving the farm raged.

"Why have you stopped?" Jack asked.

"It's a red light."

"There's nobody about. And you're the police."

"I'm off duty," she reminded him. Just saying the phrase made up her mind and she pressed the phone icon on her satnav screen.

"Who're you ringing?"

"My sergeant."

He'd be asleep but hopefully he'd have the phone close enough to wake him. It rang eight times.

"Pippa?" he said gruffly. "Do you know what time it is?"

"Yes but I really need to talk to you. I've done something."

"Like what?" he asked. His voice cleared. "Are you okay?"

"I'm fine, but I'm in a situation." She explained it as quickly as possible. Maley didn't interrupt once. "So I'm on my way to Moore Avenue with Mr Martin in the car."

There was a pause that concerned her.

"Are you insane?" he asked finally. "You've taken a witness – who may also be a murder suspect – away from the crime scene?"

"It's not me," Jack said.

"Am I on the speaker, Pippa?"

"Of course," she said testily. "I'm driving to Rachel's flat and I'm scared I've done the wrong thing."

"Of course you've done the wrong thing. What were you thinking?"

"Ken, you weren't there. I saw Munro go for him. She shot him with a crossbow."

"Twice," Jack put in.

"And her car is the one abandoned on Moore Avenue. She was in the Range Rover that chased Jack's Insignia through town earlier this evening. A separate witness corroborated the story and saw the cars in an altercation at the services."

"This is madness," Maley said.

She heard movement and a female voice said something she didn't catch.

"What's the address?" asked Maley.

She told him. "Why?"

"Because I'll come to you. If Mr Martin is telling the truth, then you're doing the right thing. If not, I'll be there as your supervising officer." He let that hang for a moment. "You might need the support."

"Thank you, Ken."

"Yeah. Just be bloody careful, Pippa."

# Chapter 40

It took Rachel a moment to find her keys in the mess of her bag and then she was standing in the warm hallway and Keel was closing the door quietly behind him.

He gave her a gentle push towards the stairs.

"Up you go."

She went and tried to think through a plan. What should she do if she found the box? Would Tilly be safe;

would they let her, Naomi and Anya go? If she didn't find it would Keel drag her to the party house and put more people into danger?

Her plan hadn't formed by the time they reached her floor. He leaned against the jamb as she unlocked the door then followed her into the flat. He closed the door gently behind him.

"Remember what I said. No funny business."

She breathed in the mixed scents of coffee, her perfume and Tilly. The thought of her being held somewhere clamped a cold hand around Rachel's heart and hammered home how much was at stake.

"Put on the lights."

Rachel kicked off her shoes and looked at herself in the mirror when she flicked on the hall light. The night had taken its toll on her now dirty and dishevelled dress. Her hair looked wild and her make-up was smudged. A livid mark covered her right cheekbone. Blood had streaked and dried on her knees. She padded into the lounge and switched on the lamp by the sofa.

Keel leaned into the three rooms that opened off the lounge – her bedroom, Tilly's bedroom and the bathroom.

"We're going to search the place," he said. "To expedite things, I'll do one room and you do another. If you find the package, don't pretend you didn't. You can't barter your way out of this."

"I won't, I promise."

"You check the bathroom. I'll check the girl's room."

"No, I'd rather–"

"I don't give a fuck what you'd rather."

She hated the idea of him rummaging through Tilly's toys, clothes and treasures, but what could she do?

"Okay," she said meekly.

Rachel went into the bathroom and checked everywhere she could think of – even under the floor mat – but didn't see the package. After a last glace around she went out and leaned through the doorway of Tilly's room.

Nothing had been strewn around but the room didn't look right – the duvet was lumpy and askew on the bed, and her toys were in the wrong order on the little chair Tilly couldn't fit into anymore. Keel was on his knees going through a chest of drawers.

"Anything?" he asked when he noticed her.

"Nothing."

"Me either." Keel stood up and checked his watch. "These rooms were a long shot though."

He brushed past her back into the lounge. She stopped in the doorway and stared into Tilly's world.

"Rachel," he called and startled her. When she turned he was standing by the sofa. "Where do you put your handbag when you come home?"

"By the table near the sofa."

He lifted the table up to reveal a small handful of crayons. He put the table back. "Not there."

"I wouldn't have taken it into the kitchen."

"The lounge or bedroom?"

She tried to remember but all she could see was Tilly doing some colouring at the coffee table.

"Either," she said.

He walked to her bedroom door and looked in, then turned to face her.

"You check in here, I'll do the lounge. And if you find anything…"

"I'll tell you," she said quickly. "I promise."

Rachel went into her bedroom and looked around desperately. Then she saw the cordless phone on the bedside cabinet the side she didn't sleep on. She used it for alarm calls now – the shrill ring forced her to move on those mornings she just wanted to turn over.

She checked Keel was absorbed in his search then pulled the door to. She walked around the bed and squatted beside the cabinet. Did she dare do this? She picked up the handset and put her thumb over the speaker to suppress any noise.

Her heart felt like it was blocking the base of her throat and she quickly dialled 999.

"You stupid bitch." Keel stood in the doorway. He threw something at her.

Rachel ducked as the phone from the lounge shattered against the wall and plastic fragments scattered across the carpet. He came round the bed quickly and grabbed her hair.

"Which service do you require?" asked a voice from the handset she held.

Keel pulled her to her feet and Rachel screamed. He threw her across the bed and she slid off. The phone clattered out of sight. Keel stalked round to stand over her.

"I saw the light on the phone in the lounge." His voice was steady and firm. "Didn't you realise that would happen?"

She could taste blood and started to panic but then saw the metal bar under the bed. A safety bar from the washing machine the installers hadn't taken away, she'd always planned to use it if she was ever confronted with burglars. It was about a foot long and as she reached for it, it felt reassuringly heavy.

"Up," Keel said. "I've had enough now."

As he grabbed for her wrist she swung out her arm. The angles were all wrong but she wouldn't have a chance like this again. The bar connected just above Keel's left ankle with a resounding crack and he cried out. Rachel scrambled up as he fell towards the window.

He slid to the floor and she jumped over his legs. He reached for her but missed and Rachel faced him from the doorway.

"Don't move," she warned and brandished the poker, "or I'll brain you."

Keel rolled up his trouser leg to check his ankle. He prodded at the skin then glanced at her with a studied look of indifference.

"I take it you have a plan?" He sounded like he was mocking her.

"Of course."

He straightened his trousers. "Made in the last five seconds?"

She felt frustrated he could see through her so easily. "You're not the only one who can think on their feet."

He cleared his throat. "How do you see this panning out, Rachel? Tell me because I'm interested. Are you planning to trade me for your daughter?"

"No," she said sullenly. She didn't have a clue what to do next and even though the thought of caving in his skull appealed, it wouldn't help Tilly. "Get on your feet."

He didn't move. She swung the poker as close to his head as she dared and it whistled through the air. He didn't flinch but got up slowly.

"Through here," she said and backed into the lounge.

He held up his hands and followed her. She directed him to stand by the sofa.

"Tell me where Tilly is."

He laughed and put his hands down. "That's your plan?"

"Where is she?" she demanded and her voice cracked as her anger bloomed.

"I don't know," he said in a sing-song voice.

"You'd better tell me."

He mimicked her and it pushed her over the edge. Anger clouded her judgement and she raised the poker and rushed at him.

Keel grabbed her wrist and bent it back then pulled down quickly. She cried out and let go of the poker. He folded her over his right knee and her breath left her. He shoved her into the coffee table and she fell over it, scattering papers, crayons and various cups and saucers from the tea set across the floor.

It took so long to draw a breath Rachel thought she would vomit. Heat ran up and down her arms, dragged across her scalp. She rolled onto her back and put her knees to her chest as she gasped for air.

Keel sat on the sofa and watched her impassively.

It took her a while to sit up.

"I warned you," he said.

She nodded but couldn't speak.

He shook his head. "You're an idiot but you've got balls, I'll give you that."

She grunted at him.

"Did you find the package or not get a chance to check?"

He waited until she shook her head then he went into her bedroom. She heard drawers and the wardrobe doors open. He came back into the lounge a few minutes later and sat on the sofa.

"You're running out of time here," he said and steepled his fingers. "Worse for you, I'm running out of patience."

"I don't know where it is," she said. "You have to believe me, Keel."

"Whether I do or not is irrelevant. The people I work for won't be satisfied until they have it."

She tried to cast her mind back to what felt like days ago but was mere hours; the worry she'd lost her keys, then Glen fobbing her off again. Rachel had her shower and Tilly borrowed her phone to...

Her phone.

In the poor light of the porch Rachel had assumed the box was part of Tilly's Little Buddies collection. What if Tilly had assumed the same when she got the phone and taken the box. But if that were the case wouldn't the bastards who had Tilly have found the box themselves? Maybe not. If she could convince Keel of her theory he might take her to her daughter.

\* \* \*

"Tilly might have picked it up when she took my phone."

His attention perked. "You don't have a phone."

She looked at him like he was a reluctant learner and he didn't like it. "No, because she's got it."

"You don't have one registered," he said.

It was standard operating procedure to check as soon as they found her address. Rachel nodded and sat up, grimacing with the movement.

"My stupid ex-husband fucked up the billing so I've got a pay and go."

Shit, he thought. Another in the painfully long list of mistakes he'd made this evening. He took out his phone.

"What's the number?"

He typed as she spoke and put the phone to his ear. It rang six times and went to voicemail. He redialled and the same thing happened.

"It must be switched off."

"I doubt it. It's probably set on silent."

"How likely is it she took the box?"

"It's very likely. She collects these toys called Little Buddies and the box looks just like one of the ones they'd come in."

He wiped the corners of his mouth with his fingertips – a meditative twitch he'd long ago picked up. If Wilson had the girl then it shouldn't take them long to find the package.

"So if we find the phone we find the box?"

He activated the Finders app on his phone and typed in her number. It only took a moment for the red dot, representing Rachel's phone, to appear on the Google map of Moore Avenue. He zoomed in and saw his own phone tagged next to it.

"It's here," he said. "Perhaps it got dropped. Where else did you go?"

"Only to the car park."

"Put your shoes on," he said and stood up. "We're going for a little walk."

# Chapter 41

The house slept around them. Pipes ticked and something above them creaked.

"Straight downstairs," Keel said quietly. "Retrace your route from earlier."

"Okay," she said and there was a tone in her voice he didn't like. It wasn't petulance but it wasn't far off.

He held her elbow before she moved away. "Remember what I said about co-operating."

"Of course."

He followed her at a short distance because the poker incident had surprised him and seemed to be yet another regrettable slip-up in this evening of disasters. He didn't want any more.

Keel scanned the floor as they walked. The carpets ran tight to the walls and there was no furniture. There was a low table on the landing and he checked below it. Two large windows looked out over the front and rear aspects but the windowsills of both were clear. A flight of stairs went up to, he assumed, the flats with balconies where he'd seen the tent earlier.

"We went straight down," said Rachel as she stood at the top of the stairs.

He jutted his chin to gesture her on and they went down to the next landing. It was laid out the same as the previous one.

"You didn't go off into the hallway?"

"No."

"And your daughter wouldn't run up any of them?"

"Why would she do that? Where's she going to hide?"

He shrugged. "Keep going."

She led him down to the foyer. A chair stood under the mailbox system and there was nothing under it. They both checked the black and white tiled floor.

"I can't see it," Rachel said and sounded frustrated.

"Try the car park."

"Then what?" she asked. Her hands made frightened, flighty motions.

"Then we have a major issue if you don't find it."

Rachel opened the front door and Keel's phone vibrated. He took it out to see Wilson's name on the screen.

"Wait here," he said to her then went down onto the driveway.

"You are still functioning then, Keel?"

He bit his lip. "I apologise, Mr Wilson."

"Are you in possession?"

"Not quite."

"Not quite?" Wilson sighed. "You've been on operation a while now, Mr Keel. Where are you now?"

"At Rachel Turner's flat."

"What on earth are you doing there? I don't have to tell you this sounds like a royal fuck-up, do I?"

He couldn't deny it. "It sounds worse than it is."

Wilson paused for an uncomfortable length of time. "I'm in the area and will be with you shortly. Please restrain Ms Turner."

The call ended and Keel looked back at Rachel in the doorway. Wilson being on site wasn't the 'personally involved' Keel had expected and this absolutely wasn't a good sign. He felt tension across his shoulders and didn't like it.

Rachel nodded her head as if to prompt him. "Well?"

He worried the inside of his cheek. "My boss is on his way."

She came down the steps with a hopeful expression. "Is he bringing Tilly?"

"He didn't say." Keel turned on the torch app and grabbed Rachel's arm. She tried to shrug him off so he held tighter. "Trace your steps to the car park and, for your sake, you'd better hope we find it there."

He swung the torch in a wide arc as he walked to try and light as much of the driveway as possible. They reached the car park without seeing anything and there was nothing under her car. The air seemed to crackle with tension.

Rachel ran a hand through her hair. "What're we going to do?"

\* \* \*

Jack's heart raced and he looked at the clock. Even though Pippa drove quickly it didn't seem like they were getting anywhere with one street quickly looking like every other.

"How far?"

She didn't look away from the road. "Not far now."

"Can you go faster?"

"The streets are empty but if someone pops out between parked cars and I'm doing fifty or sixty without blues-and-twos, we're going to come to a complete stop."

"Yeah," he said, acquiescing.

"I'm going as fast as I can."

"I know," he said, "I'm just worried."

\* \* \*

Rachel sat on the bottom stair and idly picked at the grazes on her knees. It felt like she'd been here for hours but knew it had probably only been twenty minutes or so. Keel leaned on the front door frame as he stared out into the night. He'd barely moved while she couldn't stop fidgeting as nervous energy rattled through her.

She heard an engine and Keel straightened so quickly it startled her.

"Come here," he said.

She went without question and saw the flare of brake lights as a car pulled to the kerb. Keel opened the door and guided her out. The air felt very crisp and she hugged herself to retain the warmth of the foyer.

"Don't do anything stupid," he said.

"You don't have to keep telling me," she said and didn't bother to hide her annoyance at his reminder. "It's my daughter we're talking about."

A dark Range Rover reversed into the driveway and stopped beside Munro's broken Fiat. A tall, thin younger man with close-cropped hair and a dark Crombie coat got out of the driver's side and walked around the front of the car. He nodded at Keel then opened the passenger door. Reflections of the streetlight and moon danced off the darkened glass.

The man in the passenger seat glared at Rachel fiercely enough to make her feel uncomfortable. She hugged herself tighter.

"Keel," said the man.

"Mr Wilson."

Wilson slipped out of the Range Rover. Tall and in his late fifties, he had a full head of grey hair, pronounced cheekbones and thin lips. With his overcoat and scarf, he looked like a distinguished man on his way home from the theatre.

He reached into the footwell for a black cane and limped three steps from the car so the man in the Crombie coat could close the door.

"Rachel Turner, I presume?"

He spoke quietly and she could hear traces of the Black Country in his voice.

"You've led us a merry dance." He looked her up and down and the wave of discomfort she felt left goosebumps in its wake. "Are you sure it's her?" he asked Keel without looking away from Rachel.

"Yes."

Wilson put both hands on the cane handle and leaned on it. "You're curious about my leg?"

"No," she said.

"Oh I can tell you are. Everyone is. I was in a conflict and some bastard shot me in the spine. The shrapnel took out some nerves."

Rachel didn't know how to respond so she kept quiet.

"Enough about me though, let's talk about you and the item you have that I've been engaged to recover." The friendly edge to his voice slid away. "This has gone on for long enough so please hand it over."

"She doesn't have it."

Wilson turned his gaze slowly towards Keel before looking back at Rachel. "And where is it?"

"I think my daughter has it."

"Tilly?"

Hearing him say her name made Rachel angry and she wanted to shout at him and tell him not to talk about the little girl.

"Tilly apparently took Rachel's phone and the package," Keel said. "We suspect she thought it was a toy. According to GPS the phone is on the premises but we can't find it or the package."

Wilson leaned forward. "So where's Tilly?"

# Chapter 42

Rachel couldn't quite process what he'd said.

"What?"

"You don't get to ask the questions, Rachel." Wilson shifted his weight and winced. "Christ. You'd try the patience of a saint."

She needed to understand the situation properly.

"I asked what you said," she repeated.

Wilson glanced at Keel who shrugged. "I want to know where Tilly is."

Rachel watched his face as she tried to determine if he was playing or not.

"You have her," said Keel carefully.

Wilson shook his head slowly. "That was all smoke and mirrors, Mr Keel."

Rachel felt a sudden charge of anger that heated her veins and screamed at Wilson. His expression changed as she jolted forward and hit him in the chest with her forearms. It felt like hitting a brick wall but she had some momentum and he stumbled back. Keel wrapped his arms around her and lifted her off her feet. She kicked out as he pulled her against his chest and turned her flailing legs away from Wilson. Her heel connected with his shin and she did it again. He took a wider stance as he backed away.

Wilson fell and Crombie came around the Range Rover and looked at his boss then at her. Keel pulled her back towards the house and she kept kicking.

"Stop it," he hissed in her ear.

She couldn't. Anger fizzed through her like an electrical charge. "He hasn't got her."

"I heard."

He'd linked his fingers over her chest and she knew it would be virtually impossible to break his grip. That reminded her of Kim's 'keep it simple, stupid' so she stopped struggling and kicking.

"I'm calm," she said and hoped her voice reflected her lie. "Let me go."

"And have you go off like a wildcat again?"

"I won't."

"After everything that's happened this evening, Rachel, you surely can't expect me to believe you."

She didn't say anything, content to save her energy. Keep it simple, stupid.

Crombie helped Wilson to his feet. When the older man was finally upright, he snatched his cane back and leaned on it. He glared at Rachel with a thunderous expression.

"You don't know where the fucking thing is, do you?" He shook his head. "We need to make her remember."

"How can I, when I'm having to bloody hold her back?" Keel said.

"I'm not fighting," she said and made a fist with her right hand.

"Don't question me," Wilson said.

"I'm not questioning you…" Keel said.

Rachel let her middle finger protrude slightly from her fist and punched the back of Keel's left hand as hard as she could. The first blow made him grunt and she kept punching with as much effort as she could muster. He took a dozen blows until he had to let her go.

She kicked at his shins and then sprinted towards Wilson. He brought the cane up as if intending to whip her across the face, but she feinted right and went to the left. He swung at empty air and now she had a clear run to the pavement.

\* \* \*

The shouting woke Naomi Marshall.

It had been a long night. Rachel's panicked phone call that she'd been let down once more by shitty Glen had at least given Anya the delight of her best buddy to play with. Both kids were hyped by the fireworks – at the display and then, later, from those annoying neighbours over the back – and the candy floss and tent building. Anya asked if they could sleep in it but Naomi had no intention of that happening.

The girls went to bed at ten with solemn promises they would go straight to sleep. Naomi had a long hot bath listening to some kind of commotion in the car park and by the time she got out, all she could see different down there was a badly parked Fiat.

Now she rolled over and checked the clock. It was almost four thirty. Annoyed, she got out of bed and looked out the window.

The Fiat had a 'Police Aware' sticker on its rear windscreen and a Range Rover had parked to block it in. A skinny bloke in a Crombie coat stood with his arms folded as he looked at something – the people who were shouting, she assumed – close to the building and out of her sight.

Above the noise, she heard the pantomime whispers of Anya and Tilly. It sounded like they were in the lounge, which opened onto the balcony, where the tent was set up.

Naomi went into the lounge. The room was cold with the balcony door wide open. The girls stood on tiptoe at the handrail as they tried to see the cause of the commotion.

"Anya Marshall," she said loudly and both girls jumped.

"Sorry, Mummy," said Anya and she came into the lounge and grabbed Naomi's hand. "Come and see. There are people arguing."

Tilly took her other hand. Naomi let herself be led. They'd put two cushions, a couple of Barbie dolls, some Little Buddies figures and a tea set in the tent. A selection of Anya's stuffed toys, as well as a stone gargoyle they'd picked up from a garden centre, sat on the handrail.

"How long have you two been out here?"

"Not long," they chorused.

The girls let go so they could lean over the handrail to watch the entertainment. Naomi leaned over too. The man in the Crombie coat walked towards the house as the older man lifted his cane. A woman sprinted into view as if running for the pavement. Something about her looked familiar, and then Tilly cried out, "Mummy!"

# Chapter 43

Rachel stopped so quickly at Tilly's cry she almost toppled. She looked up and saw the faces peering over the handrail and felt a wave of relief that was quickly crushed as Keel looked up too.

"Clever girl," he said and glanced at Rachel. "She's still got your phone, hasn't she?"

Crombie walked towards her and Rachel knew she had to keep her options open.

"I think so," she said and walked towards Keel.

Crombie mirrored her and made sure to keep himself between Rachel and Wilson.

"The GPS registered here," Keel said, "because she never left."

"So why didn't you intercept her before?" Wilson asked.

"I would have done except you said you had her."

Wilson shook his head. "This has proved a very disappointing task for you, Keel."

Rachel watched their exchange. She didn't know the issue between them but it couldn't hurt to try and fuel the fires.

"Let me get her down," she said.

Wilson looked at her. "I think not."

"Could she throw the package down?" Keel asked.

"And what if your ability to catch is as bad as your deductive reasoning?" Wilson asked. He jerked his head toward the balcony.

"Don't," Rachel said. "Seriously."

"What're you going to do, Rachel?" Keel asked. "This is the end of the line."

* * *

"We need to go inside, girls," said Naomi.

Something felt wrong about all of this, and she didn't want either of the girls to see it but both of them gripped the handrail so tightly she couldn't pry them loose.

Naomi watched Rachel walk towards the house and willed her friend to look up and try to acknowledge her in some way but Rachel didn't.

"Stay here," Naomi said and tapped Anya gently on top of her head.

"Okay." The girl's attention didn't stray from the car park for a second.

Naomi got her mobile from the lounge and went back onto the balcony. She dialled 999.

* * *

"I'm getting fed up standing here," Wilson said, "and this cold air is playing havoc with the shrapnel. Do your bloody job, Keel, and get the package."

"Let me," Rachel said to Keel. "My friend's not going to open the door to you and she's probably already called the police."

"I could throw you on the ground and threaten to bash your skull in against the gravel. I'm sure she'd open the door then."

"Most of my neighbours would hear you too."

Keel glared at her and she didn't break his stare. Finally, he nodded. "Fine. We both go up."

"I go to the door."

"Don't push your luck, Rachel."

She gave him a wide berth as she crossed the car park and let herself into the building. She tried to pull the door shut quickly enough to shut him out but he was too quick for her and put his foot in the gap.

"Nice try," he said.

She let go of the door and he came through it.

"Lead the way," he said.

221

She could run screaming up the stairs and implore her neighbours to call the police but decided it was too risky a proposition. It all seemed impossible and her heart sank with every step she took. She hated the feeling that she'd somehow come through everything this evening only for it all to turn to shit now. Kim drummed into them to never give up but she was finding that harder to do as her options narrowed with each step.

"Which number does your friend live at?"

"No." She shook her head. "I'll tell you when we get there."

"You're not going to tell me her name either, I presume?"

"You presume right."

They went up another flight in silence. It took ever more effort to lift her feet as no glorious insights came to her. There was, it seemed, no stunning plan to get them away from here safely.

"So what happens then?"

"That all depends."

"On what? Whether or not I comply? Or whether my friend does?"

"I'd say it all depends on what Mr Wilson wants to do."

"He's your boss, is he?"

"In this instance."

"Have you always been freelance?"

"Do you always ask questions?"

"Only when I'm dealing with bastards."

"Nice. Of course, it all depends on whether your daughter has the package."

A sudden horrible thought occurred to Rachel. What if Tilly had opened the box and realised it wasn't a toy so thrown it away?

* * *

Pippa took a turn sharply enough that the tyres squealed in protest.

Jack gazed out the window and tried not to think too much about what they might find at Rachel's.

"We're nearly there," Pippa said.

She was driving faster now and parked cars flashed by. He watched a muscle twitch on her jawline.

"You're worried, aren't you?" he said.

"Uh-huh. I'm worried you're wrong and that they're somewhere else and everything's fucked."

"What if I'm not wrong?"

"Then I'm worried we're too late and everything's still fucked."

* * *

They stopped on her landing

"You stay here," Rachel said.

"But this is your floor." He was close enough she could hear him breathe.

"I know. I'll go up alone because my friend will open the door for me. I'll get the package and come down to you."

"Right," he said and twisted her arm. She tried to pull free but he stepped back and turned her hand down and pushed her fingers up. She cried out as the muscles in her forearm burned with pain.

"Quiet," he said. "Don't say another fucking thing."

She bit her lip to stop crying out. Tears sprang to her eyes.

"Are we on the same page?"

She nodded, desperate for him to let go before he broke her shoulder, wrist or fingers. Or maybe all three.

"Upstairs," he muttered and led her up the next flight without releasing his grip.

She stumbled on a couple of steps but his hold kept her upright. She tried to keep quiet but couldn't help the occasional pained squeak. He shoved her against the wall at the top floor landing and she fell against it then rubbed her shoulder. The pain felt deep. She looked hard at him but her tears made it difficult to focus.

"You almost broke my arm."

He nodded. "Let's go see your friend."

\* \* \*

Naomi slipped her phone into her dressing gown pocket.

She'd told the operator everything she'd seen and stressed the fact Rachel was alone and being harassed by at least two men. The operator promised they'd get a patrol out as soon as possible.

"Mummy!"

The girls were still peering over the handrail and Naomi rushed across the lounge towards them.

"What's up?"

"Rachel's gone."

It felt like an icy hand had stroked Naomi's shoulders. "Are you sure?"

Tilly turned. Her cheeks were pink and her eyes glistened. "She went under the house with the man with black hair."

Naomi realised she meant they'd gone out of sight of the balcony. "Perhaps they've come in from the cold?"

Tilly nodded as if she really wanted to believe. "Can I go and see her?"

"Perhaps later, love, when she's finished playing with her friends." She tapped them both gently on their heads. "Let's go in. It's getting cold and it's really very late."

"But we haven't finished the tea party yet," said Anya and pointed to the animals and gargoyle. "They'll be sad if they don't get their tea."

"You can finish it tomorrow before school."

"Aw, Mummy…"

There was a knock at the front door. Naomi turned slowly to look towards it. The girls out on the balcony hadn't heard it.

"Okay," she said. "Five minutes then I'll be back."

* * *

Keel stood a few feet from the door and watched her. Her hands shook and she felt sick. Having him here so close to her baby, to Naomi and Anya, repulsed and terrified and angered her in equal measure.

Rachel knocked again being careful not to do it so loudly she'd wake the neighbours.

The door opened a crack and she looked into Naomi's eyes. Her friend looked panicked.

"Hey, Rachel."

Rachel glanced at Keel then back at her friend and hated herself for dragging Naomi into this.

"I need you to do something for me."

"What's going on?"

"I promise I'll tell you later but just do this one thing for me and I'll leave you alone."

"I rang the police."

"Okay."

"Did I do the right thing?"

"Yes, thank you." She glanced at Keel who watched her impassively. She looked back at Naomi. "What did they say?"

"They're sending someone over. Are you coming in?"

"God no," Rachel said quickly and watched relief spread across Naomi's face. "Can you get Tilly's rucksack? I need to check something."

Naomi frowned then moved away from the door. Rachel leaned with both hands on the wall and breathed deeply. She stayed that way until Naomi reappeared in the gap.

"I found it."

"Great. Can you search through it for a brown package?"

Naomi stepped back and Rachel shifted her position so she could see her friend. Naomi went quickly through the rucksack and held up a mobile.

"Is this yours?"

"Yes."

"Do you want it?"

"No. Just the brown package. It looks like a Little Buddies box."

Naomi delved a little further. "Got it," she said.

"Excellent," Rachel said.

Keel rolled his index fingers in a hurry-up gesture. "Get it off her."

"And what happens then? Will you take me back downstairs on our own?"

He nodded but that didn't stop her feeling sick.

"I need to hear you say it," she said.

"You can't demand anything."

"Maybe not," she said, "but the police are on their way. I'll tell her to keep the package and lock the door. Then I'll make a lot of noise."

He looked at the door across the hall. "I have no intention of going into your friend's flat."

Knowing she wouldn't get more, Rachel looked into Naomi's wide eyes. "Pass it through."

"Are you sure? I heard everything. Do you really want me to give it to you?"

She hoped her friend took comfort from the smile she struggled to form.

"Yes. Then shut the door and lock it tight. Don't open it again unless it's a police officer."

"Are you going to be alright?"

"I'll be fine."

"I'm worried," Naomi said but handed over the box anyway. Their fingers touched briefly. "Take care."

"I will. Lock the door."

# Chapter 44

Keel took the package off her and slipped it into a pocket in his parka coat.

"Let's go," he said and jerked his thumb towards the stairs.

Rachel nodded and felt a black cloud of anxiety envelop her. He now had what he wanted so she was surplus to requirements. Worse, he knew where Tilly was. But what could she do? She might outrun Keel on the stairs but Crombie would be waiting for her outside.

"Be careful on the stairs, Rachel. No funny business."

She went down the flight and Keel kept two steps behind her.

"What's going to happen when you give Wilson the package?"

"I have no idea. I was hired to deliver it to him so once it's in his hands my involvement is over."

"And what about me? What about Jack?"

"I imagine Munro has enjoyed dealing with him. As for you, I can't imagine it's going to be pleasant."

"What if he asks you to hurt me before you hand it over?"

"Then I do it. We're not friends, Rachel."

They walked down to the foyer in uncomfortable silence and he pushed her through the front door. She stumbled on the steps but managed to keep her balance. Wilson and Crombie looked up from their conversation.

"And?" Wilson asked.

Keel held up the package.

"Well done," Wilson said and came towards them. Crombie walked alongside him.

Keel put his hands between Rachel's shoulder blades but she shook him off.

"Don't push," she said. "Just tell me where you want me to go."

"Down the steps and head for Mr Wilson."

She looked around desperately for a way out. The hedgerow and trees blocked the escape route to her left and Crombie had angled himself to block the gap past his Range Rover. The only alternative was to circle the house again which didn't seem wise. The sense of futility angered her.

"Move," Keel said.

"Why don't you just fuck off?"

He didn't reply but pushed her. She let her anger with him build and it seemed to seethe and burn in her throat with a sharp metallic taste.

Wilson stopped by the corner of the building and Crombie stepped into her path and grabbed her arm.

\* \* \*

Pippa braked sharply and almost didn't make the turn into Moore Avenue. The car bounced up the pavement and back onto the road and Jack gasped with pain as he lurched to one side.

"Sorry," she muttered.

"No, speed is good."

She saw the Range Rover and recognised the number plate. "There they are."

"And it's parked by the driveway."

Pippa pulled up at the kerb by the swing park her nephew loved.

"Why are you stopping here?"

"So if anyone's there they don't see us."

She braked, switched the engine off, undid her seatbelt and opened the door, all in one fluid movement. Jack fumbled with his seatbelt.

She got out and picked up the jack handle. Jack joined her at the front of the car and they crossed the road. Trees blocked most of Rachel's building from view except where parted branches afforded brief glimpses of dark windows. Moonlight reflected off some of the panes.

She heard people talking, at least two males plus a female. She tapped Jack's arm and he nodded. Once they were past the trees, whoever stood in the driveway would be able to see them.

\* \* \*

Crombie pulled her against him and she let it happen then clawed at his cheek when she was close enough. Her nails raked him and she pressed as hard as she could. He instantly let her go and rounded on her. Four ragged streaks cut bloody tracks across his cheek. He put his hand over them and glared at her.

"You bitch," he said and backhanded her.

Her cheek exploded with pain and she dropped to her knees which sparked even more pain. Everything seemed to hurt and something whistled in her ears.

"Mummy!"

Rachel looked up and could just see the top of Tilly's head over the balcony. She wished Naomi would take her inside to spare her all this.

"Get up," Crombie spat.

She let him pull her to her feet then he twisted her around and held her in front of him. She wondered if he was close enough that she could elbow him in the throat.

"I wouldn't hold her like that," said Keel with an amused smile. "You've spent so long in front of your laptop tracking people digitally you've forgotten what things are like in the real world. She's dangerous and will kick you in the bollocks or punch you in the throat as soon as look at you."

Crombie kept hold but moved her out of range. "Don't try it," he said.

"I would kick you in the cock," she said, "if I thought you had one."

"Nice," said Wilson and cleared his throat. "I think this concludes our business, Mr Keel."

"It does mine," Keel said.


# Chapter 45


"Excellent," said Wilson and gestured at Crombie. "Get her in the car."

Rachel struggled but Crombie dragged her easily towards the Range Rover.

"Stop!" a voice cried.

He whirled around and pulled Rachel with him. She saw a tall blonde woman in a red duffel coat rushing up the driveway towards them.

"Get back against the car," the woman called.

Crombie stepped towards the Range Rover more in confusion, Rachel thought, than a desire to obey.

"You need to walk away," Wilson called to the woman. "We haven't got time for nosey neighbours."

"I don't think so. I'm PC Pippa Vincent and you're in a lot trouble."

"Me, officer?" Wilson smiled and pointed at his chest. "I think you'll find this is a domestic issue between those two people by the car. And are you even on duty?"

Crombie pulled Rachel closer as if to use her as a human shield.

"Stay where you are," Pippa advised him.

"Mummy!" Tilly called.

"I'm okay," Rachel called without looking up. "Go inside."

"You're Rachel?" Pippa asked.

Rachel looked at her astounded someone else she didn't know knew her name. "How do you know?"

"I have Jack with me."

The news that he was okay gave her a boost of energy and Rachel bent forward so her behind pressed into Crombie's groin. When he stepped back she used the space to kick at his ankle. He let go of her as he tried to jump out of the way.

Wilson came away from the building and Pippa held out her hand. "Get back," she shouted.

* * *

Naomi tried to pull Tilly away from the handrail but the little girl held on with all her might. Tears streamed down her cheeks.

"Mummy's in trouble."

"I know. The police will help."

The woman in the red duffel coat yelled, "Get back!" and her words echoed.

Tilly jumped back with a yelp and bumped Naomi which pushed her into the railings. Tilly put her hands out to break her fall and she knocked the gargoyle.

It wobbled for a moment then dropped out of sight.

* * *

Keel watched the woman who might or might not have been the police come up the driveway.

He hadn't been paid for this. So long as he could get away from Rachel, who'd assuredly implicate him, now was the time to vanish.

Movement near the end of the driveway caught his eye and he saw Jack hobble off the pavement. Keel's stomach tightened. How could Munro have failed? Had he killed her too?

He didn't have time to worry about that. He knew his only exit from the property was the driveway and while he could take Jack out easily, he had no idea how accomplished the PC was and Rachel had been a source of constant surprise since he'd first encountered her.

Wilson was edging towards Keel. "Now what?"

"No idea."

"I pay you for solutions, Keel."

"I'm not on the clock anymore."

Wilson moved away from the house and the PC yelled, "Get back!"

"Fuck's sake," Wilson muttered to Keel. "I'll bloody pay—"

He didn't finish. Keel didn't realise what took a chunk out of Wilson's forehead until the stone gargoyle hit the gravel. The head cracked off and rolled to one side as a plastic teacup bounced under the Range Rover. A fine mist of blood coated Keel's face and he saw droplets on his eyelashes.

Someone screamed.

Wilson dropped to his knees and his eyes rolled up as the open wound in his head gushed blood. He fell forward and the package lay by his now open hand in a widening red pool.

The woman in the duffel coat recovered herself enough to run across the driveway.

Rachel stared at the ruin of Wilson open-mouthed. Jack came up the driveway as quickly as he could hop.

Keel seized the moment. He grabbed the blood-soaked package and ran, angling himself away from the policewoman who paid him no attention anyway. Rachel saw him though. She shouted "Keel!" but he kept moving.

# Chapter 46

Keel passed Rachel before she had a chance to react but he heard the scuff of her shoes on the gravel behind him almost immediately.

He aimed for the driveway entrance. Jack stood and made fists. Keel felt a flash of anger at him and decided to go through him rather than round. He dropped his shoulder at the last moment and lifted him off his feet. Jack landed in a heap and Keel kept going.

\* \* \*

Rachel didn't know where the energy to chase Keel came from. Her legs felt leaden with fatigue and her breathing was laboured but she couldn't give up.

She watched Keel barrel through Jack and heard the impact before her friend collapsed and rolled onto his back.

"Jack!" she called, without stopping.

"Rachel," he wheezed. "Don't go after him. Pippa's the police, they'll stop him."

"I can't let him get away," she said and then she was past him and onto the pavement. Keel had run out of sight but she could hear his soles slapping on the tarmac.

\* \* \*

A car turned into the street from Keel's right and the headlights glared in his eyes. At this time of the morning a car wasn't likely to be good news, so he went across the road towards the park he'd sat in at the start of the evening.

He ran between two cars and took two quick strides over the pavement and onto the grass. His left foot slid out from under him and he lurched, but he managed not to fall. He ran onto the soft play surface and between the swings, yanking the chains as he went in the hope the movement would throw her.

Beyond the back fence was a run of terraced houses to the left. To this right, dozens of glassless windows stared from the blank face of an old factory unit. A hint of dawn in a line of night sky suggested an alleyway between the houses and the factory.

The park rose slightly to an eight-foot-tall fence and he ran faster at it, knowing a good leap would take him most of the way up it and he could scramble the rest.

Keel jumped and his fingers closed around the chain-link. Using the momentum, he pulled himself up and tried to get purchase with his feet.

He vaulted the top but landed badly and his left knee turned with a loud crack. It felt like someone had driven a screwdriver into it and the pain flooded his head for a moment. He looked back through the fence and saw Rachel running off at an angle then he saw why.

"Fuck," he shouted, angry with himself for missing the gate.

If she hit it hard enough to swing it into his good leg then it'd be game over.

\* \* \*

Rachel hit the gate hard and the chain-link dug into her palms. The gate swung around and she heard Keel kick it back. She managed to almost get through before it caught her right shoulder and chest hard. The collision knocked her flat and she gasped for breath as Keel got slowly to his feet.

\* \* \*

Keel limped as he followed the gravel path alongside the fence.

There was definitely something wrong with his knee and he wasn't going to be able to run anymore. But if Rachel was winded and he could get away now, he didn't have to rush too much.

A brick wall to his left marked the end of the gardens to the houses he'd seen earlier. Ahead was another slope and he made his way carefully down it, favouring his right knee all the way. The slope ended with a low wall and he sat on that to drop himself into the alley. The garden walls were high and blocked out the moonlight and the factory cast deep shadows that hid almost everything else from view.

He followed the cobblestone path into the darkness.

\* \* \*

Rachel got to her hands and knees wheezing and just saw Keel before he dropped out of sight.

When she was sure she could stand up without fainting or being sick she followed the path and went down the slope. She could hear him in the darkness and his footsteps echoed against the high brick walls.

She'd used this alley a few times and knew it ran straight for twenty or thirty yards then slanted to the right for another twenty or thirty before coming to the next street.

\* \* \*

Rachel got up quicker than he'd expected and Keel quickened his pace as much as he dared on the treacherous cobbles.

The alley was so dark he could barely see anything and he didn't want to put his foot into a hole or gap because it felt like it wouldn't take much for his knee to be completely incapacitated.

He put his hand on one wall and took as big a stride as he could. The dark seemed to shift around him, throwing off his senses. The sound of Rachel's pursuit ebbed and flowed until he couldn't tell if she was almost upon him or a long way off.

The alley took a slight turn and the shadows were pushed back by weak orange light that might have come from the next street over. If that was the case, he might be able to lose himself there if only his knee held up. It might also be that she knew the alley so she could cover it quicker than he ever would.

He looked around. The house wall to his left was solid and two-storeys high. The factory wall had a row of barred windows at street level and two doors.

What if he went into the factory and hid in there until the heat died down?

The first door had a construction company warning sign attached to it. He tried the handle but it didn't move. Keel put his shoulder to the door but it didn't budge.

He tried the next door which was a few paces away. An old sign marked 'Office' was nailed to the top rail. A newer sign below it warned of deep excavations. He tried the handle but this one was locked too. Determined to get in, he put his shoulder to it and this time it worked. With a loud crack the door opened wide. The protest of the hinges echoed around him.

He stepped into the gloom and kicked the door shut behind him.

* * *

Rachel slowed down when the commotion began but it stopped before she reached the point where the alley turned. Cautiously, she peered around but couldn't see anyone. Then she noticed the broken door.

With her back to the house wall, she made her way along and half expected Keel to leap out at her as her heart hammered with tension and fright.

She got to the door and kicked it open. It swung wide and caught on something, leaving an open maw into the gloom of the factory interior. She could just make out a short narrow corridor with two-tone walls and a stairwell at the end of it. There wasn't enough light for her to see if anyone was there.

Had he gone in?

She stepped into the corridor. It smelled awful, as if something had crawled in here to die. A short-handled broom had been left by the door and she picked it up. The brush head remained on the floor and there was a ragged end to the shaft where someone had snapped it off. It wasn't brilliant but it felt good to have a weapon.

## Chapter 47

As her eyes adjusted to the gloom, Rachel could see four doors opening off the corridor.

Her heart raced and her throat clicked when she tried to swallow. Keel was injured, clearly, but he was also dangerous and she needed to be careful. She raised the broom handle like a sword.

She stopped at the first door and held her breath to listen intently. She could only hear the thud of her own heartbeat. She tried the door handle but it was locked.

The second door was locked too. Now her nerves were jangling and she could hear the pulse of blood in her ears so clearly it seemed as though all of Hadlington could as well.

By the time she stood in front of the third door her shoulders felt bunched from the tension, but she couldn't stop now. Even if she turned and walked away there was nothing to stop him coming after her.

She put her hand on the handle and strained to hear anything out of the ordinary. In her mind's eye she saw him waiting patiently ready to jump out and overpower her, and that pumped adrenaline through her.

Rachel stepped back far enough that if he came through quickly he couldn't grab her and she wedged the broom handle against her side.

She leaned forward and tried the door. It gave with a slight click. She gave it a push and leaned back and the door swung open slowly. The hinges creaked and grit caught underneath. Nothing moved. Her chest felt tight and she licked her lips as she waited.

Keel came out of the darkness in a rush and threw something that shattered against the wall behind her. She screamed and almost dropped the broom handle but it caught against her coat and she managed to keep a grip on it.

He limped along the corridor holding the wall for support. Rachel took a moment to recover then realised he was going up the stairs and potentially away.

So she ran.

He went up the gloomy stairs and pulled himself up by gripping the banister. His left leg dragged. Rachel kept her distance but stayed with him and held the broom handle upright so she could use it straight away.

The first landing had a meshed window that let in some light and he went out of sight for a moment then she heard the scuff of his shoes on more steps. She followed him up two more flights of stairs and soon the ragged sound of their breathing echoed in the enclosed space.

A corridor opened up from the final flight of stairs and the ceiling had been removed. Most of the roof was missing too so moonlight filled its length. Keel ran for a door at the far end with a sign on it that read 'Down to Shop Floor'. His stride broadened as he limped past doors marked 'Accounts' and 'Production' and 'Engineering'. She knew she had to keep up because there would be a hundred places to hide on a shop floor. She focussed on moving her legs even though pain flared in her thighs and calves. Her whole body felt like it had reached the end of its tether.

The gap between them opened and Rachel could feel her pace ebbing away.

* * *

Keel risked a glance over his shoulder and was glad to see Rachel dropping back. Whatever he'd done to his knee got worse with every stride and he didn't know how long he could keep this pace up. He'd gain a big advantage if he reached the door before she caught him, and if he got onto the shop floor, the job was finished. Even if the area had been stripped clean there would be plenty of places to hide away in and sneak out when she'd gone by.

If he shed the parka on the street and kept his head down, he could calmly walk away. Nobody would pay him attention and even if they did, who could prove he'd ever been on Moore Avenue?

The door was five or six paces away now. He held out his hand ready to grab the handle and push.

Three paces.

His knee clicked and failed to hold his weight, and he stumbled against the door. It clattered open and he fell through.

* * *

Rachel watched Keel fall through the door into an area where glass panels in the roof let in a lot of moonlight.

He yelled and seemed to be holding on to something.

Lifting her legs now was a trial, but with gritted teeth she willed herself on.

Closer to the door she could see he was hanging in the air. The staircase that should have been there had been removed. Scaffolding had been erected a few feet from the wall and he'd been able to grab the outermost bar.

Rachel held on to the door jamb. The drop was at least two storeys and the ground was littered with rubble and debris. Keel was swinging slowly but grunting with the effort and clearly not going anywhere.

She bent forward on her hands and knees and tried to fill her lungs as her chest heaved from exertion.

Keel shifted his hands so he faced her. "Now what?" he said. His breathing was as heavy as hers.

She looked at him. "Now I get the police."

He swung his good leg to try and catch the scaffolding pole in front of the door by Rachel.

"Don't," she said.

"I'm not trying to escape," he said with panic. "I'm trying to get a leg hold. My arms aren't going to hold me here forever."

"Who wants you to hold yourself up?"

Keel's initial frown dissolved into a smirk. "As if you'd let me fall."

"Why shouldn't I after everything you've put me through?"

"You're not a bad person, Rachel. Look down, I'd never survive that drop."

His smirk made her angry and she felt it bloom hot across her chest as she stood up. She tapped the broom handle against her leg and fought a sudden urge to do something horrible. But the urge got too much and she swung the handle against the scaffold pole six inches from his foot.

Keel's smirk slipped.

She hit the pole again, closer to his foot this time. The smirk disappeared altogether as he shifted his hands to get a better grip. She jabbed the jagged end of the handle at his foot and forced him to swing free.

"You bitch," he shouted, clearly shocked. "What the fuck are you doing?"

"The same as you did to me."

She braced her feet against the sides of the door and pulled the broom handle up quickly. It clanged against the pole a foot or so from his left hand.

Keel's eyes went wide. "Fuck you," he shouted.

"Shall I do it again?"

"Could you live with it?" he asked quickly. He tried to look concerned but it didn't wash. "Could you live with yourself if I fell and you knew you'd caused it?"

"You tried to kill me tonight," she shouted at him. "You came to my home and threatened my daughter."

He had to shift his hands and she could see the strain of the effort in his face. His breath came in short, sharp bursts.

"It was business, not personal. Not like this."

"Fuck you, Keel. Tonight's been personal for me."

"Rachel."

She hit the scaffold pole close to his hand.

"Rachel," he pleaded and his eyes were wide with terror. "Please…"

She revelled in his fear. They both knew he wouldn't survive the fall but nobody else was there to be witness to what she did.

"Rachel!" He raised his voice but she barely heard him.

Her fingers were white where they gripped the broom handle. If she hit his left hand as hard as possible he'd have to let go. Could he support himself one-handed? In her mind's eye she saw his fingers slip on the metal; she watched him fall and almost heard his scream. She saw Tilly drawing at the coffee table and calling Rachel in to share a cup of tea with the toys. She thought of their life in the flat and of them being a family.

"Rachel?" Keel sounded desperate.

She looked at him and tried to shake the murderous thoughts out of her head. What had she been thinking? Had she really contemplated killing him?

She stepped back from the doorway and he swung his leg onto the scaffold bar and breathed out heavily. "Thank you."

Footsteps rang out and she glanced over her shoulder to see the woman in the red duffel coat come up the stairway. Two policemen in uniform were behind her.

"Stay where are you!" Pippa ordered.

"I'm not going anywhere," said Rachel. She leaned against the wall and dropped the broom handle.

Pippa stopped beside her while the policeman went to the doorway. "Are you okay?"

"I've been better," Rachel said as she watched Keel get dragged into the corridor and bundled to the floor.

"I'm sure you have. You're safe now."

"Yeah. What about Tilly?"

"She's safe, my colleagues are looking after her. She doesn't know what happened with the falling statue."

"The man's dead though?

"Most definitely."

"And Jack?"

"He's as well as he can be. There's an ambulance en route."

"He got shot with a crossbow."

"I know."

One of the policemen pressed on Keel's shoulder. "You do not have to say anything…"

"There's a brown package in one of his pockets," Rachel said. "That's what all this is about."

Pippa looked at the officers. "Search him, Adams."

"Have you got anything sharp on your person?" Adams asked while the other finished reading his rights. Keel didn't respond to either of them.

"Take that as a yes," said Pippa. "Be bloody careful."

Adams put on latex gloves and handed a pair to Pippa before he searched Keel's parka. It didn't take him long to find what he was looking for. He gave it to Pippa and she showed Rachel the box.

"Is this what you meant?"

"Yes. So what happens now?"

"Let's get you back, shall we?"

# Chapter 48

Sergeant Maley interviewed Rachel at the station with a duty solicitor by her side. The room felt too small and smelled of sweat and fear. The plastic chairs were uncomfortable and everything about the bland room seemed tired and sad, from the decrepit wall tiles to the chipped table between them.

Maley quickly explained the interview procedure then asked her to tell him in as much detail as she could remember what had happened.

She told him everything and the tears came before she'd even got to her experiences at Fowler's Field. She kept herself under control even when she told him about Stephens and answered his questions as clearly and fully as she could.

Maley kept circling back to two questions in particular. Did she know Keel or Wilson and what was in the brown package? He asked her so many times that in the end she snapped, "Well do you know what's in the package?"

He admitted he had no idea.

It took a little over an hour. Once they had finished, Maley explained they would need to see her again and allowed the solicitor to lead her out of the interview room.

"Is there anything you want?" the duty solicitor asked.

"Could I borrow your phone?"

The duty solicitor handed hers over and left Rachel to stand in a corner for a bit of privacy. She dialled Naomi.

"Rachel! It's so good to hear your voice. A policewoman explained what was going on and asked me to keep Tilly here."

"Thank you. Is she okay?"

"Still asleep. Her and Anya were so excited about all the goings-on, I couldn't get them to go off."

"Thank you for this, Naomi."

"You need to tell me what happened."

"I will."

"I'll come down when you're ready and bring a bottle of wine so you can tell me the whole story."

Rachel handed the phone back to the duty solicitor.

"I'll leave you now," the solicitor said, "but you have my card, and when they need to talk to you again, which they will, make sure I'm involved."

Pippa came up to her as the duty solicitor left. "Is everything okay, Rachel?"

"I think so. I'd like to go and see Jack, if that's alright?"

"I'm sure it is, just give me a moment."


# Chapter 49


Pippa Vincent sat at her desk as the sun rose over Hadlington and watched the night fade in shades of purple as orange hues cut through the mist of the morning. From here she could just see the treetops of the wood bordering Fowler's Field.

She finished her coffee, which was almost palatable when it cooled down and you hadn't drunk anything else all night, and checked through her paperwork. She'd been given some reports coming in from her colleagues checking out the site and as unbelievable as they seemed, all of them bore out what Jack and Rachel had told her.

After signing in the package as evidence, she'd gone up to the interview room to watch Maley question Rachel. Maley also spoke to Jack at Hadlington General Hospital and neither of their stories changed, tallying completely apart from the period of time they'd been split up.

Pippa hadn't expected to be in on the interviews having been told, in no uncertain terms, she was in trouble. Maley kept telling her she'd done the right thing at the wrong time and she tended to agree with him but she hadn't followed procedure and had broken a lot of rules.

After checking in with Rachel when the duty solicitor left, Pippa had been sent upstairs to finish her report and await a meeting with Inspector Michaels.

He had passed through the office twenty minutes before as the first shards of dawn lit the sky. He'd nodded at Pippa when he passed her desk but didn't say a word. A man and woman went into the office a few minutes later but Pippa had no idea who they were.

The sun glared in through the windows, showing handprints and smears on the glass, when Maley came into the squad room. He sat across from Pippa, put his elbows on the blotter and clasped his hands.

"How're you doing, kid?"

"I'm as nervous as buggery."

He nodded with pursed lips. "Have you written your report?"

"Yes, and filed it too."

He smiled. The inspector's door opened and Maley looked over Pippa's shoulder. She turned in her chair. The man who'd gone in left and closed the door behind him. A few moments later the door opened again and Inspector Michaels leaned out.

"Glad you're here, Ken," he said. "Could you and Constable Vincent come in please?"

Pippa stood up with a grimace. "Surname only," she said. "Now for the bollocking to end all bollockings."

"Just remember," said Maley quietly. "Whatever else he does, he can't kill you."

She smiled and followed her sergeant into the office. Michaels stepped out of the way to allow them through the door then closed it. A woman sat in front of the desk.

"This is Susan Brown," Inspector Michaels said. "Susan, this is Police Constable Pippa Vincent and Sergeant Ken Maley."

Susan Brown wore a navy blue trouser suit and her white-blonde hair was pulled into a severe bun. She stood up and held out her hand.

Pippa shook it and felt tension run through her. The fact she had no idea what department Brown worked for made her think this might be an even bigger bollocking than she'd originally feared.

Michaels gestured for them all to be seated then walked around the desk. He sat beside Brown and steepled his fingers against his chin.

Pippa clasped her hands in her lap to stop them dancing.

"Ms Brown and her colleague work for British Intelligence and want to have a word," Inspector Michaels said.

Pippa pressed her hands together more tightly. British Intelligence? Her palms felt clammy.

"Thank you, Inspector," said Brown and cleared her throat. "I've read your report about this evening, Constable Vincent, and I've also seen the transcript of the interviews you, Sergeant Maley, carried out with Rachel Turner and Jack Martin. They're very consistent."

Pippa didn't know whether to nod or ask if she meant to suggest some kind of conspiracy of lying. She decided to keep quiet.

"It would seem Mr Martin had no idea about the package so I think we can safely discount him. Ms Turner might well have been aware of it though she clearly had no idea of its purpose."

Pippa nodded, unsure of where this was going.

"My colleague has already removed the package from your evidence suite into our custody with the kind permission of Inspector Michaels."

Pippa felt, rather than saw, Maley start at this information. "Can I ask–?" he began.

Inspector Michaels cut him off. "No."

Brown looked from the inspector to Maley. "I can't tell you much," she said, "because it's a matter of national security and a somewhat delicate situation. You will both be asked to sign paperwork relating to the Official Secrets Act, which my colleague is just preparing now. While we wait though, I can tell you that the package was a hard drive which contained highly sensitive data. This was being processed at a data company in Hadlington and an employee, a Mrs Barbara Gilbert, was concerned that the information might be leaked."

Maley and Pippa exchanged a glance.

"Several foreign agencies were interested in this data and Wilson was a well-known information broker on the black market. My colleague and I will take the package back to London under secure escort. Other than in taped interviews with us you are not to refer to it again."

She looked at Inspector Michaels. "Thank you for the time and the loan of your office."

"My pleasure," said Michaels and got to his feet.

They all shook hands. Brown opened the office door then looked back into the room.

"Thank you both," she said. "It's not an exaggeration to say that without your input tonight, the United Kingdom could have faced quite a serious data breach."

Maley waited until the door closed then turned to Michaels. "What the hell happened there?"

Michaels shrugged. "You know as much as I do, Ken. I've got to sign the paperwork too."

"Do you think she was MI5?" Pippa asked.

"She wasn't specific and I don't think you ought to ask questions like that. Either way, we all clearly heard what she said so I suggest you act on it. Now get out of here. Finish your reports then bugger off home."

"Am I suspended?" Pippa asked.

"Not to my knowledge," Michaels said. "Now get some rest and be back for tonight's shift."

"I told you," Maley said to her. "Now get going."

\* \* \*

Jack's bed was a general ward next to the window. The other five beds were occupied by much older men, some of whom read while others stared into space. He hadn't seen her enter the room and Rachel watched him for a moment as he stared out the window. He looked sad. His left upper arm and right hand were heavily bandaged.

She sat at the empty chair beside his bed and the leg shifting on the floor startled him.

"I didn't see you," he said. He winced as he moved his arm when he shifted to face her. "I'm not very comfortable."

"You don't look it. They told me you were fine."

"These aside," he said and moved his arm a little, "I'm just knackered. I think I've dozed for about five minutes."

"Me too."

"How are your knees?"

"I'll live."

He looked like he wanted to say something but didn't. She knew how that felt. She wanted to talk through the experience to try to figure out what had happened beyond what Sergeant Maley and PC Vincent had told her but now didn't seem the time.

"How long are you in for?" she asked finally.

"Just a day or so for observation."

"Then home?"

He shrugged and the corners of his mouth turned down. "Back to Bristol, yes."

248

"Are you okay about that?"

"Of course, it's just…"

He let the sentence taper away and Rachel was happy to let him do so. His news about Luisa had come out under extreme circumstances and maybe he needed time to process how open he'd been with a relative stranger.

"It's been a time, hasn't it?" she said, trying to change the subject.

He nodded and looked relieved. "How's Tilly?"

"I saw her for five minutes, kissed her and stroked her hair but she was dozing. I'm going to get her after I leave here."

"Say hello to her for me."

"I will, Jack, I promise. But why don't you call round before you head back? I'm sure Tilly would love to throw you a tea party."

He nodded and offered her a smile. "That sounds lovely, Rachel."

She frowned. "You haven't been to many little girls' tea parties have you?"

# Acknowledgements

Writing is a solitary process but I appreciate everyone who helps out, in one way or another, to bring the story to life. In this case, many thanks and much love go to:

Mum and Dad; Sarah, Chris, Lucy and Milly; Nick Duncan, Sue Moorcroft, Julia Roberts, Caroline Lake, Jonathan Litchfield, Kim Talbot Hoelzli, Katrina Souter, Louise Styles, Ian Whates and the NSFWG gang, Steve Bacon, Wayne Parkin, Peter Mark May, Richard Farren Barber, Steve Harris, Phil Sloman, James Everington, Ross Warren, Penny Jones and Jim Mcleod; Laura, Barry and Bob Burton; The Crusty Exterior and all who sail in her; my friends who've championed the books; EVERYONE who's bought a copy (thank you so much) and EVERYONE who's told a friend about my writing. Many thanks also to the entire team at The Book Folks.

David Roberts and Pippa for the Friday Night Walks, the endless support and encouragement and those plotting sessions that tie up most of the loose ends.

And as always, Alison and Matthew, without whom none of this would make much sense.

If you enjoyed this book, please let others know by leaving a quick review on Amazon. Also, if you spot anything untoward in the paperback, get in touch. We strive for the best quality and appreciate reader feedback.

editor@thebookfolks.com

www.thebookfolks.com

## Also by Mark West

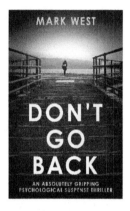

Beth's partner Nick can't quite understand why she acts so strangely when they return to her hometown for the funeral of a once-close friend. But she hasn't told him everything about her past. Memories of one terrible summer will come flooding back to her. And with them, violence and revenge.

After separating from her cheating husband, Claire begins to feel watched. She nearly gets run over and someone daubs a hangman symbol on a wall near her house. As letters begin to get added to the game, she'll need to find the identity of her stalker before they raise the stakes.

## Other titles of interest

When the body of a young woman is discovered under the floorboards of an isolated house during its renovation, questions are raised about DCI Jack Harris' own potential connection to the site. Will he clear his name or will his reputation be forever besmirched in the rural Pennine community?

A THRILLING MURDER MYSTERY WITH A BIG TWIST

NO REFUGE

NICOLA CLIFFORD

Reporter Stacey Logan has little to worry about other than the town flower festival when a man is shot dead. When she believes the police have got the wrong man, she does some snooping of her own. But will her desire for a scoop lead her to a place where there is no refuge?

Printed in Great Britain
by Amazon